Oric and the Web of Evil

Lesley Wilson

Cataloguing-in-Publication entry is available from the National Library of Australia.
ISBN: 978-0-9954220-4-9 (paperback)
          978-0-9954220-5-6 (ebook)

Other titles by Lesley Wilson:
Oric And The Alchemist's Key (2015)
Oric And The Lockton Castle Mystery (2016)

Publishing Consultant: Linda Diggle – www.bookboffin.com
Editor: Val Atkinson
Internal Layout and Formatting: www.authorsecret.com
Cover Design: Spiffing Covers
Social Media Assistant: Slyv Kerslake – sylv.net

Acknowledgements

My grateful thanks go to dear friend Val Atkinson, who painstakingly edits my books. Her knowledge of the English language, energy, and good humour are second to none. Val, you bring many a smile to my face with your entertaining and informative post-it notes attached to my manuscripts.

Many thanks also go to:

Sylv Kerslake, my dedicated PA who looks after my social media and keeps on coming up with fabulous ads. You are always there when I need you, Sylv.

Linda Diggle of Book Boffin, who organises my publishing and deals with many Amazon issues on my behalf. Her valuable input sees my books in print with the minimal amount of effort on my part. Linda, you save me many sleepless nights.

Spiffing Covers for all three of my book jackets in the Oric trilogy. Any future books I write will certainly have your incredible artwork on their covers.

Bookworm associates Sandy Paull, Jodie Zammit and Daryl Barnes. As fellow authors, I appreciate your support. Our long, literary lunches are wonderful.

And to my family, Miles, Amanda, Gerran and Taneesha, you inspire me. Bless you all.

Finally, my lovely husband, Mike, who is always on hand to help in any way he can. Love you babe.

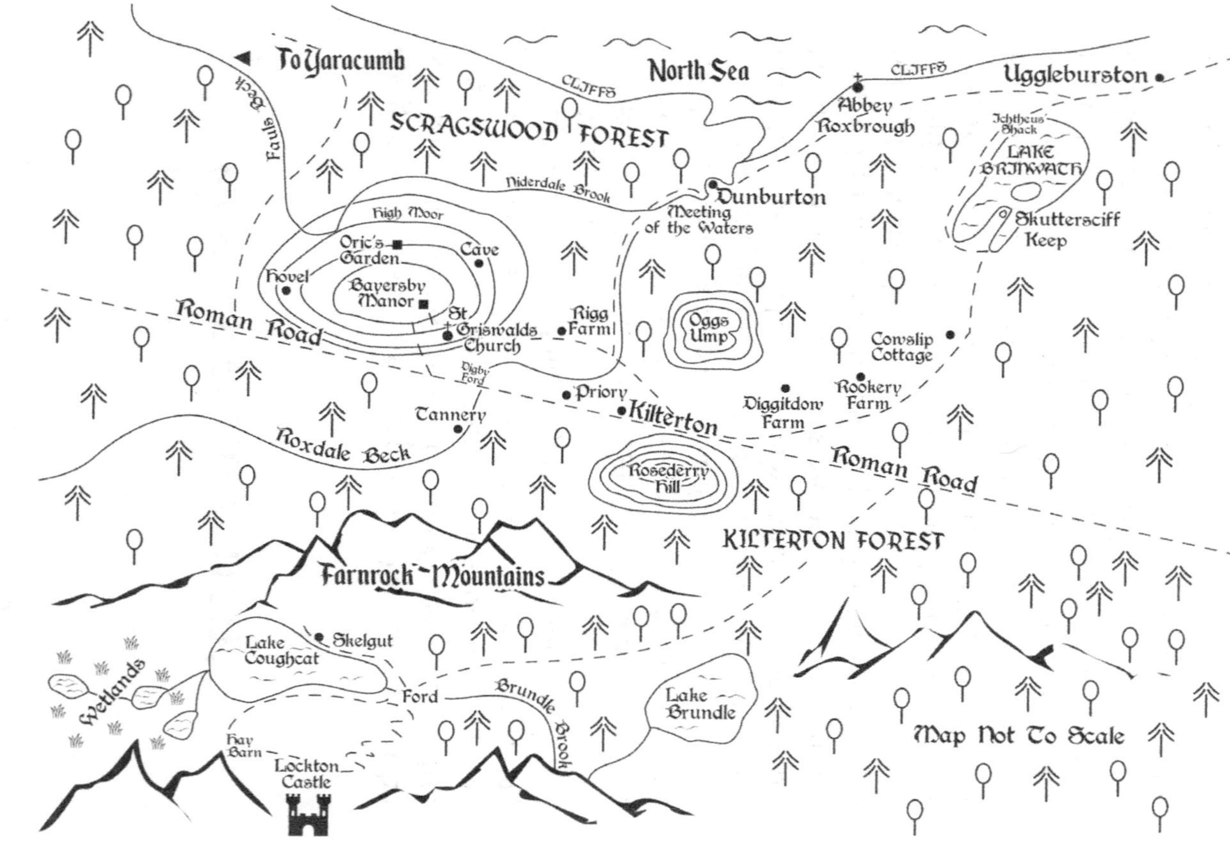

To Yaracumb
North Sea
CLIFFS
Uggleburston
SCRAGSWOOD FOREST
Fauls Beck
Abbey Roxbrough
Ichtheus' Shack
LAKE BRINWATH
Niderdale Brook
Dunburton
Meeting of the Waters
Skuttersciff Keep
High Moor
Oric's Garden
Cave
Hovel
Bayersby Manor
St Griswalds Church
Rigg Farm
Oggs Ump
Cowslip Cottage
Roman Road
Digby Ford
Priory
Kilterton
Diggitdow Farm
Rookery Farm
Tannery
Roxdale Beck
Rosederry Hill
Roman Road
KILTERTON FOREST
Farnrock Mountains
Lake Coughcat
Skelgut
Ford
Brundle Brook
Lake Brundle
Map Not To Scale
Wetlands
Hay Barn
Lockton Castle

Prologue

Marauders sack Dunburton Manor, killing all the inhabitants. Out on an errand, orphaned boy Oric returns home to find his mentor and friend, Deveril, near to death. The old alchemist presses an ornate key into Oric's hand. *"This key unlocks the secret to great wealth. You must promise to keep it safe. If it falls into wrong hands untold disasters could occur."*

Clutching the key, Oric runs away from the blazing house. With no place to go, he wanders the countryside until he stumbles upon the home of Sir Edred and Lady Myferny of Bayersby. Apothecary Ichtheus takes the boy in and teaches him the skills of healing and herbalism.

Several years pass before Oric discovers the meaning of Deveril's words and the mystery behind the key with the double knots engraved upon its shaft.

-oOo-

Sir Edred, Lord of Bayersby, hears rumours of disease at Lockton Castle. Keen to stop the infection from spreading, he sends young Oric to investigate the pending epidemic. Wolfhound Parzifal is sent with Oric for protection. The last thing Oric expects after his four-day ride to the castle is the den of iniquity into which he plunges.

Sick of the ruthless killing of landowners in a bid to take over every estate in the county, several older mercenaries in Sir Ragnald of Lockton's employ turn against their lord. Sir Ragnald discovers their murderous plot and poisons the culprits. Thus, the rumour of an epidemic emerges.

Suspicious of underhanded dealings, Oric makes a clandestine reconnoitre of Lockton Castle and discovers a small door hidden away behind a wall tapestry. He tries Deveril's key in the lock and is astonished when the door springs open. Two parchments scribed in Latin, a language Oric has not yet learned, lie alongside a ruby ring. Afraid of discovery, he thrusts everything back in place and locks the door.

-oOo-

After receiving a thrashing from his father for committing various misdemeanours, the Bayersby heir, Guwain, runs away from home. Oric is amazed to find the youth asleep in one of Lockton Castle's turret rooms.

Bannulf, a mercenary soldier who has also become disenchanted by the ruthless killings, manages to evade his employer's wrath and warns Oric of Sir Ragnald's intended challenge for Sir Edred's manor. Bannulf also explains how Guwain believes he is Sir Ragnald's guest when, in fact, he is to be used as a hostage. With Bannulf's aid, Oric escapes the castle and returns home to warn Sir Edred of the impending danger to Bayersby Manor.

-oOo-

During Sir Edred's annual jousting contest, Sir Ragnald investigates the Bayersby estate. He learns the Lord of Bayersby maintains a poorly equipped and badly trained defence force. The popular lord's major concerns lie in the running of his wealthy estate, and the care of his serfs and cotters. Sir Ragnald hardly believes his good fortune when Guwain runs away from home and asks to join his party. He orders his son, Joffrey, to keep an eye on the youth. A reasonably cordial relationship develops between the two boys – until Guwain learns that he is to be used as a bargaining tool against his own father. He is further incensed when, on the day of battle, he is secured to his saddle with rope.

Ready to do battle, Sir Ragnald musters his army and makes the four-day journey from Lockton Castle to Bayersby Manor.

Far from enjoying the element of his planned surprise, Sir Ragnald runs full tilt into the worst ambush of his life. Plumes of flame erupt on either side of his compact column of men. Mostly all of them are incinerated. At the head of his army Sir Ragnald escapes the inferno, but is felled by Sir Edred who lies in wait.

At the back of the column, in charge of Guwain, Joffrey misses the worst of the blaze. Realising he has little choice but to run for his life, he cuts Guwain loose and makes for the forest with a few of his father's remaining mercenaries.

-oOo-

Keen to inspect the spoils of his successful battle, Sir Edred plans to spend the short Yuletide holiday looking over the newly-won Lockton Estate before deciding what to do with it. However, Mother Nature has other ideas. Copious amounts of snow fall, and the attending Bayersby folk are trapped indoors at Lockton Castle for five weeks.

The castle, situated on a mountainside plateau, consists of two double-storey stone buildings set at right angles to one another. One square, three-storey castellated tower joins the two wings together at the centre, and circular turrets at each end of the buildings provide private sleeping quarters for family members and guests. Rugged mountains form an impenetrable barrier to the rear of the castle. A wide moat around the base of the castle walls provide a deterrent to would-be marauders. Across the drawbridge, a stout portcullis gave access to the inner bailey.

Oric remembers the two parchments he stumbled upon during his first visit to the castle. He retrieves them from the secret hiding place in the women's bower and hands them over to Ichtheus. He is shocked to learn the words are written by his father, Askell. During Oric's infancy Sir Ragnald had attacked Lockton Castle. The family escaped and rode for many days, eventually seeking shelter with the Lord and Lady of Dunburton.

Shortly afterwards Oric's parents succumb to a horrible malady, and he is left in the care of Deveril, the Dunburton Alchemist. Before Askell passes away, he leaves his will in Deveril's safekeeping and asks that Oric not be informed of his situation until he becomes of age.

Happy with his life as an apothecary and his relationship with ladies' maid Dian, Oric is appalled at the news. He begs Ichtheus to keep the contents of his father's will secret. Harbouring a strong sense of what is right, Ichtheus refuses Oric's request and informs Sir Edred.

A consummate gentleman, Sir Edred takes everything

in his stride. In a ceremony before his entire entourage, he announces Oric's rightful tenure of Lockton Castle.

Everyone is delighted except for Guwain. The Bayersby heir is eaten up with jealousy and swears to unseat Oric at the first opportunity.

Dian is devastated because she believes she is now too humble to deserve Oric's friendship, and she becomes subservient. Oric is perplexed by her attitude, but he is unable to persuade her otherwise.

Early February brings warmer weather to the district and a slow thaw begins. Keen to start the farming year at home, Sir Edred and his party set off on the rigorous journey back to Bayersby Manor.

Dian tries to sneak away from the castle without saying goodbye but, tipped off by Master Ichtheus, Oric challenges her as she rides out through the castle gate. He gently accuses her of leaving without bidding him farewell and asks her why.

Dian explains that it is not her place to seek out a gentleman of high rank. She pledges her undying loyalty and asks what else Oric desires.

Desire! Oric's love for Dian threatens to set him alight. He seizes her cold hand and kisses it. Unable to force a friendship Dian does not wish to pursue, Oric promises to remain at her service should she ever need him.

Guwain observes Oric and Dian's painful parting and calls out in a derogatory tone. He lewdly promises to warm the maid's bones on chilly nights in Oric's absence.

As a lord in his own right with a rank exceeding Sir Edred's, Oric no longer needs to show deference to anyone. He threatens to kill Guwain if he harms one single hair on Dian's head.

In a face-saving exercise, Guwain sneers and suggests there are plenty of other willing females keen to provide him with entertainment. Despite his bravado, Guwain is afraid of Oric, for he believes the new Lord of Lockton will remain true to his word.

Oric is comforted by the knowledge that Guwain will not return to Bayersby Manor with his parents. As punishment for various misdemeanours, Sir Edred has arranged for his wayward son to refine his attitudes under the tutelage of the Roxbrough Abbey monks. Guwain will remain at the abbey, posing no threat to Dian or any other young female, until he learns to behave like a gentleman.

Apothecary Ichtheus, Oric's mentor and friend, is last to leave. He embraces Oric and promises to visit the castle again as soon as he can.

Sir Edred's wolfhound, Parzifal, bounds out of the bushes. A parchment attached to his collar dislodges and falls to the ground. Oric picks it up and reads it.

'I can think of no good reason to drag Parzifal back to Bayersby against his will! He is more your dog than mine and will likely pine away without you. Consider him my gift to you.
I am at your service should you ever need my assistance.
I wish you well, my lord.
Edred, of Bayersby.'

Sir Edred also leaves behind two donkeys and a fine gelding named Jester. Overwhelmed by his former master's generosity, Oric blinks rapidly to stem tears that brim his bright blue eyes. Dashing them away, he grabs Parzifal's collar and strides back toward the castle's open drawbridge.

CHAPTER ONE

Lockton Castle

Wandering listlessly into the bailey, Lockton Castle's dismal atmosphere closed around Oric like a damp shroud.

Gatekeeper Rory, wanting to keep on the good side of his new master, all but curtsied. "Will I close the portcullis now, your worshipfulness?" he asked.

Oric gave a curt nod. The obsequious, bandy-legged little man made his flesh creep.

Rattles and clanks issued from the gate's tortured mechanism, setting Oric's teeth on edge. "For the sake of sanity, Rory, do something with that wretched gate! Maintain it properly or seek employment elsewhere."

Rory popped his head out of a narrow window half way up the gatehouse wall, reminding Oric of a ferret in a rabbit hole. He tugged on his forelock. "Aye sir, yes sir. Will there be anything else you require, sir?"

"Get someone to help you cleanse that stinking moat before someone dies from the fumes issuing from it." Many extra people in residence during Yuletide had caused human waste to outweigh the quantity of clean water.

"Aye, sir, I will get on to it straight away, sir."

Death had come too close for comfort on one or two occasions lately, and Rory intended to keep on Oric's good side. He tightened the rope around his baggy breeches, praying a similar scenario would not include his neck any time soon.

Securing the winch, Rory thrust home the timber locking-device for what felt like the thousandth time. Words he had heard from the Bayersby people, for the duration of Sir Edred's sojourn, rang inside his head. *'Rory let me in! Rory let me out!'* Clang, clang, the bell beside the gate resounded from morn 'til night. With the departure of the Bayersby folk, very few people remained at the castle, and Rory hoped not to hear such demands again for a long time.

Lazy and good for nothing much Rory muttered to himself. "I suppose I had best get on with fixing this portcullis. Ain't no other silly beggar going to do it." He parted his droopy black moustache and spat on the ground. "No doubt yon stinking moat will present me with another problem an' all."

Wind moaned around the castle's weatherworn battlements, and Oric shivered in the early morning chill. Determined to make the best of his new situation, he climbed the flight of stairs that gave access to the castle's main living quarters. Pushing open the iron-studded timber door, he entered the cold Great Hall. Emotionally drained, he pulled a high-backed chair up close to the fire and chafed his hands before the meagre warmth. Tongue lolling, wolfhound Parzifal looked up at Oric with unadulterated adoration.

Before the recent discovery of his father's will, life had offered Oric everything he ever dreamed of. His work as assistant apothecary to Master Ichtheus satisfied his ambition, and folk in the Kilterton and Bayersby districts respected him for his medical skills. He made a little money from his stall, selling herbal remedies at the weekly Kilterton market. His life in Sir Edred's manor remained enjoyable most of the time, and he savoured his relationship with ladies' maid Dian. Now, for the sake of family honour, he faced the terrifying prospect of managing the near destitute Lockton Castle estate and everything else the position demanded.

Oric's friends Ned and Joe chose not to return to Bayersby Manor with Sir Edred. They bounded into the Great Hall, looking for Oric. Concerned over the boys' decision to remain at the castle, Oric questioned them closely.

"Are you sure you want to relinquish a life of comfort and safety with Sir Edred in exchange for an unknown future with me?"

Ned's dark eyes sparkled mischievously. "Of course, we want to stay with you, sir. If we leave, who will look after you?" He poked Joe playfully in the ribs. "What say you, young-un?"

Joe nodded his head vigorously. "Oh aye, my lord. I agree with Ned."

"And I am mighty glad to have you both. Though all I can offer at present is a roof over your heads and a poor supply of food. I might be able to pay wages eventually, but I have no idea how far away that day will be."

The boys had suffered many hard times in the past and they were prepared to rough it in the future, especially if they could remain with Oric. Joe, with his spiky black hair, dark eyes and thin, undernourished frame, was tougher than he looked. Ned, a year or so older and a good deal more robust, looked after the smaller boy. Their loyal, brotherly attitude toward one another warmed Oric's heart.

Stable boy Walter and two kitchen maids, Faylinn and Genevieve, also begged leave from Sir Edred and Lady

Myferny to stay with Oric. Including Rory and Hamish, eight people now inhabited Lockton Castle. Not enough to run the estate, but at least it was a start.

Needing a moment of quiet, Oric left the Great Hall and headed toward a small place of worship in a corner of the bailey. Faithful as ever, Parzifal loped along beside his beloved master. A gentle push opened the chapel door, and Oric eased his way into the fusty building. Tangles of cobwebs stretched from one dust-encrusted pew to the next, and Oric surmised no-one had used the chapel in many a long moon. No icons graced the interior, and the only decoration on the carved timber altar came from roosting birds. The unloved, rundown feel of the place added to Oric's feelings of inadequacy.

Morning light struck through a blue and gold stained-glass window above the altar, projecting pools of bright colour on to the dusty flagstones at Oric's feet. Enjoying the moment of peace, he knelt and bowed his fair head in prayer. The list of people he deemed worthy of God's blessing was long and, in the asking, he lost track of time.

The chapel door banged open, admitting an icy blast of wind. "Ah – there you are, my lord!" Ned bowed low in deference to Oric's new status. "Me and Joe have been seeking you everywhere. We are keen to learn what you want of us, sir?"

Oric scrambled to his feet. "You can start by not bowing every time you set eyes upon me! How am I supposed to carry on a conversation with someone who is bent double most of the time?"

Joe's thin face appeared around the door jamb. "Can I come in here an' all, your lordship? 'Tis pouring rain again and I am getting a soaking, hanging about outside." To prove his point, he shook himself like a wet dog, sending drops of moisture on to the flagstones.

"Aye, come on in, Joe, and for pity's sake, shut the door to stop the draught." Oric brushed dust from his breeches. "Sit down, both of you, I have something important to say." He paced up and down the aisle before coming to a stop in front the pew on which his friends sat. "We need to get one or two things straight."

Ned's face paled. "You ain't planning to send us away, are you, your lordship?"

"No! Of course not, but I cannot continue with the two of you bowing and grovelling, and calling me 'your lordship' all the time. How long have we been friends?"

"Ever since you rescued us from Master Figg's clutches," said Joe. "Up 'til then my life was miserable. I care not what work I must do, but I ain't going back to picking folks' pouches. Nor shall I work for a mean-minded villain like moneylender Figg again."

"Listen well, both of you. If you wish to remain here, call me Oric like you always have. I might have inherited a castle and a title, but I am still the same person."

Joe leaped to his feet and squeezed his skinny arms around Oric's waist. "Do you really mean that, sir?" Realising what he had done, Joe hastily stepped back, his face redder than a setting sun. "Oh, heck, m'lord… Er, Oric. I got carried away – please forgive me."

"Nothing to forgive, young fellow," smiled Oric, hugging the small boy's shoulders.

"If calling you Oric is all I must do to keep my place at Lockton Castle," said Ned, "you have my word upon it."

"I am indebted to you both. However, before you swear life-long allegiance to me and my cause, you had best listen to what may lie in store."

-oOo-

Joffrey rode into the near derelict village of Dunburton. He made a cursory inspection of the high street and, finding the settlement deserted, he ordered his men to set up headquarters in the only cottage with a half decent roof.

Sleet and frost now replaced the mild autumn weather, the cottage-roof leaked, and a fire on the central hearth afforded little warmth. Joffrey's followers did not suffer winter's biting chill gladly, and their bellies rumbled with hunger. Tempers soon frayed.

"How long do you intend to stop in this Godforsaken hole?" growled the eldest mercenary. "Can we not find somewhere more comfortable to bide?"

Joffrey narrowed his tawny, cat-like eyes in a deep scowl. "Nice idea, my friend, but who will pay for such luxuries? In case you failed to notice, I am fresh out of funds." He shrugged his wide shoulders. "If my way of doing things is not to your liking, clear off and fend for yourself!"

"Aye, I might just do that!" snapped the soldier, but he failed to follow his words with actions. Instead he wrapped himself more tightly in a moth-eaten blanket and huddled closer to the fire.

Joffrey lay face down on a pallet of damp straw and buried his dark head in his folded arms. Fighting overwhelming emotion, he mourned the loss of everything he held most dear. *If only my father had done things differently he might be still be alive, and I might now be on my way home to Lockton Castle.*

A desire to seek revenge for his father's death throbbed within Joffrey's breast, but he lacked the courage or the wherewithal to do anything about it. Rolling on to his back, he stared through a grimy window embrasure. A small spider crafted a web from one side of the opening to the other. Creatures trapped within the gossamer threads struggled to break free. Joffrey observed the insects with malevolent interest, and an idea began to formulate in his mind. Instead of making a head-on challenge to recover his Lockton Castle estate, he decided to spread a web of evil across the district. Little by little, he would suck the lifeblood out of Sir Edred and his cohorts. *Once I have broken the mighty lord, I will regain my tenure of Lockton Castle.* Unaware of Sir Edred's changed circumstances, Joffrey finally drifted off to sleep.

CHAPTER TWO

Skelgut

Annie Brody leaped from the bed she shared with her wheelwright husband and fell over a brood of chickens in her haste to investigate a noise outside. She eased open the cottage door, allowing a blast of winter air to enter the already chilly room.

"Gawd help me," she sniffled. "'Tis cold enough to freeze the leg off an iron pot!"

"Shut the door, woman!" hollered Jeremiah Brody. "I am near froze to death!" Kicking a stray chicken off the bed, the wheelwright drew a threadbare coverlet over his head.

"Quit squawking, husband – you are worse than a clutch of chickens. I ain't leaving this doorway 'til I see what is going on."

Fancy-looking people on horseback rode along the pathway between the lakeside and Skelgut's row of tumbledown cottages. Cartloads of older folk, children, and servants followed the horses. Dogs of all sizes yapped and snapped at each other, hackles bristling, as they jostled to keep up with their masters.

Clad only in her under-shift and no footwear, Annie's teeth chattered; nevertheless, she refused to budge until the last cart disappeared around a bend in the road. Blue with cold, she returned to bed and shoved her icy feet on Jeremiah's bare backside. "Well! What do you make of that?" she demanded, hogging more than her fair share of bedclothes.

Jeremiah wriggled away from his wife. "Od's blood woman, your feet are colder than the chunks of ice what floats in the lake."

"'Tis not my feet I refer to, y' great lummox! I want to know who all them fancy folks are. Where have they been and where are they going? We ain't seen the likes of them hereabouts for many a long day. Maybe they been visiting Lockton Castle."

"If they be as fancy as you say," said Jeremiah, yanking at the bedcovers, "Sir Ragnald must have come into a goodly sum to entertain such folk. Maybe now would be a good time to demand payment for the last pair of wheels I made for his highfalutin lordship."

Annie hunkered further down the bed, worried what might happen to Jeremiah if he followed up his threat. "You need to be careful, husband. Sir Ragnald will, like as not, set his bully boys on us if you press him for payment."

"Bully boys or no, I ain't doing no more work for that pinchpenny 'til I see the colour of his money!" Jeremiah wriggled on the thin straw pallet, which formed the only padding between his bones and the bed's wooden frame. "If those people you saw came from the castle, I wonder which poor beggar met his maker to provide our horrible lord with the money to fund his carousing." Jeremiah paused thoughtfully then added, "Always assuming he returned to the castle – I ain't seen hide nor hair of him lately and, as far as I know, neither have any of our neighbours."

Lacking energy and enthusiasm to begin another miserable, hungry day, Annie and Jeremiah remained in bed. Huddled together for warmth, they dozed until a frantic knocking at the door of their cottage jerked them awake.

"Now what?" squawked Annie, pushing her husband to the edge of the bed. "You had best go and investigate before someone breaks down our door."

Jeremiah scraped greasy strands of dark hair away from his pale face and, pulling a pair of breeches up over his nightshirt, he grumbled his way to the door and cracked it open. Desdemona Whittle, gossip and trouble maker, dithered on the doorstep.

"What d'you want?"

"If you let me in, I will tell you something you might like to hear," smarmed the thin, mousy-haired woman.

Intrigued, Annie scrambled out of bed and wrapped a frayed shawl around her shoulders. "Come away in, Mistress Whittle; we will sup a drop of broth together." She kicked at a pile of rags under which her young son slept. "Get out of there and stir some life into the fire, lad!"

Desdemona viewed Mistress Brody's unkempt appearance with distaste. The woman was a smelly disgrace with her dark, matted hair, and eyes gummed with sleep. The dirt floor of the Brody's cottage, liberally spattered with droppings from a milk cow and a few egg-laying chickens, had clearly not seen a broom in a long time. "'Tis hard to find decent rushes to freshen a place up these days." Desdemona cocked her head spitefully, "Even though I says it myself, I usually manage to keep my floor clean."

Lacking energy for a fight, Annie allowed Desdemona's barb to go unanswered.

Fourteen-year-old Ruben Brody eyed the visitor with profound dislike. He had been on the receiving end of her sharp tongue more than once, and he resented the woman's presence in his home. Squatting beside the central hearth, he pushed twigs into a pile of ash. Charged with keeping logs of wood at a low smoulder throughout the night, he hoped sufficient heat remained to produce flames. But the ashes were colder than a two-day corpse.

Jeremiah glared at his skinny offspring then clipped his ear. "Stupid boy, you let the fire burn out again!"

"Seems I ain't able to do owt right in this place," Ruben snivelled. "If I let the fire burn too low, I am in trouble. If the flames blaze high, I cop a clout for burning overmuch fuel." He hurled a bundle of dry kindling onto the hearth and bashed a flint against the stonework to create sparks.

Annie shoved her feet into a pair of old boots and disappeared with a jug to fetch water from the lake. She returned moments later to add more liquid to a thin lentil and onion broth. Flames licked around the blackened iron cauldron in the centre of the fire, and steamy bubbles eventually popped on the surface. Annie scooped ladles full of liquid into four wooden bowls, and handed them around. The broth tasted watery, but at least it was hot.

Jeremiah gulped down a couple of spoonfuls, then stared pointedly at his unwanted visitor. "Well, now, Mistress Whittle, are you going to sup at our table, making the most of our fire – or are you going to tell us what you *think* we need to hear?"

Smoke from the hearth billowed into Desdemona's face, causing her to cough and sneeze. "I was fetching fresh rushes from the lakeside for my cottage floor." She wheezed and wiped away streams of tears. "And who do you suppose I bumped into?"

Annie rolled her eyes. "I have no idea, but I am sure you are going to tell us."

"Oh, aye – I got a real shock and no mistake. I ain't seen the woman for a long time. Not since she flew the coop at the castle."

"What woman?" Jeremiah roared.

"Mistress Foley, of course, her that used to be Sir Ragnald's housekeeper. I walked along beside her for a step or two and she told me she spent Yuletide at Lockton Castle with the new lord."

Annie threw her empty bowl into a wooden bucket. "God help us woman! Getting information out of you is like drawing teeth. For pity's sake tell us – who *is* the new Lord of Lockton?"

Her feathers ruffled, Desdemona simpered. "Well it ain't Sir Ragnald, that's for sure. I am told he bit off more than he could chew with his last little foray."

"What do you mean?" Jeremiah growled, his interest aroused.

Desdemona lowered her voice, and glanced furtively from side to side. "By all accounts, men were catapulted into the air on spouts of flame. Mistress Foley reckons the smell of scorched flesh was akin to the odour of spit-roast pork. She told me Sir Ragnald escaped the initial onslaught, but he met his maker at the hands of a fellow named Sir Edred. The carnage was so terrible, folks believe the battle was won with the aid of sorcerers. Ragnald's son, Joffrey, vanished after the event an' all."

Annie's grey eyes grew round with fright and her face paled under its layer of grime. "Sorcerers? I want nowt to do with any form of wizardry."

"I am far more concerned over the disappearance of Sir Ragnald's son," thundered Jeremiah. "Cartloads of sorcerers would prove no match against that evil young viper."

The three-legged stool proved a challenge for

Desdemona's bony backside and she shuffled about, trying to find a more comfortable position. "According to Mistress Foley, Sir Ragnald's son was not one of the charred bodies the Bayersby men buried after the event." She narrowed her bulbous brown eyes. "I give not a tinker's cuss what happened to Joffrey, just so long as he don't fetch up here again."

Jeremiah scratched his bristly chin. "If Sir Ragnald and Joffrey ain't coming back to Skelgut, who is to be master of Lockton Castle now?"

"Mistress Foley reckons the new master is a young apothecary by the name of Oric."

CHAPTER THREE

Oric Appoints a Steward and a Reeve

February behaved true to form, blanketing the countryside in a thick layer of snow. Strong winds blew icy drifts against Lockton Castle's walls, and no-one ventured outside unless it was necessary. Supplies of food and firewood dwindled, and the eight hungry inmates huddled together around the inglenook fireplace in the Great Hall.

Everyone rubbed along well, except for gatekeeper Rory. The man proved workshy and sneaky, filching extra food when he thought no-one was looking. His efforts to clean out the moat ground to a halt at the first sign of inclement weather and so did his personal hygiene. "I ain't stripping off my clothes to plunge bits of my person into a bucket of water what needs the ice broken first. Nor am I going near that cesspit of a moat again 'til the weather warms up." He hogged more than his fair share of the fire and moved away only at mealtimes.

Hamish, another ex-member of Sir Ragnald's workforce

also remained at the castle. The burly Scot had fallen from his horse before Yuletide and snapped his leg. The broken ends of his shinbone protruded through his flesh and he dragged himself around with the aid of a pair of makeshift crutches. Unless the wound received treatment soon, he would spend the rest of his life as a cripple – always supposing he survived at all. Oric attempted to explain the situation, but his words fell on deaf ears.

"Och, aye, and who is gonn'e fix me? Tell me that, young fella. Ah see no miracle workers hereabouts."

"I have mended many broken bones in the past," said Oric, crossing his fingers behind his back. He had assisted Master Ichtheus to perform the operation several times, but he had not yet attempted the job by himself.

Worn down by pain and the inability to get about as he would like, Hamish grudgingly allowed Oric to look at the twisted limb.

"This break will not be easily fixed, but I reckon we can get you moving without your crutches given time. Come summer you may be able to ride a horse again."

"In that case what are we waitin' for? Get on wi' it, lad. Where d' y' want me to sit?"

Oric prepared wide strips of leather and left them soaking in warm water, whilst Ned fetched the stable boy, Walter. Exuding confidence for the sake of his patient, Oric rolled up his sleeves. "You cannot sit for this procedure, Hamish, you must lie full length on the table."

Having witnessed Master Ichtheus' bone-setting techniques in the past, Ned instructed Walter to take a firm grip on Hamish's brawny shoulders. He nodded briefly to Oric, and grabbed the patient's feet.

"Brace yourself," warned Oric. "This may hurt."

"Aye, lad, I am ready."

Oric felt for the broken ends of bone and, before the big Scot had time to protest, he forced the two pieces of shin into alignment.

Hamish screamed and passed out.

"Keep a firm hold on him boys, in case he regains consciousness and tries to move." Working quickly with the strips of wet leather, Oric bound the area around the break. "As the leather dries," he explained, "It will shrink and hold the leg in place until the bones knit together." The operation complete, Oric helped carry Hamish to a straw pallet beside the fire. Cared for by kitchen maids Faylinn and Genevieve the big Scot soon regained consciousness. He sat propped up against pillows, wiry red hair awry, grinning like a callow youth as the girls plied him with hot broth from a spoon.

Satisfied with his work, Oric issued instructions for Hamish's care. "If he develops a fever, let me know at once. Keep him still, for he must not put weight on his injured leg for several weeks."

The foodstuffs Sir Edred had left behind dwindled, and everyone's rations were reduced. Bad weather froze the land as hard as iron, preventing Oric from foraging for edible roots and plants. Braving the raw winter conditions, Ned, Joe and Walter ventured outdoors to hunt down a deer. Butchered and frozen away in Lockton Castle's dungeon, the joints of meat provided many welcome meals.

Unable to work outside, Oric wandered into the castle library. Books lined the walls, and an oak desk stood in a corner of the room. A rough wooden box looked out of place beside the desk, and Parzifal cocked his leg against it.

"Give over y' stupid mutt!" Oric yelled, swiping at the dog's backside. "Since this box appears to be the only seating in here, kindly refrain from pissing on it." He shoved Parzifal out the door and yelled for Joe to let the dog outside into the bailey.

A ledger marked '*Household Accounts*' attracted Oric's attention. He lifted the leather-bound tome on to the desk and blew a thick layer of dust from the cover. No recent entries had been made inside the book; nevertheless, the outdated information interested Oric. Items of expenditure pertaining to the kitchen, stables, and the estate in general were written in a neat hand. Another column indicated which stores were running low and how soon they would need to be replenished. To bring the figures up to date would be a waste of time, for the storerooms were all but empty. Still, the book would provide excellent guide lines for the future management of the Lockton Estate.

Oric's next find was a weighty bible. A green and silver crest with a wolf rampant above a double knot stood out against the book's black leather cover. The first page recorded marriages, births and deaths. Reading to the bottom of the births column, Oric's heart missed a beat. *Oric, born to Askell and Isolda Stidolph 25th September 1384.* He gasped and, bringing a shaky hand to his forehead, he stared at the handwritten words. Could this be the information he craved? If so, he now knew his family name and his age. In seven months' time he would turn seventeen years-of-age.

Information inside the back cover of the bible led Oric to believe his great-grandfather had built Lockton Castle. No further recordings appeared after thirteen-eighty-four, and Oric wondered if Sir Ragnald had illegally seized the estate around that time.

Gathering his wits together, Oric made a firm decision. Now he knew exactly who he was and where he came from, he would take the bull by the horns and manage the Lockton Estate properly. But he could not do it alone.

Returning to the Great Hall, Oric beckoned to Ned and Joe and tipped his head toward the far end of the vast room, out of earshot of Hamish and the others. "Take a seat, lads, I need to talk to you."

Ned and Joe pulled worried faces. "Has something bad happened?" asked Ned.

"No, nothing to worry about." Oric lowered his backside on to the bench opposite to his friends and folded his arms on the table top. "I have been doing some thinking and I would like you, Ned, to act as my Steward."

Stunned, Ned's mouth fell open. "You would trust me with the financial affairs of your estate?" He scratched at his mop of black hair. "Even though you know of my criminal past?"

"It is because of your past I am offering you the position. That evil moneylender, Esica Figg forced you to steal from folk against your will. When Sir Edred offered you a new start, you jumped at the chance to better yourself. Sir Edred knows you and I are friends, and he encouraged you to remain at Lockton to help me start a new life. I want to continue with my career as an apothecary, so I will need someone reliable to manage the estate. I would like that person to be you, Ned."

Ned's mind whirled. As steward, he would be expected to oversee farm work, collect rents, and keep ongoing accounts of the castle's finances. Workmen and servants would fall under his care, and he would be responsible for keeping the castle supplied with food and drink. All of that aside, he could not read or write too well. "Nay, Oric, I am not up to the job. Best ask someone cleverer than me."

Oric jumped up, knocking over the bench. "Of course, you can do the job! You are the wiliest person I know, and I can think of no-one better qualified for the post."

A warm glow spread through Ned, turning his face rosy pink with pleasure. "Since you believe I am up to the challenge, I will do my best to not let you down." He smiled wryly, "You may need to help me with the paperwork from time to time – just until I can improve my scholarly skills."

Joe's thin face crumpled in deep concern. "Have you a job for me, Oric? I ain't got no place else to go."

Oric swiftly put Joe's mind at rest. "You will join Ned and learn to read and write. I need you to pick up those skills as quickly as possible, for I want you to act as the district reeve."

"But the peasants usually choose their own reeve," cried Joe. "How will they take to a stranger telling them what to do?"

Since I believe no local person is up to shouldering the responsibility, *I* am offering you the post, Joe." Oric handed over a long, white stick he had found among other tools in the stable. "This pole is the reeve's badge of office, carry it with you wherever you go so people will know who you are."

Frowning, Joe ran his fingers up and down the stick's smooth surface. "What exactly does the job entail?"

"A reeve is responsible for getting the peasants to start work on time. He also stops them from making off with the estate's produce. The reeve usually reports back to a bailiff, but until I find someone suitable for the job, you will need to keep me informed of what is happening around the district."

Blowing out a huge breath, Joe nodded his head. "I will be the best reeve ever."

Delighted with the boys' reaction, Oric put his arms around their shoulders. "Come my friends, let us announce our good news."

Everyone congratulated the two new appointees, except for Rory. He put on a good face, but the boys' addition to the

Lockton hierarchy infuriated him. *Am I fit only for opening and shutting a gate, and shovelling filth out of the moat?*

-oOo-

Winter loosened its grip on the countryside and daylight hours lengthened. Oric arose at dawn, and ate a frugal breakfast of dried peas, boiled and mashed into a pulp. Filled with a sense of purpose, he strode across the bailey to the stables. Already up and about, Walter was halfway through his daily chores.

"Morning, Walter. Saddle Jester for me please."

"Aye, sir." Walter grinned, wondering what kind of mischief the stroppy horse would inflict upon his rider today.

The sun rose bright and warm over the horizon, Oric mounted Jester and set forth to reconnoitre his property. The further he rode, the less he liked what he saw. Not only had Sir Ragnald neglected the castle, he had allowed weeds to overtake the farmland, pastures had clearly not been mown for a long time and Brundle Brook, which fed Lake Coughcat, was filled with the dross of many seasons. With minimal knowledge of husbandry, Oric hoped the castle library might provide him with enough information to help Ned run the estate efficiently. One thing he did know – ploughing and planting needed to commence immediately.

Chopping sounds greeted Oric when he returned to the castle. Ned and Walter wielded axes in the outer bailey, and Joe ran back and forth to the woodshed to stack the logs. The pile of firewood, depleted over the winter, had grown considerably in Oric's short absence.

"Can you spare me a moment, please, Ned?" Oric slid down from Jester's back and, true to his wicked form, the horse jerked his head around and nipped his rider on the arm. Oric hastily jumped aside. "Oish! What am I going to do with you, you wretched beast? I swear you are the devil in disguise!"

Ned propped an enormous woodcutter's axe against the wall and strolled to where Oric stood beside the horse. He smothered a chuckle and wiped his brow on his sleeve. "I could give the horse a whack if that would help."

"No need," laughed Oric. "'Tis my own fault for turning my back on the animal. Besides he rarely nips hard." He took a handful of oats from a barrel inside the stable door and offered them to Jester on the flat of his hand. "There is a more pressing matter I need to discuss with you, Ned. I want to know how the folk of Skelgut fare but, for the first visit, I think it best if you and Joe go in my stead. If the villagers believe you are wayfaring workers, they are more likely to talk freely." Oric subconsciously rotated the ruby ring he wore on his finger. "If our local peasants and tenants cannot be persuaded to produce food this summer, everyone in the district may well starve come next winter."

"I agree," said Ned, "but we need to tread carefully. I fear the villagers may be hostile."

Oric's shoulders drooped. "Who would blame them after the privations they suffered under the regime of Sir Ragnald?"

Crossing the inner bailey, Oric saw two people unloading items of foodstuff from a cart and into the kitchen. "Who are you, and what is your business here?" he demanded, making a mental note to chastise Rory for allowing strangers into the castle unannounced.

"Hark at yon hoity toity young lord," exclaimed the larger of the two fellows. "He has got the bit between his teeth since last we saw him." A battered, twin-horned helmet sat atop the visitor's unruly brown hair, and pieces of frayed black ribbon tied off his plaited beard. An assortment of ill-fitting leather clothing hung from his huge frame.

"That is never you, is it, Bannulf?" Oric's spirits lifted at the sight of his old friend.

"Aye your lordship, none other."

"Wait 'til I talk to those boys in the outer bailey – they never said a word about you being here!"

Bannulf chuckled. "Nay, 'tis my fault Ned and Joe remained silent. I wanted to surprise you and swore them to secrecy." The old warrior nodded toward the stables, "As we speak, Sir Ragnald's ex-squires Erik and Arnald are settling in a bull and two milking cows. A couple of sows and a boar are already ensconced in the pigsty. Sir Edred said to tell you a small flock of sheep will be coming your way once the lambing season gets underway." Bannulf pointed to chickens and a cockerel in a separate cage. "In the meantime, these little beauties should provide you with plenty of fresh eggs."

Overwhelmed, Oric grasped Bannulf's hand and pumped it up and down. "Man, you are a sight for sore eyes! Thank God you abandoned Sir Ragnald when you did. Without your input, Sir Edred would have lost his manor and the Bayersby folk, including me, would all be dead."

"I grew heartily sick of the bloodshed Sir Ragnald inflicted; though it took a while to convince Sir Edred of my good intentions." Observing Oric's weight loss, Bannulf added, "Master Ichtheus is worried sick, thinking about you. We would have travelled to Lockton sooner but for the terrible weather." Bannulf hefted a stout wooden box down from the cart. "He packed this container of medicaments to keep you going until you can concoct some of your own. We also brought sacks of seeds and rootstock to start up a new herb garden."

"I am glad of fresh supplies," said Oric, placing his hands on his concave stomach. I needed to take my belt in several notches to hold up my breeches. Everyone at Lockton has shrunk in size since last we met."

Bannulf looked Oric up and down. Topping six feet tall, wide-shouldered and muscular, the golden haired, blue-eyed youth portrayed the proud lineage of his Saxon ancestry. What he had lost in weight he had gained in stature.

"Who is your companion?" asked Oric, nodding his head at a second fellow unloading more bulky items from the cart.

The youth dropped his load, and unwound a strip of cloth from around his head. "Have you forgotten me already, your lordship? 'Tis I, Josh Cole, and mighty glad am I to arrive here in one piece." He eyed Oric belligerently. "You could not have found a more inaccessible spot had you searched the length and breadth of the country, and the road from the valley to the castle is terrible! We had the devil's own job driving the oxen and other livestock up here."

Oric laughed and gave his friend a hug. "It seems you are better in health than temper," he laughed. "How fares your sister, Dian?"

"She is well enough." Josh dragged more items from the cart. "But she is run ragged, helping Lady Myferny to look after Sir Edred."

Oric frowned. "What ails Sir Edred?"

"He has gout, but he refuses to listen to his apothecary's advice. According to Master Ichtheus, Sir Edred continues to gorge on rich food and drinks too much. If he continues along this path, he is unlikely to improve." Josh shook his head. "As far as we can tell, he worsens with every day that passes."

The sky darkened, and fat drops of rain spattered on the ground. "Come, let us finish unloading the cart," interrupted

Bannulf. "If these sacks of wheat, beans and barley seeds get a soaking, they will be of use to neither man nor beast."

With everything safely loaded into the kitchen, Josh braved the wet conditions outside once more to take a swift turn around the outer bailey. Stepping back indoors, he confronted Oric. "I see no evidence of a herb plot, my lord. I thought you might have an area of ground dug over by now." He gave Oric a sideways glance and sighed deeply. "Oh, never mind, once I get settled in I will make a new garden and plant all the seeds and roots Master Ichtheus has sent."

"Settled in!" Oric cried. "What do you mean – settled in?"

Bannulf grinned and bounced on his toes, "Lady Myferny reckons you could do with some extra workers. When Erik and Arnald heard we planned to return to Lockton, they asked to come along an' all. The castle was once their home, albeit not a very happy one under Sir Ragnald's tenure. We are here to stay, my lord, if you will have us."

"Of course, I will have you and welcome," cried Oric. "I have sorely missed you both. Besides, Lockton is in a sorry state of disrepair and I need all the help I can get. But who is caring for my hut and herb plot since you are come to Lockton Castle, Josh?" Oric had enjoyed stolen moments with Dian in his moorland garden near Bayersby Manor and he hoped his special place would not become derelict.

"My younger brother says he will look after your garden," said Josh, pulling a wry face. "Who knows, Mother might allow my younger siblings to join him. Conditions in your old hut are cramped, but anything is better than the filthy hovel my brothers and sisters live in at present. Our parents are nowt but drunkards, and Father spends most of his earnings as an odd job man in the Kilterton Inn. The children are always hungry, and I believe they deserve a better life. Bayersby Manor is close by so Dian can keep an eye on them."

Mention of Dian twisted a knife in Oric's heart. If she visited his old herb garden, would she recall the friendship they enjoyed before his inheritance changed their lives forever?

CHAPTER FOUR

Ned and Joe Visit Skelgut

"I hope this donkey is sure-footed," said Ned, digging his fingers into Otty's thick mane. Every bend along the way revealed views of the valley far below and, terrified of heights, Ned's stomach churned with nerves.

Melted snow followed by weeks of torrential rain had turned the pathway to and from Lockton Castle into a quagmire, and black clouds threatened more rain.

Mounted on the donkey behind Ned, Joe squeezed his eyes shut and clung tightly to his friend's back. "What do you reckon the villagers in Skelgut will make of us?"

Ned pulled his shabby doublet closer to his chest. "We look like a pair of no-account vagabonds, so I doubt folk will pay us much attention."

At the bottom of the steep track, the boys congratulated themselves upon their safe arrival. "I ain't looking forward to our return journey," said Ned, loosening his grip on Otty's mane for the first time since the beginning of the journey. "When the weather improves we must clear a better pathway between the castle and the village. Something tells me we will be making many trips back and forth in the future."

Gusts of wind rippled the surface of puddles in the track between Skelgut's row of dismal cottages and Lake Coughcat's shoreline. "Ain't much area between the water's edge and folks' homes!" remarked Joe, eyeing the grey, wind-ruffled white caps on the lake. "If I lived here, I would never sleep nights for fear of a flood."

A crack of thunder followed by a vivid streak of lightning caused both boys to jump and duck.

Ned glanced left and right along the deserted street. "Do you reckon anyone still lives here? I see no sign of human life."

"What if the villagers are all dead?" Joe whimpered. "Oric heard folk were near starvation."

"'Od's blood! What a terrible thought." Ned's stomach roiled at the very idea. "I hope they are all indoors, sheltering from this miserable weather."

Engrossed with their observations, the boys failed to hear Skelgut's wheelwright creep up from behind. "What is your business here?" Jeremiah Brody bellowed, brandishing a pitchfork perilously close to the boys' faces. "We ain't keen on strangers skulking around our village."

Startled, Ned almost lost his seat on the donkey. "And we ain't keen on folk shoving a pitchfork at us neither. Put it down before you do someone damage."

A smaller, red-faced version of the fork-brandishing individual raced out of the wheelwright's rundown premises. Tossing a heavy wooden mallet from hand to hand, Ruben Brody squared up to Ned and Joe. "Do not dare to threaten my father!" he yelled, "or I will have a piece of you."

"Get back inside, boy, I can handle this." Jeremiah glared at his son and continued to make jabbing motions at Ned with the fork. "There ain't nothing here for wastrels. Clear off afore I run the pair of you through."

The altercation took place outside Archie Pender's abode and, hearing angry voices, the old man shrugged into his cloak and hastened outside. A faithful servant of Oric's parents, Archie had spent Yuletide at the castle with the new lord, and he recognised Ned and Joe immediately. "Hold off, Master Brody! I can vouch for this pair, they are from Lockton Castle."

Jeremiah lowered his fork. "Are you telling me this raggedy-arsed pair are our new masters?"

"No, I ain't!" snapped Archie. "But they serve our new lord."

Prickling up like a cat in the face of a mad dog, Jeremiah yelled, "If you know so much, how come you ain't shared this titbit of knowledge with the rest of us villagers?"

"Because you never asked," huffed Archie. "I could be dead for all you lot care. Why should I come out in the cold to knock on your doors to give out information?"

Ned groaned. "So much for keeping our identity secret."

Lornika Fentwhistle, self-proclaimed fortune teller and herbalist, peeped through a crack in her cottage door. Nothing much happened in the village these days and this current disturbance promised a much-needed diversion. Covering her carrot-red hair with a shawl, she shoved her feet into a pair of large boots and scurried along the road toward the group of noisy people.

Doors up and down the street creaked open, and more folk braved the weather to investigate the upset. In awe of Mistress Fentwhistle, the villagers allowed the tall, thin woman to push her way between them.

"Stand back, Brody. You are naught but a rabble-rousing ignoramus who knows nowt about owt." Mistress Fentwhistle placed both fists on her bony hips and thrust her beak-like nose close to Ned's face. "So, young feller-me-lad! What brings you and your little friend to our village?" She smiled unpleasantly, her beady green eyes gleaming with curiosity. "You had best come to my house before these yokels tear you both limb from limb."

The sign, hanging from a gibbet-like structure beside Mistress Fentwhistle's garden gate, informed Ned and Joe they were about to enter Langend Cottage. Written below the cottage name were the words: *Lornika Fentwhistle. Herbs and potions for all ailments. Fortunes told.*

Hitching Otty to a fence post, the boys scrutinised the woman's odd-looking house. The dwelling, surrounded by a sizeable parcel of land, was the best maintained property in the village. A neatly clipped thatch roof dipped toward the ground at each end of the building and stout timber shutters covered two narrow windows.

Lornika kicked off her boots outside her arched front door and indicated that Ned and Joe should do the same. "No point treading muck into the house causing me extra work, is there?" She smiled benignly, exposing pink gums and two rows of small teeth.

Uncomfortably aware she trod a fine line between fortune telling and witchcraft, Lornika pursued her clients with caution. She possessed no real skills in either profession, but she eavesdropped on conversations and used things she overheard to her advantage.

A shiny black raven swooped down from the cottage rafters and landed on Lornika's shoulder. "Beware, strangers! Beware, strangers!" The bird dug its clawed feet into the woman's shawl, and preened her hair with its shiny black beak.

Lornika poked her finger in amongst the raven's sleek feathers and scratched his pimply skin. "My bird is better than a guard dog, but he will do you no harm." She indicated a high-backed settle beside the brazier, and invited Ned and Joe to sit down. "Make yourselves at home, I will bring you some refreshment." Lifting a large brown bottle from the table, she poured two drinks into leather vessels, and handed one to each of her visitors.

The elixir, concocted from the seeds of corn roses gathered from summer hedgerows, acted as a mild sedative. Eased into a pleasant, soporific state, Lornika's clients talked about themselves without realising how much information they imparted. In awe of Mistress Fentwhistle's cleverly constructed predictions, folk parted with money and goods they could ill afford.

Flashing Ned and Joe an insincere smile, Lornika proffered more drink. "Should you ever require medical assistance, I have the ability to cure many ills. I also have an extensive knowledge of lunar and celestial patterns. Folk travel from miles away to hear my weather predictions." Pictures of moons and stars dotted across Mistress Fentwhistle's lime-washed walls backed up her story.

Bleary eyed, Ned and Joe sipped more elixir and smacked their lips. Feeing relaxed and sleepy, they told Lornika everything she wanted to know about the new Lord of Lockton.

In a mellow mood, Ned gazed through cracks in the shutters. Daylight was fading. Shocked, he jerked his body upright, and jabbed Joe's leg with his heel. "How long have we been here? Wake up, Joe! I have changed my mind about spending a night in the village. We must hurry if we are to reach the castle before dark."

Before Ned and Joe had time to gather their scrambled wits, they stood shivering on Lornika's doorstep. Joe pulled on his boots and brushed a hand across his eyes. "I feel a bit funny. Kind of dizzy in the head."

"Maybe you stood up too suddenly." Loath to admit he felt much the same, Ned unhitched Otty from the gatepost. He swung into the saddle and hauled Joe up on to the donkey's rump. "Hang on little 'un, a brisk ride will soon clear your head."

Half way home, Ned reigned the donkey to a sudden halt. "Y' know what, Joe? We ain't got any information worth passing on. Mistress Fentwhistle revealed precious little about herself, save she professes to be a fortune teller." Silently berating himself, he added, "Oric ain't going to be impressed with us."

Joe huddled closer to his friend. "What about that evil-looking raven? I ain't never heard any creature talk like it did. Maybe Lornika Fentwhistle is a witch, and the bird her magic spirit."

"I am more concerned about the villagers' less than friendly welcome." Ned clicked his tongue to move Otty forward. "Thank goodness Archie stepped in when he did. Without his help, I reckon we might be manacled to a cart in some out of the way hay barn right now."

CHAPTER FIVE

Change of Master

Joffrey idled away two of the most miserable months of his life. The Dunburton cottage he called home continued to leak, despite all efforts to patch up holes in the roof with interwoven sticks coated with mud. Henchmen Cadwin and Leofrick gathered firewood from around the village and dragged it indoors, but the rotten wood proved too damp to remain alight and everyone shivered throughout the long, cold winter nights.

On the point of starvation, all but two of Sir Ragnald's mercenaries rode out of the village, leaving Joffrey's plan to undermine and demoralise Sir Edred in tatters. After all, what could three weak and dispirited fellows do to unseat the mighty Lord of Bayersby?

A few shrivelled onions, gathered from cottage gardens, and a clamp of turnips provided Joffrey and his two loyal supporters with their only food.

"I ain't sure how much more of this vegetable stew I can stomach," grizzled Leofrick.

Cadwin glared at the unkempt mercenary. "If you got

off your lazy arse and helped me to snare a rabbit or two, we might all enjoy a more varied diet."

Sick of his henchmen's constant bickering, Joffrey left the cottage interior to sit on the doorstep. He longed to get away from Dunburton with its dismal rows of derelict dwellings, but he had nowhere else to go and no money to pay travelling expenses.

Hawkers had long since ceased to pass through the deserted village, and Joffrey was surprised to see a plump, well-dressed fellow drive a smart horse and cart along the road. The newcomer reined his conveyance to a stop abreast of Joffrey and doffed his hat. "Greetings, my good fellow! I have driven a long way today and I am weary. Can you direct me to a comfortable inn?"

Joffrey considered the fellow's expensive clothes and sniggered. "No fancy accommodation around here, my friend! Kilterton is the next settlement to the west, and you have left it too late to arrive there before dark." Not wanting to miss the chance of making a copper or two, Joffrey offered to share his humble abode. "You are welcome to rent part of my accommodation – if you wish."

"That is very civil of you, young sir." The short, fat man wobbled down from his perch on the cart, and thrust out a pale, podgy hand. "Amery Trundle at your service."

"Pleased to make your acquaintance. I am Joffrey."

Once inside the cottage, the newcomer's face fell. "'Od's blood, sir, my pigs back home live in better conditions than this!"

But there was no longer any 'back home'. An ill-educated medicine man and barber, Amery Trundle had dispensed one too many bad potions along with indifferent haircuts. His last patient died an agonising death and Amery fled in the dead of night before the victim's relatives could call the magistrate. Already having one summons against him for causing a local dignitary to suffer a horrible eruption of the bowels, Amery believed he would hang as penalty for killing a client. Would he be safe staying in Joffrey's ghastly hovel or should he press on?

Joffrey sensed the fat man's hesitation. "Take it or leave it, my humble abode is all there is on offer hereabouts."

"In that case I have little choice but to accept your offer."

Before fleeing his home, Amery had thrown logs and bundles of kindling on to his cart along with other useful possessions. His supply of dry timber made a better fire than Joffrey and his men had enjoyed in a long while.

Keen to further improve his comfort, Joffrey inspected Amery's cart.

Apprehension tingled along Amery's spine; most of his life savings sat in a box at the bottom of the cart. An emergency supply of silver coins was sewn into the hem of his tunic. Facing three men to one, he had no chance of making a run for it. Amery decided to bluff it out and turned on the charm. "I have an ample sufficiency of food and I would be delighted to share it with you."

Comforted by the fire and a belly full of salt beef and stewed vegetables, Amery overindulged on his own liquor. Drink loosened his tongue and he shared his woes. He awoke the following morning with a sore head and little recollection of the night before.

"I have a small favour to ask of you," said Joffrey, handing Amery a bowl of leftover stew.

Amery squinted at the lithe, swarthy young man. "What kind of favour do you have in mind?"

"I want you to kill someone!"

Amery choked on a spoonful of turnip. "You want me to do what?" He had killed only one person in his entire career, and that was unintentional. "I will do no such thing!"

"Oh, I think you will." Joffrey flapped a sheet of parchment under Amery's nose. "Last night, in your drunken state, you signed this confession. It describes how you *deliberately* poisoned the fellow at Roxbrough. If you refuse to do as I ask, my men will return you to that town, and hand you over to the magistrate."

"I thought we were playing a gambling game," Amery bleated, wringing his clammy hands. "'Od's blood, man, you even won money from me."

Joffrey curled his lip into an unpleasant sneer. "Perhaps next time you sup with strangers, you will drink less copiously, and still your tongue."

Blood drained from Amery's face. Sick to his stomach, he nodded and awaited Joffrey's instructions.

"Kill Sir Edred of Bayersby, and I will allow you to go about your business. Fail, and I shall see you dance at the end of a hangman's noose."

-oOo-

Severe weather kept the Bayersby folk indoors and, bored with enforced inactivity, Sir Edred continued to over-indulge on rich food and home-made wine. His gout flared up, and he took to his bed.

Ichtheus spread comfrey root on squares of leather, and wrapped the poultices around Sir Edred's swollen feet. The remedy brought some relief, but Sir Edred refused to give up his rich food and copious quantities of liquor.

In desperation, Ichtheus presented his master with a sprig of dried gout-wort to hold against his feet, but Sir Edred tossed the herb to the ground. "Get away from me, you foolish old goat, I swear your horrible medications are making my condition worse."

Determined to see Sir Edred well again, Ichtheus summoned up his courage and voiced his opinion. "My Lord, if only you could moderate your intake of rich food and drink, your condition would surely improve. My poultices are soothing, but to affect a cure we must tackle the problem at the source."

Struggling to sit up in bed, Sir Edred turned a horrible shade of puce. "How dare you tell me what I can and cannot consume. I have followed the same regime for years without suffering any ill effect."

"Aye, sir, but you are not as young as you once were. Your body no longer copes with excess as well as it used to."

The timely arrival in the bed chamber of Sir Edred's wife, Lady Myferny, saved Ichtheus from further expletives. "My Lord, we have a visitor who may be able to help you." She indicated the fat little man at her side. "May I introduce Master Freeman, renowned healer and herbalist."

-oOo-

The late winter countryside resounded with the hoarse cries of young boys as they prodded teams of oxen with pointed wooden goads. Ploughmen tilled at least one field each day, and returned home at dusk to feed and stable their beasts, muck out dung, and clean the ploughshares. The stinking business of digging in manure, both animal and human, followed ploughing before crops of wheat were sown.

Peasants worked long days, broadcasting seeds across the fields by hand. Bundles of brushwood tied to horses' tails were dragged across the earth to cover the seed. Until germination took place, every available man, woman, and child spent all daylight hours banging drums, clapping hands, and shouting to scare away birds intent upon eating the seeds.

Meanwhile, Sir Edred remained indoors in a darkened room. Attended by his manservant and fed a daily dose of plausible lies from his new healer, he flatly refused to see Ichtheus or any inhabitant of the manor other than his wife. After a particularly dreadful night, Sir Edred's attendant approached the apothecary.

Ichtheus hastily put aside his pestle and mortar. "What is the latest news on your master's condition?"

"No improvement. In fact, I believe Sir Edred is worse. He no longer eats, but he drinks the foul mixture that Master Freeman concocts." The servant scrubbed at his weary face. "I reckon the stuff is making him worse."

"How so?" Ichtheus demanded.

"Master Freeman heats crushed seeds over a brazier, and encourages Sir Edred to inhale the smoke. Sir Edred reels in a dizzy fashion before falling into a stupor. When he awakes, he rants and raves like a mad man until Freeman repeats the treatment."

Ichtheus tapped his fingers on the table. "An attack of gout should not make him so ill. Is he still determined not to see me?"

A snort and a small head-shake from the manservant said it all.

Worn out with worry and loss of sleep, Ichtheus confided in Mistress Foley. The housekeeper had arrived at the manor a few months before Yuletide, and Ichtheus had taken a dislike to her. However, over time, he had developed a certain respect for the woman. She was a stickler for getting things done properly, and she cared for the serfs' welfare as no other Bayersby housekeeper had ever done before. And she kept her own counsel.

The housekeeper sat down beside Ichtheus. "I have seen such peculiar behaviour only once before after a fellow imbibed overmuch henbane."

"Aye, I believe you are right, and I dread to think what other filthy potions Master Freeman is pouring down Sir Edred's throat."

The kitchen door flew open, stopping Mistress Foley's reply.

Lady Myferny rushed across the room and grabbed hold of Ichtheus' hand. "Come quickly, Master Apothecary! There is something terribly wrong with Edred."

Ichtheus raced for his master's bed chamber, but he arrived too late to help the Lord of Bayersby. "Find Master Freeman and lock him up," he yelled. "The man is murderer."

Dian did all she could to comfort Lady Myferny, but the beautiful woman was inconsolable. Her violet eyes poured tears as if from an unstoppable source, and her pale hair flew around her head as she tore at it in misery. "I sh-sh-should have listened to Master Ichtheus, but Edred was adamant he did not want our apothecary near." Another torrent of sobs racked her body and, in a similar teary state, Dian guided her mistress away from the room of death and into the women's quarters.

An extensive search of Bayersby Manor confirmed that Master Freeman had vanished, along with his horse and cart, and who knew what else.

-oOo-

Amery Trundle reached for the incriminating parchment that held his confession for past misdemeanours, but Joffrey snatched the page away. "How do I know the deed is done?"

"Oh, the mighty Lord of Bayersby is dead, right enough." Amery showed Joffrey a gold ring engraved with Sir Edred's initials. "Would he give me this family heirloom voluntarily? Not on your life! I dragged it from his finger as he drew his last breath. Before anyone realised what had happened, I was on my cart heading back to Dunburton." With a crisp nod, Amery held out his hand. "Now, if you would hand over my confession note, I will be on my way." He slipped the ring into a small pouch. "Methinks I will keep this little token as payment for services rendered." A smile split his shiny, pink face. "After all, you would not wish to be caught with such an incriminating piece of evidence, would you?"

"Your name will be mud," scoffed Joffrey. "Sir Edred was a popular fellow and every law-abiding fellow in the district will be after you."

Amery sniggered, "Do you imagine for a single heartbeat that I gave my real name? Sheesh! I am not the fool you think me."

"Where will you go?"

"I am hardly likely to impart the truth, am I? Suffice to say, I shall put as much distance between this godforsaken place and myself as swiftly as possible." Amery ran his hands over the gold-brocade tunic stretched across his belly. "I had hoped to retire in my home town, but now I must seek a comfortable life elsewhere. And what does one more death matter if it gains my freedom?" Amery tried to snatch the incriminating parchment from Joffrey's fingers. "I will take that now, if you please."

Joffrey jerked the parchment away. "I do not please. You ain't getting your hands on this until you part with the money you bragged about."

Sweating profusely, Amery shook his head and stood his ground.

At Joffrey's nod, his henchmen moved forward, each grasping one of Amery's arms. "Take him back to Roxbrough."

"All right, all right, you can have my money!" Afraid for his life, Amery unpacked his cart and handed over his life savings. He chose not to mention the Lord of Bayersby's silver hidden in his pouch or the coins sewn into his tunic hem.

Joffrey grabbed the box of coins, and dropped the parchment onto the fire.

With a great sense of relief, Amery watched the page burn. Mustering what little dignity he had left, he repacked his cart and settled his leather hat firmly on his head. "If you will excuse me, I shall be on my way." He climbed onto the driver's seat and urged his horse to trot away from the ghastly Dunburton township.

Elated, Joffrey returned to the cottage. He was no longer a pauper, and Sir Edred was dead. Tawny eyes glinting, Joffrey confronted his two henchmen. "Cadwin, Leofrick – ride to Bayersby Manor first thing tomorrow and ingratiate yourselves with Master Guwain. Discover what he plans for the future and report back to me."

-oOo-

Lady Myferny spurned any idea of burying Sir Edred in St Griswald's graveyard. The church, a short walk from Bayersby Manor, had fallen into a state of disrepair and the overzealous priest, employed by Sir Edred to educate countryfolk in Godly ways, had driven away every parishioner brave enough to attend his services. Local folk now believed the church to be haunted, and they blamed spirits and ghouls for Father Chrispian's sudden and unexpected disappearance. Most people had avoided St Griswald's ever since.

"I shall have Sir Edred's remains interred in the newly constructed Kilterton Priory," Lady Myferny confided to Dian. "It is further to travel when I wish to visit my husband's tomb, but the beautiful building offers a peaceful and dignified resting place for my beloved husband."

Embalmed, the Lord of Bayersby lay in the priory until Guwain could be brought back from Roxbrough Abbey. Upon the heir's arrival home a few days later, Father Fransiscus, Kilterton's young priest, performed the funeral ceremony. The folk of Bayersby and Kilterton paid their last respects and returned to their homes, satisfied Sir Edred had been given a decent send-off. All were concerned about their future, for no-one liked change.

Unable to run the estate on her own, Lady Myferny confronted her son. "Now you are Lord of Bayersby, you must remain at home. Hopefully you have gleaned sufficient knowledge from your father to successfully shoulder your responsibilities."

Guwain puffed out his chest. "Have no fear, mother, I shall do a better job than my sire."

Strutting around the compound, Guwain barked orders to all and sundry. He chased the female serfs, mercilessly pinching their bottoms and tweaking their hair. The girls complained to Mistress Foley who in turn spoke to Lady Myferny. Lady Myferny chastised her son, but he laughed in her face. "I am lord and master now, dear Mother. These people are my servants and I shall treat them as I see fit."

To protect herself from Guwain's unwanted attentions, Dian stayed close to her mistress, but she needed to enter the servants' hall at mealtimes. Guwain blustered and bellowed wherever he went and, hearing him coming, Dian avoided him as best she could. Nevertheless, after a mid-day meal, Guwain accosted her in a narrow passageway.

Dian bobbed a curtsey, "Excuse me, sir, I am needed in the women's quarters."

Guwain was having none of it.

Unable to push past him, Dian attempted to retreat the way she had come.

Guwain backed her up against the wall. "Why are you in such an uncommon hurry? Come on, girlie, I only want a little kiss." He brought his fleshy lips down hard upon Dian's mouth.

Dian jerked her head to one side.

Guwain grasped hold of her jaw and forced her face close to his. "I am your lord and master, you would do well to obey my orders."

Nauseated by the smell of raw onion and sheep's cheese on his breath, Dian attempted to pull her head away.

"So, you think to play the hoity-toity miss with me, do you?" Guwain leered. "I know your type – you tease with your flashing eyes then squeal like a stuck pig when confronted by a real man." He pressed his body against Dian until she thought her spine might snap.

Sticking out his tongue, Guwain licked Dian's neck. Close to her ear, he whispered, "You ain't the innocent you pretend. I watched you with the apothecary's assistant." He traced his forefinger down Dian's cheek, "I wager *Sir* Oric no longer wants you now he is a high and mighty lord." Guwain fumbled with Dian's clothing. "I suggest you be nice to me unless you want to lose your position as ladies' maid."

Repulsed and terrified, Dian struggled to break away from Guwain's sweaty clutches but he held her tight.

Walking by the entrance to the passageway, Ichtheus

noticed the frantic activity. "What is going on here?" he roared, striding toward the disturbance.

Guwain backed off abruptly, and Dian collapsed on to her knees.

"I caught this wench stealing money," he stated. "I warned her, if she is caught doing such a thing again – she will be thrashed like a common thief, ladies' maid or no." Dusting himself down, Guwain turned on his heels and swaggered away.

Ichtheus helped Dian to her feet. "Oh, you poor girl! What has that wretch done to you?"

Dian looked like a small deer trapped in the sights of a huntsman. "Please, do not concern yourself, Master Ichtheus. Everything is fine." Hugging herself tightly, she hurried off along the passage.

The situation at Bayersby Manor deteriorated. Employees who dared to cross their new lord were dismissed on the spot. With no steward, bailiff, or reeve to direct work, chaos reigned.

-oOo-

Joffrey's two henchmen dismounted and led their horses through Bayersby Manor's open gate. Inside the compound chickens ran loose and pigs rooted up clarts of mud wherever they chose. A few serfs trailed about with no apparent purpose, but no-one came forward to enquire what the strangers' business might be. Cadwin and Leofrick secured their mounts to posts in the compound and entered the manor house to seek out the young lord.

CHAPTER SIX

Oric Seeks Help

The pain in Hamish's leg subsided and the big Scot sat at the kitchen table, helping to prepare vegetables for the main daily meal. Possessed of a wry sense of humour, he teased maids Faylinn and Genevieve mercilessly. Glad of his help, the girls bore his gentle ribbing with good humour. When his daily chores were finished, Josh often dropped into the kitchen to chat with Hamish and Oric.

Talking together over a pot of ale, Ned slanted a knowing look at Oric. "Looks like Josh and Faylinn are becoming more than just friends."

"Is that so?" Bound up with his own thoughts and worries, Oric had not noticed the budding romance.

"Aye, I saw them holding hands in the kitchen when they thought they had the room to themselves." Ned laughed, "Good luck to them I say, we could do with a few joyful happenings around here."

Oric grinned and nodded, delighted to hear the young couple were getting along well. But their happiness made his longing for Dian hurt more than ever.

-oOo-

Strong winds blew March out. April brought warmer days and the Easter festival. Josh strode into the kitchen with a dead peahen dangling from his fingers. "There you are girls," he said, swinging the weighty bird onto the table with an almighty thwack. "Do you reckon you can pluck, stuff, and cook this beauty for our Easter feast?"

"Take it to the cellar before you fill the kitchen with feathers," cried Faylinn. Josh retrieved the bird, and Faylinn followed him down stairs.

The Lockton folk worked as a team, digging, planting, and caring for the animals. Two sows gave birth to healthy litters and the chickens, well fed on kitchen scraps, laid sufficient eggs for everyone to enjoy. The rooster excelled himself, and several broody hens sat on clutches of fertilised eggs.

With Ragnald's long-ago assault on Lockton Castle in mind, Oric asked ex-warrior Bannulf to organise instructional combat sessions. "Our number might be small, nonetheless, we need to hone our skills to defend the castle, should the need arise."

Bannulf wholeheartedly agreed and drilled everyone in the art of swordsmanship and archery. Target practice took place two or three times a week in the outer bailey and from the ramparts of the castle. Determined to pull their weight in the face of any threatened danger, Faylinn and Genevieve joined in and became passable archers.

After the apothecary's shared working conditions at Bayersby Manor, Oric revelled in the peace Lockton Castle offered. He commandeered one of the turrets and spent many happy hours concocting new medicaments and recording new recipes in his journal.

Most days Josh worked in his large garden on the plateau outside the castle walls. Colewort, catmint and comfrey grew alongside feverfew, mint and dock. Rosemary and thyme, grown at Faylinn's request for culinary purposes, perfumed the garden. Carrots, cabbage, peas, beans, beetroot and onions marched in neat leafy rows alongside the herbs.

Visiting Josh's garden for fresh supplies, Oric complimented his friend. "You are a marvel, Josh. I am amazed at how quickly you have turned this piece of rough ground into a show piece." A sheepish grin spread across Oric's face, "I feel guilty stealing so many of your herbs."

Josh leaned on his hoe. "Nay, Oric, that is what the garden is for. No point working the plot as nowt but a show-piece. All thanks to a mixture of sunshine and rain, the seeds Master Ichtheus supplied have germinated well, so there are more good things to come. Pick away to your heart's content."

"I should soon have everything required to cover most medical conditions without needing to forage in the countryside quite so often." Oric said. "My next concern is to obtain enough bottles and jars in which to store my concoctions."

"Is there not a potter in the village who will supply you?" asked Josh.

Oric frowned. "Who would know? Last time I visited Skelgut, the villagers remained surly and unhelpful." He drew in an exasperated sigh, "I suppose there is nothing for it but to return and try to talk folk around."

As good as his word, Oric saddled Otty and put a halter and leading rein on one of the oxen Bannulf had brought from Bayersby Manor. He rode down to Skelgut, leading the docile ox along behind. Dismounting in the middle of the village, he approached a group of peasants gathered together outside the inn.

The inn was in a remarkable state of repair, and the landlord had the largest girth in the district. During the summer months, Gregor collected elder flowers from which he brewed wine. Folk always found ways of getting their liquor and Gregor swapped drinks in return for labour, and whatever foodstuff his patrons had to offer. Travellers occasionally rested at the inn overnight and supplied Gregor with small amounts of money. Thus, the landlord and his family fared better than their half-starved neighbours.

In stark contrast to the inn, cottages and workplaces along the high street looked tumbledown and shabby. Oric's heart ached for the poor souls forced into such abject poverty and he strengthened his resolve to do something about it.

"Could anyone use this fine beast to plough a furrow or two?" he shouted, leading the ox forward.

The villagers mumbled amongst themselves, but no-one raised a hand.

Oric let out a frustrated sigh. "Does anyone around here own a serviceable plough? It is almost too late to plant seeds, but we must try to raise some crops, or we will all be in dire straits come next winter."

The Skelgut blacksmith stepped forward. "Aye yon fellow is right. If we fail to pull together we will lose everything we have worked for over the years." He chafed his upper arms where his biceps had deteriorated from lack of use and good food. "Lord knows, most of us are close to starvation." Pushing back his shoulders he glared at the peasants. "Some of you folk have ploughs but, since I have not seen any of them in my forge for some time, no doubt they are in a poor state of repair. I am willing to hone your ploughshares and repair farm tools in exchange for a morsel or two of food." Spotting wheelwright Brody skulking at the back of the crowd, the blacksmith beckoned him forward. "Hey, Brody, you could fix folks' carts if you put your mind to it."

"Aye, that is all very well for you to say," cried Mistress Brody. "But someone needs to pay for our labours."

"Feeling sorry for ourselves ain't going to solve our problems," retorted the blacksmith. "If we sit on our arses doing nowt – nowt is exactly what we will get. I for one am sick of going hungry and watching my family fade away before my very eyes."

A semi-circle of people crowded in upon Oric and, unable to back away because of the lake's proximity, he put out his hands and gently pushed folk away. "How about I cancel all tithes to the castle until every family is back on its feet? I am unable to pay craftsmen for work, but my steward will keep a record of earnings until the funds become available. Meanwhile I can provide foodstuff from my kitchen garden until you all become self-sufficient again. In return, meadows must be mown, fields ploughed, and crops sown. Many orchards around the district are choked by weeds. Prune and fertilise the trees; let us produce abundant crops of fruit next autumn. Come up to the castle and get vegetable seeds. Thanks to the generosity of Sir Edred and Master Ichtheus, the Bayersby apothecary, I have many varieties to give away. If anyone is unwell, I will supply medicaments free of charge. However, I need pots in which to store my ointments and potions; if anyone knows of a potter hereabouts, please ask him to contact me."

The villagers mumbled amongst themselves, most nodding, a few frowning.

Oric ploughed on. "We also need to increase our herds of cows, sheep and pigs. Whoever owns animals suitable for breeding, get them together and produce new stock."

"A few beasts might still roam about the outlying farms,

but we folk in the village ate most of our animals to stay alive." Mistress Brody glanced at her husband. "We have one cow of calf bearing age, ain't we, Jeremiah? If someone can come up with a bull p'raps our Buttercup will produce an offspring."

The innkeeper's wife put up her hand. "I have a healthy rooster, if anyone wants to put him among their chickens."

"That is all well and good," shouted an old codger, spots of angry colour reddening his cheeks. "After we flog ourselves half to death, how do we know this fellow ain't going to take everything like Sir Ragnald did?" He eyed Oric scathingly. "Besides, what would this fancy young lad know about husbandry? I doubt he has done a hands' turn in his entire life."

"Yes, I have shortcomings," Oric retorted. "But I am willing to learn. If we work together we can undo the damage Sir Ragnald did when he lived in the castle. My ambition is to return Lockton to the thriving estate it was when my ancestors lived here." Having little else to add, Oric tethered the ox to a tree, and remounted his donkey. "I will be off now, but please know you are welcome to visit the castle any time you like."

Desdemona Whittle listened to Oric from behind her open door. Waiting until he left the village, she stepped out into the street. "Who does he think he is, coming down here from his fancy abode, telling us villagers what to do?" Her dark eyes glittered with malice. "I for one am not about to take notice of a thing he says."

"Since when did you take notice of what anybody says?" exclaimed Mistress Brody. "I reckon we should give the new lord a chance. We ain't got nowhere else to go and, if we are to survive another winter, we need help from somebody."

Village hypochondriac, Master Plunket, screwed up his pimply face. "Yon new fellow professes to be an apothecary.

He might do a better job than Mistress Fentwhistle. The last potion she dispensed for me did my innards no good at all." He rubbed his belly, and farted. "Truth be told, she made me feel worse – I ain't moved a stool for days and I feel like my guts are about to burst."

Mistress Brody wrinkled her nose and stepped away from the gaseous odour. "If you propose to prove your point, Master Plunket, I urge you to return home to make your mess."

Lornika Fentwhistle's worst nightmare suddenly became a reality. Since Master Plunket appeared to be impressed with the new Lord of Lockton, many other villagers might feel the same way. If that was the case, she could kiss goodbye many of her clients along with her paltry income. Playing for time she said, "Perhaps we should wait and see what the Lord of Lockton does next."

Everything the young fellow had said made sense to forester, Barda. "You lot can please yourselves," he growled. "If no-one wants to take advantage of yon ox, I will put my hand up. I should have begun tilling my strip of land long since, but I killed our one and only beast to feed the family." He elbowed his way out of the crowd, grasped the ox's halter and headed off toward his smallholding on the outskirts of the village.

Local potter, Zane, kept his own counsel until everyone else had voiced their opinions. Getting by on what he could grow, trap, or scrounge, he longed to get back to work. "I might fire up my kiln again, if the young lord is willing to make potions for the good of us all. I will take a walk up to the castle directly and discuss how many pots and jars he needs."

"What kind of miserable churl are you?" demanded Lornika. "When I asked you to make pots for me you refused.

And I have money to pay you, whereas this new upstart from the castle has not."

"Do not name-call me, Mistress Fentwhistle! Your reputation is not all it might be." Having imbibed one of her potions with catastrophic effect, Zane harboured a deep distrust of the woman's abilities. "When I begin potting again, none of my wares will contain your poisonous potions, Mistress, payment or no."

Village urchins tittered and capered about. Concerned the situation might turn nasty, parents dragged their offspring away. Others also drifted back toward their homes.

"Wait," screeched Lornika. "If others are offering their services free, I will tell fortunes without charge – for a limited period."

With an anything-for-nothing attitude, Desdemona Whittle stepped forward. "In that case, you can begin with me. 'Tis time I got summat for nowt."

Lornika crooked a finger. "Follow me, Mistress Whittle."

A crease of satisfaction quirked the corner of Lornika's mouth. Fed with outrageous predictions, the village gossip would do more damage in a half day than an army of doubters.

CHAPTER SEVEN

Winds of Change

Lornika Fentwhistle's tomcat spent the night terrorising the local rodent population. Come dawn, he yowled at the cottage door, with the remains of a large brown rat dangling from his jaws. Lornika prised the corpse from the cat's mouth and gathered up her pet. "What a clever little fellow you are." The cat purred and nuzzled his mistress' chin.

Lornika observed the villagers going about their daily chores. "Just look at them, Master Puss. Judging by their overactivity, the things I said about the new Lord of Lockton fell on deaf ears. Silly fools are falling over themselves to do his bidding. Nobody ain't been near me for a fortune reading or a potion since he came to the village. At this rate, I foresee my business grinding to a halt." Disgusted with her traitorous neighbours, Lornika retreated inside her cottage and dropped the cat none too gently onto a chair.

Rusted ploughs materialised, as if by magic, from folks' barns, and villeins rounded up oxen and one or two cart horses from outlying farms. The blacksmith inspected ploughshares, and ordered the best of them be yoked to the oxen. Worn farm implements were dragged into the forge for repair. Jeremiah Brody scrutinised a cart with broken wheel spokes and, with the aid of the owner, pushed the battered conveyance into his workshop. Zane dusted cobwebs from his potter's wheel, and fetched a barrowload of good quality clay from his favourite place along the lakeside. Meanwhile, goodwives worked on their vegetable gardens, employing more vigour than anyone had witnessed for many a long moon.

-oOo-

Guwain lolled on a dais in Bayersby's Great Hall. Barely past breakfast he had already downed overmuch ale. Picking up a carafe beside his elbow, he tipped the last drops of liquor down his throat. "Hey, serf, fetch me another pot. And, if you wish to avoid a flogging, be quick about it."

"Aye, sir, at once, sir." Desperate to avoid punishment, the youth took off at a gallop.

In deep mourning, Lady Myferny remained in her room surrounded by her female attendants. Consumed with sadness at the loss of her beloved Edred, she paid little attention to her son's objectionable behaviour.

The late, unexpected arrival of two strangers did nothing to ease the unhappy situation.

Guwain stared at his visitors. "What d'ya want? I ain't in the mood for socialising."

"We ain't here to socialise," smarmed the smallest of the pair. "We are here to ask for employment."

Guwain looked the thin mousy-haired fellow up and down, thinking him too puny to engage in any form of physical activity. "What kind of posts are you seeking?"

"We heard you are short on workers, and we can turn our hands to most things."

"Aye, but we ain't prepared to labour for nowt," chipped in the thin man's swarthy, barrel-chested colleague. "We want paying the going rate for whatever task we take on."

Cadwin slanted a look at Leofrick fit to fell a horse. The fellow lacked tact and Cadwin wished he would shut his mouth. Master Joffrey had ordered them to ingratiate themselves, not put Guwain's back up.

In a state of agitation, Mistress Foley hastened across the room toward Guwain's dais. Observing her master's black expression, she curtsied deeply. "I am sorry to disturb you, my lord, but cook has absconded with most of the kitchen utensils. She reckons they belong to her and she has gone to seek work elsewhere. In her absence, I know not who will prepare your evening meal."

Guwain clenched his fists. "Can you not see I am busy, seek out my mother instead of pestering me with women's work."

"With respect, sir, Lady Myferny is in no state to cope with anything at present."

Guwain leaped to his feet, sending his chair crashing off the dais. "Ye gods woman, can you not cook?" He pounded his fist upon the table, causing the housekeeper to jump with fright. "Get yourself back to the kitchen and produce something edible for the evening meal."

Cadwin and Leofrick exchanged nervous glances. They remembered Mistress Foley from her time as housekeeper at Lockton Castle. But had she recognised them? If so, Master Joffrey's plot to infiltrate Bayersby Manor would end abruptly. To their great relief, the housekeeper returned to the kitchen without a hint of recognition.

Guwain jumped down from the dais. Fists planted on

his hips, he confronted his visitors. "So – who are you, and what are your skills?"

"We can to turn our hands to most things, your lordship." Cadwin smirked at Leofrick. "Though my large friend, here, is better at using his brawn than his brain."

"If that be the case," said Guwain, "all my problems are solved. Since you are blessed with so many skills you can act as my steward." Barely glancing at Leofrick, he added. "Yon muscle-bound half-wit will do well as your bailiff."

Thus, the new Bayersby employees moved into the castle. Using threats and bully-boy tactics, they extorted money and goods from the local peasants and villeins. Guwain received an income, but Joffrey received more. Pleased with their work, he doled out wages to keep his two henchmen on side.

At the end of each day, Cadwin and Leofrick joined in Guwain's nightly sessions of overindulgence and enjoyed the performances of song and dance the female serfs were forced to perform.

Dian dreaded when her turn to entertain came around. Utterly miserable, she behaved in such lack-lustre fashion that Guwain bellowed at her. "Can you do no better than waft about like a half-starved wraith? Put some gusto into your performance or I will demote you to scullion." Turning to Cadwin he added, "Master Ichtheus once had an assistant apothecary who was totally besotted with the wench – still is as far as I can tell. But she will have none of him, for she believes she is not good enough to warrant his attentions." He flicked a hand under his nose as if trying to disperse an evil smell. "I would get rid of her, but I feel my mother needs the girl's support during her period of mourning." In truth, Guwain's jurisdiction did not extend to his mother's personal servants.

Out of his depth and not man enough to admit it, Guwain accepted the money his two new employees brought to him. He never asked them whence it came. The few Bayersby servants who remained at the manor worked each day until they dropped. Insubordination received instant and brutal punishment. Between themselves, the unhappy serfs referred to Guwain as 'The Tyrant' and crept about the manor in a vain effort to keep out of his way. A small boy misunderstood an instruction, and Guwain flogged him with a leather strap. The child's mother tried to intervene and was forced into a scold's bridle as punishment for her insolence. The iron framework encapsulated her head and a curb plate projected into her mouth, pressing down on her tongue. The poor woman could neither talk nor eat. Left in the device she would die a slow death from starvation, and Guwain held the only key.

Horrified, Ichtheus confronted his young master. "All the years I worked for your father, I never saw a child under the age of fourteen years beaten. Nor did I see the scold's bridle used. Unless you follow your father's kind-hearted example, sir, you may well find yourself without any servants at all. You have already sacked your principal assistants, and some of the lesser serfs have run away. I beg you to temper your ill humour, otherwise I foresee the demise of Bayersby Manor as we know it." In full voice Ichtheus carried on. "And that is not my only concern. Do you think it wise to allow your two latest employees free reign across the district? We know nothing about them."

"How dare you address me in that tone of voice," Guwain ranted, spittle frothing the corners his mouth. "Believe me, Master Ichtheus, your age and longevity of service are all that prevent me from throwing you out on your ear. As for Cadwin and Leofrick, I have absolute faith in them. They keep me supplied with funds; I care not how they do it, just as long as they continue to do so." Guwain flicked his hand in dismissal. "Scuttle back to your dingy lair and stick to mixing potions, old man, otherwise I will have you flogged."

Ichtheus returned to the kitchen, his usually pale cheeks flushed with anger. His fists clenched, he paced up and down the room.

Concerned for his wellbeing, Mistress Foley begged him stop and take a few deep breaths. "Dear man, if you carry on at this rate, you will suffer an apoplectic fit." She handed him a posset of hot milk curdled with wine, and stood by his side until he drank it.

"I know not what to do for the best," said Ichtheus, mopping stray drops of liquid from his beard. "Guwain rides rough-shod over everyone."

"Perhaps we should persuade Lady Myferny to leave the manor. I am sure the few remaining servants would follow her."

Ichtheus' knees suddenly grew weak, and he plopped down on to a three-legged stool. "Aye, Mistress Foley, 'tis easy to say, but I fear the manor will go to rack and ruin if we allow that to happen."

"Is the estate not already going that way? I say let the stupid boy stew in the mess of his own making. If he comes to his senses, we will return and pick up the pieces. With help from the Kilterton folk, we would soon put things right."

"I hear the villagers are suffering too." Ichtheus rubbed his chest as if it pained him. "Guwain behaves more like Sir Ragnald every day. And we all know what happened to Lockton Castle under that black knight's ghastly tenure."

-oOo-

Clad in old clothes, Joffrey saddled his horse and rode from Dunburton to Kilterton. Long haired and bearded, he hoped the villagers would not recognise him. Until he made his peace with Guwain, he risked being lynched for his part in the confrontation between his father, Sir Ragnald, and Sir Edred.

Aided by his henchmen, Cadwin and Leofrick, Joffrey planned to bring the new Lord of Bayersby to his knees – but his interest lay not in the takeover of the manor. A more pressing objective occupied his mind, namely the recovery of Lockton Castle. He perceived Guwain as the only obstacle in his way.

Arriving in the village, Joffrey dismounted outside the inn and handed his horse in to the care of a stable boy. Smoke from a fire on the central hearth hazed the inn's main room, and tallow candles in wall sconces added the sour smell of animal fat to the odour of unwashed bodies. It took a few moments for Joffrey's eyes to adjust to the gloom before he spotted his henchmen at the end of a long trestle table.

Joffrey took a seat and accepted a pot of ale from the inn's serving wench. "So, how goes it at the manor?" he asked, taking a deep draught of ale.

"Ha, you may well ask!" sneered Cadwin. "Guwain shows interest in nothing but the pursuit of pleasure. He cares not where the funds for his excessive lifestyle come from, just so long as we keep him supplied with vittles and money. In the short time he has overseen Bayersby Manor's affairs, the place has deteriorated markedly. The silly fool does not see it and I know not how much longer we can keep on providing him with what he demands. The villagers and cotters are all but on their knees."

"He is a lousy judge of character, too – just look who he chose for his steward and bailiff." Joffrey laughed, ducking to avoid Cadwin's friendly swipe. "Joking aside, do you think our grand lord is sufficiently worn down to accept some help?"

"The foolish fellow has dug himself into such a deep hole, he might be glad to take your advice." Cadwin swigged the last of his ale and summoned a serving wench to fetch him another pot. "But who would know? He is an arrogant little pig."

Joffrey wrinkled his brow. "Aye, but he may not greet me warmly after all that has happened. Unless I can persuade him my father was to blame for his misfortune and none of it my doing."

"Good luck with that idea," retorted Cadwin. "If you are not successful you might find yourself under lock and key, awaiting the arrival of the magistrate to try you."

"Thank you for that," said Joffrey, his voice laced with sarcasm. "Your cheerful input is sure to keep me going." As an afterthought he added, "Mind you pretend not to know me once you return to the manor. It would not do for Guwain to think we are in league."

-oOo-

Past caring who came and went, none of the Bayersby servants noticed a newcomer enter the compound. Intercepting a serf at the doorway of the Great Hall, Joffrey relieved the fellow of a carafe he carried. "I am an old friend of Lord Bayersby, I will deliver his liquor and give him a nice surprise."

Entering the Great Hall, Joffrey approached the dais and made a perfunctory bow. "It seems both commiserations and congratulations are due, my lord."

Bleared by drink, Guwain rose unsteadily to his feet. "How the devil did you get in here? I should kill you after what your father did to me. I never expected to be used as a bargaining tool against my own sire."

Joffrey climbed onto the dais, and placed the fresh carafe of mead on the table in front of Guwain. "I am truly sorry, sir, my father forced me to obey his orders. I am here now, cap in hand, to beg your forgiveness. I am hoping we can rekindle the friendship we once enjoyed."

"I suppose we could," said Guwain grudgingly. "But any sign of disloyalty and I will have my henchmen slit your throat."

"In that case, sir, you have my undying loyalty."

Feeling sorry for himself, Guwain whinged. "There is no-one here of my rank and standing to converse with apart from my mother, and she is in perpetual mourning." He topped up his pot of mead and sipped, glancing at Joffrey as he did so. "No doubt you have heard my father is dead."

Joffrey stared at the floor, pretending remorse. "Aye, my lord, I heard, and I am sorry for it. But I wager you are better placed than me. Not only did I lose my father, I also lost my inheritance. Since you are now custodian of my former home, I am here to suggest a compromise. I believe it may be difficult for you to run both estates efficiently, so I would like to offer my services as Steward of the Lockton Estate in your absence."

"Then I am sorry to say you are here on a fool's errand."

"How so?" asked Joffrey, somewhat taken aback.

"Because Lockton Castle ain't my property," Guwain pushed the carafe of mead toward Joffrey. "Oric is the new Lord of Lockton, and he has papers to prove it."

Joffrey's jaw dropped. "You cannot mean Oric, the apothecary's lowly assistant!"

"The very same. A will was discovered, stating that your father, Sir Ragnald, seized Lockton Castle illegally many years ago. Oric's noble family escaped, but his parents died soon after from some malady or other. Their brat survived but, unaware of his situation, he lived as a servant and, latterly, an apothecary's assistant." Guwain smiled spitefully. "Now it seems he is 'lording it' in your old home."

Joffrey's knees gave way and he winced as his buttocks contacted with a wooden bench. Oric would present a far greater challenge than Guwain. The young apothecary was no fool and, backed by the lineage of a noble family, he had a head start.

"Are you alright?' Guwain asked. "You look like a stunned rabbit."

"I have felt better," said Joffrey, reaching for the carafe of liquor. Taking a swallow of the sweet liquid, he winced as it burned its way down his gullet. "Tell me – how do you feel losing Lockton Castle to Oric?"

"I care naught for the castle or the estate. The property requires too much hard work, and by all accounts the effort affords little income." Guwain's lips stretched into a vicious snarl. "But I would do anything to see Oric discredited."

Joffrey's mind moved faster than a galloping horse. "If we work together, perhaps we can both achieve our ambitions."

"How so?" asked Guwain, his interest instantly aroused.

"I want to return to Lockton Castle; you want to see Oric deposed." One hand on his knee, Joffrey leaned forward. "To aid our cause, we must first discover Oric's Achilles' heel."

"His Achilles' heel!" Guwain scoffed. "Her name is Dian and she lives right here, under this very roof."

Joffrey experienced a lightness of spirit he had not enjoyed since his father's passing. Sir Ragnald's death was well and truly avenged, now he could concentrate on getting rid of Oric. If he could seize the girl, she might well play a major part in the fellow's demise.

-oOo-

A log crackled on the hearth in Bayersby manor's kitchen. Under normal circumstances, the sound would be soporific but, at present, nothing soothed Ichtheus' troubled mind. Chatting to housekeeper Mistress Foley at the end of the day's work, he confessed his concerns. "I wonder what Joffrey is doing here, and why is he suddenly as thick as thieves with Guwain? I thought they were mortal enemies, but seemingly not. Mark my words, that pair are up to no good."

Busy mending a tear in one of Lady Myferny's kirtles, Mistress Foley nodded. "I agree with you, Master Ichtheus. And another cause for concern is the way Joffrey stares at Dian." Agnes broke the thread with her teeth. "Methinks he may have designs upon her but, since he never puts a foot wrong, she has no cause to complain."

-oOo-

Market day in Kilterton dawned warm and bright. Exceedingly worried about the situation at Bayersby Manor, Ichtheus had no ear for the birds' dawn chorus, and he failed to notice the wild flowers in bloom as he travelled along the road. Entering Kilterton's main street, he was saddened to see how few vendors had set up stalls under the huge horse-chestnut trees that lined the thoroughfare. None of the usual market-day cacophony disturbed the quiet atmosphere, and the few folks who turned up looked miserable and down-trodden. Instead of immediately setting up his stall, Ichtheus made a bee-line for the cobbler's shop to catch up on the latest gossip.

Uther's premises appeared much the same from the outside but Ichtheus realised something was amiss the moment he stepped through the door. The cobbler stood idle by his work bench and the pile of leather used for making boots and shoes appeared sadly diminished. Ichtheus forced a cheerful smile. "Good day to you, Uther. How do you fare this beautiful spring morning?"

The cobbler barely lifted his head to greet Ichtheus. "I ain't faring well at all, Master Ichtheus, and, as far as I am concerned, the devil can take this boot-making business."

"Good gracious, man! Surely things cannot be so bad."

"Huh! 'Things', as you put it, are about as bad as they can get. I am currently working on my last order. Tanners Meerig and Lanaval are also suffering. I cannot afford to buy new leather, and neither can anyone else. Other folks are in the same state, buying naught but necessities. Since Sir Edred's demise, Guwain has tripled his tenants' rent. Outsiders have ceased to attend the market because there ain't nothing to buy. Foodstuff is confiscated and taken to the manor to feed the influx of Guwain's ne'er-do-well friends."

"Aye," replied Ichtheus. "I know not where all the disreputable men are coming from, but more trickle in every day."

"If we dare to complain, ruffians are sent into the village to beat up the ones who speak out." Uther laughed mirthlessly, "Only good thing to come out of it as far as I can see, is that the butcher's disagreeable wife is suffering alongside everyone else. For the first time in her life, yon hellcat is short of meat and money."

Ichtheus sympathised but, unable to offer any solutions, he changed the subject. "Are Egglebart and Etheldrida planning to attend the market today?"

"Oh. Aye, Eltheldrida will be here directly," replied Uther. "'Tis her what's keeping the village bairns fed with vegetables and pies. She sneaks stuff to folk without Guwain's men knowing." Uther glanced nervously from side to side. "If they catch her, she will be locked into the stock for days on end. Mind, the only thing she will suffer is her incarceration, for no-one will pelt her with rotten food. She is much loved, and the villagers will look after her until she is released."

Ichtheus tugged at his white beard. "We cannot allow this disgraceful state-of-affairs to continue. Methinks 'tis time to resurrect the Committee of Law. Let us see how many former committee members we can round up. Shall we meet at the inn around noon?"

"Nay, Ichtheus, I would not advise you to hold a meeting in a public place." Uther thrust his head outside the shop doorway and glanced along the street in both directions. "Many spies lurk abroad these days. Let us meet in the backroom of my shop, no-one will hear or see us in there."

CHAPTER EIGHT

Cottage Fire

The first day of May heralded the beginning of summer. Bright sunshine warmed the earth and showers brought forth new shoots, which coloured the brown earth with many shades of green.

Folk decorated their doorways with perfumed sprays of May blossoms, and young maids wore flowers in their hair. Neat rows of cabbages, onions, leeks, and carrots grew in the cotters gardens alongside all manner of herbs, which the goodwives used to flavour soups and stews. Stooks of hay stood in the fields to dry, and orchards shimmered with pink and white blossoms.

Bonfires blazed across the district, and farmers drove their cattle through the clouds of smoke to cleanse the animals of ticks and lice and to increase the cow's fertility. One or two young women leaped smaller fires in the hope of improving their own child-bearing abilities. Faylinn watched them and, waiting until after the last village girl jumped, she secretly took a turn herself. Her feelings for Josh had blossomed, and she hoped he might soon suggest they wed. Keen to have a family of her own, she planned to leave no stone unturned to ensure she gave birth to healthy babies.

As Sir Edred had promised, the Bayersby shepherd sent a small flock of sheep to Lockton Castle and, at the beginning of June, shearing began. Countrywomen harvested and boiled madder, woad, greenweed, and weld, and soaked hanks of spun yarn in the cooled, coloured liquids. Later in the year, the dyed threads of green, yellow, blue, and red would be woven into fabric to make winter clothes.

-oOo-

Oric spent much time hunched over a work bench in his turret room workshop. He experimented with herbal ingredients and wrote down his new recipes in his *Apothecary's Almanac*. He treasured the book, for his mentor, Master Ichtheus, had gifted it to him after the completion of his apprenticeship.

Another ancient *almanac* Oric discovered in the castle's library suggested that rue mixed with salt, walnuts, figs and juniper berries provided a possible antidote to poisons. During his time at Bayersby Manor, a group of siblings had mistaken toadstools for mushrooms. Unable to save any of the children, Oric agonised over his lack of knowledge on the subject. The mother's howls of anguish haunted him still, and he was keen to experiment with an antidote to prevent any future deaths. Salt, walnuts, and dried figs already lay in his store cupboard, but he had no rue or juniper. Oric stretched and rubbed the back of his neck. He would imbibe a small amount of the fungi himself, so the recipe needed to be followed to the letter. With that idea in mind, he wandered outside to talk to Josh.

Parzifal, who rarely strayed from his master's side, also stretched, yawned, and shambled after Oric.

Hot sunshine streamed from a cornflower-blue sky, and Josh's discarded tunic lay in a heap on the grass.

"Morning, Josh. The garden is looking good," said Oric, picking a spray of lavender. He crushed the narrow grey leaves between his fingers to release the plant's sweet perfume. "Do you have rue and juniper planted?"

"I have rue, but it is not yet fully grown. You will need to wait until June or July before it is ready to harvest. Juniper takes a few years to mature, however, I saw a few shrubs clinging to the shaly slopes of the mountain at the back of the castle. I can collect some for you if you wish."

Josh, with his freckle-dusted nose and mop of unruly brown curls, resembled his sister Dian. Reminded of his lost love, Oric experienced a deep feeling of longing for the young woman.

"How goes it?" Pulling himself together, Oric managed a small grin. "We are both so busy I barely see you these days."

"I could not be happier." Ready for a rest and a chat, Josh stopped work and rested his back against the sun-warmed castle wall. "You are pleased with my production of herbs, and the kitchen maids love the fresh vegetables I bring to them each day. What more could a fellow ask for?"

"Aye," replied Oric, his blue eyes twinkling. "And I bet one of the young ladies in question loves more than your vegetables."

A wave of hot colour flushed Josh's sun-bronzed face. "How did you know Faylinn and I like one other?"

Oric bumped shoulders with his friend. "The way your faces light up each time you set eyes on each other is a real giveaway."

"'Od's blood," exclaimed Josh. "We wanted to keep things quiet 'til we were sure of our feelings." He picked at a rough spot of wood on the hoe's handle, and cursed when a splinter ran into his thumb. "Is anyone else aware of our friendship?"

Oric laughed. "I doubt your 'friendship' with Faylinn has gone unnoticed by anyone."

The agitated arrival of Joe saved Josh from any further embarrassing explanations. "Where is Ned?" The small youth panted, sliding down from the saddle. Hauling off his red neckerchief, he mopped sweat from his face. "We need to get back to the village as soon as possible. Can someone fetch me another beast – this poor fellow has done his dash." The donkey, lathered from nose to tail, snorted for breath.

"What ails you?" cried Oric, doing his best not to panic.

Revelling in his newfound responsibility as Skelgut's Reeve, Joe often stayed overnight in the village with Archie Pender. The old gentleman with his bent back, and fluff of white hair, became the grandfather figure Joe longed for. Joe, in return, provided a willing set of muscles to deal with chores the elderly gentleman found too heavy to handle.

"I worked for Archie yesterday, but I ran out of time. Rather than trek home to the castle and return the next day, I stayed overnight with him, intending to finish the jobs today. I went to fetch water from the well first thing, and folk were running about the street like headless chickens."

"Whatever for?" Josh demanded, hastily donning his tunic.

"A crazy man accused Mistress Fentwhistle of witchcraft, saying he plans to burn her at the stake. She is trapped inside her cottage, but no-one dares go near. The fellow is standing outside her door brandishing a flaming torch and a battle axe. If she fails to go back to the woods with him, he reckons he will burn down her cottage with her locked inside." Joe tugged at Oric's arm. "If he follows through with his threat, sparks from Mistress Fentwhistle's roof could well set the entire village alight."

"Quick, find Ned," cried Oric. "Where are Erik and Arnald? Maybe 'tis time for our two squires to put their fighting skills into practice. Tell them to fetch pikes and swords. Josh, round up Jester from the paddock and help Walter to saddle him. After we leave the castle, I want you to remain behind and guard the place along with Bannulf, Walter and Hamish." Oric raked his eyes over the deserted gatehouse. "Where the devil is Rory? God rot his guts – he is never there when I need him!"

Not so fresh from his bed, Bannulf scratched his belly and yawned. "What has ruffled your feathers so early this morning?"

Oric described the situation, and warned Bannulf to keep watch with weapons at the ready. "It may be nothing, but better safe than sorry. Drop the portcullis as soon as we leave. When Rory shows his face, tell him to remain on lockdown until we return."

Stableboy Walter arrived in the bailey with Jester in tow. The horse looked ill-groomed after his free time in the paddock and getting a saddle onto his back turned into a free for all. The look in Jester's eyes was all too familiar, and Oric knew his ride to the village would be a challenge.

Ned and Josh led two donkeys from the stables for themselves, and two horses for squires Erik and Arnald. The small cavalcade left Lockton Castle with Oric in the lead on Jester. Having been on the receiving end of the gelding's flying hooves in the past, Parzifal kept a respectable distance between himself and the horse.

The journey had barely begun when Jester clamped the bit between his teeth. He arched his back, cavorted sideways, stopped abruptly, turned in circles, and remained oblivious to Oric's commands. Oric clung on to the pommel, Jester's mane, and anything else within reach. At the bottom of the hill, the gelding splashed joyfully across Brundle Brook ford. Along the lakeside he cantered in and out of the shallows until Oric's boots and leggings dripped cold water. Parzifal cavorted in the lake and yapped until Oric screamed at him to stop.

Between guffaws, Erik and Arnald shouted advice.

"Shut your mouths and mind your own business!" Oric yelled. "I have everything under control." But Jester continued to misbehave, snickering and prancing until the party of riders neared the village. At sight of the melee in the street, he tossed his head, let go of the bit, and behaved perfectly. "I cannot fathom this animal," puffed Oric. "He plays me for a fool when there is no danger, but the moment I encounter any kind of trouble he behaves like an angel."

A black-clad figure wearing a hood, and a rag tied across his face, brandished a fiery torch and a battle-axe outside Lornika's cottage doorway. Several unlit torches lay within easy reach against the wall, ready to ignite when the current torch burned low.

At sight of the man, Parzifal barked repeatedly. Froth from his mouth sprayed the fellow's legs. Afraid for the dog's safety, Oric spurred Jester forward. "Parzifal, get back!" he yelled.

The dog ignored Oric's command and continued to lunge at the madman who blocked Lornika's escape.

Terrified of the dog, the man brandished his torch and accidentally set light to the low-hanging thatch above Lornika's doorway. The dry straw bloomed bright with flames, and plumes of black smoke soon billowed forth from Lornika Fentwhistle's dwelling.

Inside the cottage Lornika screamed to be let free.

Disturbed by the racket, Jester reared up. His flailing hooves missed the arsonist's skull by a whisker. Oric drew his sword, but the man ran into the cottage and slammed the door. Bolts rasped into place, and Oric heard a heavy item being dragged across the floor.

"The walls are afire, fetch buckets and form a human chain between the lake and Lornika's place," yelled Oric, leaping down from Jester's back. "Come on, lads I doubt we can save the cottage, but we must try to save Lornika's life."

Mistress Fentwhistle's popularity had diminished since Oric's arrival at Lockton Castle; nevertheless, the villagers did not wish to see the woman burned alive. Everyone rallied to the cause.

Once the fire was extinguished, Jeremiah Brody threw his bucket on the ground and battered down Lornika's cottage door with an axe. "Where is the misbegotten scoundrel?" he yelled at the terrified female within. "Not only did he threaten your life, he nearly burned down our entire village. When I get my hands on him I will throttle him!"

Coughing convulsively, Lornika stumbled outdoors with her cat and raven clutched to her bony chest. "Lawks a 'mercy," she howled, "I ain't never seen anything like it." Red hair awry, face and clothes streaked with soot, Lornika presented a sorry sight. "Yon fellow is deranged. He tried to set my hair alight! But for my raven attacking him, I would not be here to tell the tale."

The acrid smoke snatched at Oric's throat as he entered Lornika's cottage. Burn holes in the roof exposed swatches of blue sky, but no-one remained inside. A man's sandal lay under a narrow window embrasure at the back of the cottage and Oric gathered it up. He hastened outside and thrust his find under Lornika's nose. "Mistress Fentwhistle, does this item of footwear belong to you?"

"Certainly not," snapped Lornika. "My choice of clothing may be unusual, but I have not yet taken to wearing men's apparel."

"No-one is inside your cottage. Do you know where the madman has gone?" snapped Oric. "Erik, Arnold, search the rear of the dwelling."

Lornika let go of her cat and gave the raven a leg up on to her shoulder. "I ain't got no idea where he went! Smoke inside the cottage was that thick I could barely see a hand in front of my face."

"Are you able to describe him?"

"That I can. I dragged off his hood and mask when we scuffled. His horrible features are etched upon my brain forevermore."

"Mistress Fentwhistle!" Oric roared. "You are safe now but, if we are to apprehend the villain, we need to know exactly what he looks like. We must warn everyone to watch out for him."

Lornika rubbed her sooty brow. "Looks like he hacked off his hair with a blunt knife. His black beard was straggly an' all, like he couldn't grow a proper one." Lornika gulped. "And his filthy robes reminded me of a priest's vestments."

Deeming the danger to have passed, Desdemona Whittle sidled up to the cottage for a closer look. She folded her arms under her scant bosom and nodded knowingly at Lornika. "So, Mistress Fentwhistle, how come a talented fortune teller like yourself failed to foresee this unfortunate episode?"

"I tell fortunes, and my predictions are accurate," snarled Lornika, "but I ain't no match for no crazy robe-wearers."

Erik and Arnold returned to the front of the cottage, and re-sheathed their swords. "Ain't no sign of anyone nearby," reported Erik despondently.

Exasperated, Oric waved the sandal under Parzifal's nose. "Go seek, boy!" Remounting Jester, he instructed his four companions to unhitch their mounts and follow suit. "Let us form a search party. The man cannot vanish into thin air, he must be hiding somewhere nearby."

Nose to the ground, Parzifal trotted along the lakeside. Where dense woodland met the water's edge, he stopped and barked.

Oric swivelled in his saddle to look back at Ned. "More than likely our quarry waded a short distance in the lake to kill his scent."

"Not much point continuing, then, is there?" Ned shrugged, "He could be anywhere by now."

"Nay, lads, we dare not give up so soon." Oric raked the ragged tree line with narrowed eyes. "The fellow is a danger to the entire population."

"How so?" asked Erik, a puzzled frown on his brow. "I cannot imagine he will go around burning folks' homes for no good reason. Most likely he received a bad prediction from Mistress Fentwhistle and set light to her cottage to wreak his revenge. I say we return to Lockton Castle."

Oric held back a shout of frustration. "But Mistress Fentwhistle swears she did not recognise him. I say we spread out and search the woods. He cannot have ventured far on foot with only one sandal."

The boys grumbled, but they agreed to continue looking until dusk.

At the end of an unsuccessful day, tired and grumpy, Oric and his friends regrouped on Skelgut's main street. "We can accomplish nothing more today, let us go home." Oric urged Jester into a trot only to pull him up at sight of a sooty figure by the roadside. A cat in a wicker basket yowled dismally, and a large black raven sat atop the basket with his claws firmly anchored on to the handle. "Good Lord, Mistress Fentwhistle, what are you doing outdoors?"

Lornika scowled. "My cottage is destroyed by the fire and I ain't got nowhere to go. Everything I own is ruined by water or soot."

"Will no-one in the village give you a bed until your cottage is repaired?" asked Oric.

"Folks might have once upon a time but, since the arrival of a certain person, no-one sets much store by me anymore." Lornika looked pointedly at Oric. "You could say my life in Skelgut is ruined."

Ned smirked and whispered to Erik and Arnald. "Mark my words, Oric will play the knight in shining armour."

"I heard that!" Oric growled. Climbing down from his saddle, he scooped the raven from the basket and placed the bird on Lornika's shoulder. "How would you like to stay at Lockton Castle until your cottage is repaired?" Grinning with evil intent, he helped Lornika to mount up behind Ned knowing he would not be happy.

"Here you go, lad," said Oric, passing the cat in its basket up to Joe. "You can take care of the moggy." He picked up Lornika's two small bundles of possessions and handed one each to the squires. "Now, if we are all ready, let us go home."

After one or two side steps and a couple of attempted nips, Jester finally allowed Oric to remount.

Unused to horse-riding, Lornika grasped Ned's tunic tightly. The fabric tightened around his neck and he gagged. "Loosen your hold on my clothing, Mistress," he cried, prising the garment away from his windpipe. "You have me near choked to death."

The raven upon Mistress Fentwhistle's shoulder cawed dismally. Hungry and irritable, he pecked at Ned's cap all the way back to Lockton Castle.

CHAPTER NINE

New Friends, Old Enemies

Word of Oric's benevolent tenure of Lockton Castle spread rapidly across the district, and many former inhabitants of Skelgut returned to their cottages and farms. They implemented repairs and worked the land until the estate prospered again.

Once a week, on market day, Oric loaded his medicinal supplies into wickerwork panniers on Otty's back and rode the donkey downhill to Skelgut. Throwing a cover on the ground, he set out his medicaments beside the other stall-holders.

In the beginning, folk treated their new lord with grave suspicion, for they had never seen a member of the gentry work like a common serf. Applying a policy of patience and kindness, Oric gradually won the country-folks' trust. New customers queued up to ask his advice and, as promised, Oric gave it freely along with the relevant potions and lotions.

Long summer days passed without incident, and work in the castle's garden continued in leaps and bounds. Bright and early one morning, Oric sauntered outside with a long list of herbal requirements.

Josh balked at sight of it. "I hope those are not all items you seek from this garden. We have cut so much lately the plants need a little time to regenerate."

"In that case I had best forage in the woods," Oric replied. He shouted for Walter and instructed him to harness Otty, and affix a pair of panniers to her back. Glancing furtively over his shoulder he added, "Have you seen Mistress Fentwhistle this morning? She has become uncommonly interested in my work, and she follows me closer than my own shadow. I would like to escape before she sees me."

Josh winked and cupped a hand over his mouth. "Speak of the Devil, I think we are about to have company."

Lornika Fentwhistle hastened across the drawbridge and grabbed hold of Oric's sleeve. "You were not trying to sneak off without me, were you?"

Muscles rippled in Oric's jaw as he clenched his teeth. "Of course not, Mistress Fentwhistle. Whatever makes you think that?"

"I heard you telling Walter to harness the donkey. Where are we going?"

"*We* are not going anywhere, Mistress, *I* am bound for Farnrock Forest to gather more herbal supplies." Oric imagined the peaceful time he would enjoy without his second shadow. "And I shall be gone all day."

The red-haired woman tapped her temple, "I know where the best plants grow. Much time will be saved if I act as your guide. Give me a moment to fetch a shawl and we shall set off together."

Walter had difficulty keeping his face straight. "Am I right in thinking you will require two mounts rather than just one today, my lord?"

"Correct," Oric snapped. If looks could kill, Walter would lie stone dead. "And put panniers on both animals. If the woman insists on coming along, she might as well make herself useful."

Living at the castle whilst awaiting repairs to her cottage, Lornika's dislike of Oric had changed to envy. The fellow certainly knew his stuff when it came to healing the sick and, determined to glean as much knowledge from him as she could, Lornika observed Oric's every move like a hawk with an eye to its prey. The more she learned, the better chance she had of usurping his position as village apothecary when she returned to Langend Cottage.

Lornika irritated Oric beyond measure and her raucous laugh set his teeth on edge but, true to his word, he intended to provide her with shelter until repairs to her cottage rendered the building habitable. Afraid she might kill someone with her crazy potions, Oric put up with her company in the hope some smidgeon of medicinal knowledge might rub off on her.

A short ride took Oric and Lornika into the forest behind Skelgut. Not far into the woods, an overhead canopy of leaves and branches made the atmosphere gloomy. An all-pervading smell of fungus hung in the air, and Oric slid down from Otty's back to gather up some brown mushrooms.

"You need to be careful with those things," Lornika warned. "I know not which ones are deadly, so I leave them all alone." She nodded her head primly, "And you should do the same if you know what is good for you."

"I have eaten these delicious fungi for many years!" snapped Oric. "And yet, here I am, still alive and able to tell the tale." He plucked up a mushroom and popped it into his mouth, savouring the earthy taste that pervaded his palate as much as the look of disbelief on Lornika's face.

Lornika shrugged. "Please yourself! But I ain't hauling you home if you drop dead."

Venturing deeper into the forest, Lornika began to grizzle. "Perhaps we should turn back now. I hear tell some funny things have been going on in the depths of these woods of late."

"I have not yet collected all the herbs I require. If you are uncomfortable with the situation, return to Lockton Castle."

"Nay, I will tag along. Your friends would never forgive me if anything untoward happened to you." Lornika failed to admit her reluctance to make the return journey by herself.

Lost in his own world, Oric dismounted often to collect plants as he came upon them. Where the canopy of trees thinned, an abundance of honeysuckle bloomed in golden shafts of sunlight. Many of Skelgut's youngsters suffered from sunburn, and ointment made from the pink and white blossoms soothed the uncomfortable condition. Purportedly the medication also whitened skin and diminished freckles, afflictions kitchen maids Faylinn and Genevieve constantly grumbled about. They admired high-born ladies' complexions, and they longed to look the same. Thinking to please the girls, Oric ordered Lornika to pluck all the sweetly perfumed honeysuckle flowers she could reach.

Further into the forest, Oric dug up clumps of St Peter's wort from the edge of a narrow brook to plant beside Lockton Castle's moat. Master Ichtheus suffered with chronic sciatic pain, and ointment made from the plant was recommended to provide relief. Oric planned to have some concocted before his former mentor paid the castle another visit.

Seeking different specimens, Oric chose an alternative route for his return journey to Lockton Castle. The sun disappeared behind a cloud, making the forest gloomier than ever. A spiteful wind sprang up, and the branches of closely packed trees creaked as their limbs chafed together.

Lornika urged her donkey closer to Otty. The little

animal kicked back, clouting the shins of Lornika's mount. Both donkeys bucked and tossed their riders to the ground. Freshly gathered bundles of roots and greenery scattered across the forest floor, and Otty took off across a nearby brook.

"'Od's blood, woman! Now look what you have done!" Irritated beyond measure, Oric waded through the water to retrieve his runaway donkey.

On the opposite bank, a pile of tree branches nestled together in a contrived, square shape on a grassy curve of land beside the brook. Several stout branches lashed together, with twigs and reeds woven through, made a rough shelter. Animal bones lay strewn around a burned-out fire. "What do you make of this, Mistress Fentwhistle?" Oric called, feeling a prickle of concern.

Lornika lifted her kirtle and paddled across the brook. "Looks like a hermit's den to me. They ain't renowned for their hospitality so I suggest we get out of here as quick as we can."

-oOo-

Cordelia Ramshorn returned to her woodland cottage, tired after a long day away from home. Sunset washed the sky with pink and lavender streaks, and a pale, crescent moon accompanied by a single bright star climbed the twilight sky. Blackbirds trilled a melodious goodnight to one other and Cordelia sighed with contentment. Her life had turned out better than she expected.

Widowed many moons past, Cordelia's step-children had put her out of the family home. Without relatives of her own to give her succour, Cordelia was obliged to fend for herself. A resourceful woman, she had taken to the forest and moved into a deserted, semi-derelict woodman's cottage. Over the years, she repaired the dwelling, and carved out a relatively comfortable life for herself. Her garden thrived with an abundance of vegetables, apple, pear and plum trees. She snared rabbits, badgers and weasels, which provided her with fresh meat. A fair hand with a sling shot, she downed many a pigeon to supplement her diet. A stout chicken run, installed by the forester, kept her poultry safe from wolves and foxes. Fish were plentiful in the nearby stream and the water was clear and potable. She made the animals' skins into children's clothes and shoes, and she assembled gewgaws for ladies from the birds' feathers and dried flowers. These items she sold at Skelgut market along with wines she brewed from wild berries and flowers.

Cordelia heard her two dogs baying long before she got to the cottage gate. Her skin prickled with gooseflesh not from cold but fear. She had left the cottage early that morning and strangely, a light now flickered behind the window.

Cordelia crept up to her dogs and released them. They raced, one after the other, and began jumping at the cottage door. She followed her pets, and tentatively lifted the latch. The dogs bounded over the threshold but Cordelia found no-one inside.

A few tallow candles illuminated total disarray. Everyday items were thrown about the floor, and Cordelia's few clothes lay torn to shreds on her bed. Her spare pair of boots burned in a fire, which she herself had not set upon the hearth. Clearly, whoever had wreaked the havoc was not long gone. Nothing seemed to be missing, indicating the motive behind the break-in was not theft. Cordelia kicked the door shut, and bit down upon a scream. Her disembowelled rooster dangled from the wooden peg upon which she usually hung her only set of spare clothes. Revolted, she stepped backwards and collapsed on to her bed.

"Who would do such a thing?" she whispered, gathering her dogs close for comfort. "As far as I know, I have no enemies."

CHAPTER TEN

Committee of Law

Ichtheus paced Uther's cobbler shop, awaiting the arrival of the Committee of Law members.

The shop door crashed back on its hinges to reveal ex prize-fighter Egglebart. His one eye gleamed with enthusiasm, and a wide smile revealed the gaps from his many lost teeth. Though he was no longer young, his carrot-coloured hair remained thick and his red whiskers showed no sign of turning white. "What-oh, my old friend, here I am as requested." The huge man walloped Ichtheus between the shoulder blades, almost knocking him to his knees. "What do you require of Etheldrida and me? Whatever it is, you can count on us."

Egglebart's buxom, raven-haired wife bustled into Uther's shop behind her husband. "Lawks, man, give poor Ichtheus time to draw breath," she cried, giving the apothecary a hug. "As soon as the others arrive, we shall have something to eat." Unhitching a huge basket from her arm, she plonked it down on Uther's work bench. "Folk always think better on full stomachs," she chuckled. Famous for her rabbit pies and honey cakes, Etheldrida proved a popular guest at many a function.

Next to arrive were Sir Oswold, the one-armed knight, and his dainty wife Lady Malla. No longer young enough to fight battles, Oswold ran his own smallholding on the outskirts of the village. He grew vegetables to feed themselves, with a few left to barter or sell at the local market. But his major income came from the magnificent war horses he bred for sale to young knights. Late in life he met and married Malla, Kilterton's capable, white-haired, blue-eyed midwife.

"Now we are all here," said Ichtheus, "let us repair to Uther's back room." He peeked out of the shop doorway to make sure no-one lurked outside, for he did not want anyone overhearing the agenda he was about to discuss. "Has anyone spoken to Tewdric Bascoomb? I know he was once a keen member of the committee, but I refrained from informing him of this new turn of events. Not that I have anything against the butcher," Ichtheus added hastily. "He is a mighty fine chap, but I have difficulty dealing with his wife." Ichtheus shuddered at memories of past, unpleasant associations with Helled Bascoomb. "The woman is a termagant and I have no desire to work with her ever again."

Sweeping fallen leaves away from the entrance to Tewdric's butcher shop, Helled saw Ichtheus bob his head out of the cobbler's doorway. The apothecary's stealthy movements suggested he might be up to something, and Helled wanted to know what. Like a ship with canvas a-taunt, she sailed across the road to Uther's premises.

Too late to close the door, Ichtheus faced up to the woman. "If you are seeking Uther, I am afraid he is not available at present. You must collect your boots another day." He attempted to push the door shut, but Helled stuck her broom in the gap.

"It ain't Uther I am after. But I do want to know what is going on. I seen the two couples from up the road entering in here a few moments ago. When you lot get together, something untoward is usually afoot. As a member of the shopkeepers' guild, I demand to know what you are up to." She stared unwaveringly at Ichtheus with no intention of backing down. "No doubt this meeting has something to do with the miscreants who are plaguing our district at present. And I, for one, want them stopped. Two of our best dairy cows disappeared from Diggitdow Farm last night, two beef cows vanished last week. And I want to know how much rent the cobbler is coughing up. Master Guwain's steward and bailiff are extracting more tithe money than Tewdric and I want to pay." Helled gave the door an almighty shove and pushed past Ichtheus.

Ichtheus followed Helled into Uther's back room. "Now our meeting is no longer secret, you may as well inform your husband we are here. And, since Uther's back room is so small, perhaps Tewdric can come on his own whilst you mind the shop."

"Oh, no! I ain't letting my husband loose on his own with you lot ever again, for he usually gets the thin edge of the wedge." Helled curled her lip. "Rest assured, I will return with him directly."

"So much for our peaceful meeting," muttered Uther, looking glum. "Yon woman would make trouble between a band of angels."

Etheldrida threw a cloth over Uther's stained work bench, and set out the contents of her basket. "Let us not wait 'til the Bascoombs return before we eat. At least without them we can enjoy our meal in peace."

Not a crumb of food remained by the time Helled and her rotund butcher showed their faces.

"Fancy organising a meeting without me," Tewdric blustered, then looked contrite. "But I understand your reason for secrecy." Used to Helled's vitriol, never mind who was on the receiving end, Tewdric knew why he was not a popular addition to village functions. His only pleasure in life came from his thirteen-year-old twin daughters, Lunette and Novena. Totally opposite to their unpleasant mother, Tewdric revelled in his girls' company. Together they netted butterflies, picked and pressed wildflowers, and caught sticklebacks from the pond behind Diggitdow Farm. In spring, they gathered slimy ropes of black-spotted frogspawn to take home and keep until little frogs developed and hopped away. If it wasn't for his girls, Tewdric would also like to hop away.

As always in Helled's presence, verbal altercation soon broke out and, exasperated beyond measure, Ichtheus banged a hammer on Uther's work bench, and called for silence. "Pay attention everyone. Guwain's bully boys are terrorising the folk of Bayersby and Kilterton and we must try to stop them, for they are bleeding folk white."

"I hear Sir Ragnald's son has moved into Bayersby Manor an' all," rumbled Egglebart. "How come he ain't been sentenced to death for his part in the challenge against Sir Edred?"

Ichtheus snorted. "He claims his father forced him to do what he did in the battle against Sir Edred, and Guwain believes him. Thus, he has escaped arrest and trial. Mark my words, yon crafty viper is up to something."

"Guwain has already squandered his father's fortune," growled Egglebart. "And I wager he is relying on someone to extort money from tenants hereabouts to support his extravagant lifestyle. If it is Joffrey, I cannot fathom what the fellow's long-term intentions are."

Sir Oswold harrumphed. "Guwain is naught but a toss-pot incapable of making decisions. Unless we wish to see our livelihoods disappear, we must do something to stop him from further ruining the estate. If necessary, we should muster Sir Edred's army again."

"But how do we prove that Joffrey is the culprit?" cried Uther. "And, if that be the case, is he not working for Guwain? To do battle against our own lord and master would be classed as treasonous. We could all face the death penalty if we go down that road."

"What say we ask Oric to return to Bayersby Manor for a short time?" Etheldrida suggested. "Everyone loves and respects him. He might be able to talk some sense into Guwain."

"Ha, what would that lily-livered little squirt know about men's business?" sneered Helled. "We need someone with clout, and plenty of it."

Ichtheus bristled up. "Oric far outranks Guwain. And, since he has his own estate to manage, I doubt he will have the time or the inclination to return to Bayersby."

"How is Lady Myferny coping with all the upset?" asked Lady Malla. "Poor dear soul must be sick at heart."

"Mistress Foley and I are extremely worried about her." replied Ichtheus. "She rarely shows her face outside the women's quarters these days. We would like to see her leave the manor along with all her female servants. Those poor girls are expected to fetch and carry and provide entertainment for Guwain and his rabble all hours of the day and night. Dian is especially vulnerable."

"Whatever for?" gasped Etheldrida. "Dian is one of the best workers at the manor."

"Guwain is singling her out because she rejected his romantic advances." Tension knotted Ichtheus' belly because of his inadequacy. Outnumbered, he could do little to help the girl. "She is the butt of his jokes, and he demands that she accomplish the most menial of tasks. Lady Myferny provides the maid with some protection, but for how much longer I know not. I fear for the ladies' sanity, unless we can persuade her to flee to one of her sisters' homes."

"Are you suggesting we abandon the district to Guwain and Joffrey's rotten ministrations?" demanded Egglebart.

"Far from it," replied Ichtheus. "What I am suggesting is a tactical retreat." His blue eyes gleamed more brightly than they had in a long while. "We need to sneak people away from Bayersby a few at a time, until only Joffrey's evil entourage remains. Give a man enough rope, and he will eventually hang himself. When that happens, we will pick up the pieces."

"Are you insane?" Helled screeched. "I ain't leaving my property to the mercy of yon Bayersby mob."

"Nay, Mistress, I am thinking only of the vulnerable servants at Bayersby Manor. Strong people like you and Tewdric are needed to keep an eye on the village. You must do everything in your power to thwart the usurpers without putting your lives at risk. Evil rarely outshines good and I am convinced everything will right itself eventually."

"In what way do you suggest we 'thwart' these usurpers?" Helled demanded.

Etheldrida emitted a snort of disgust. "The same way you 'thwart' everyone you meet. You portray the poor, downtrodden trader to perfection – keep up your act and the villains may not bother you. If they press you, offer them beef instead of money and lace the carcasses with a potion to make them sick. Not enough to kill, but sufficient to make Joffrey and his men horribly unwell. If the potion is sufficiently slow acting, no-one will link their indisposition to your meat." Etheldrida winked at Ichtheus. "I am sure our illustrious apothecary can help out in that department."

"As owners of our own property, Sir Oswold and I will refuse to pay Joffrey's tithes," Lady Malla stated. "Besides, we live far enough away from the village to not draw attention to ourselves."

Helled curled her lip. "Oh, aye, very nice I am sure, my lady. But what will you be doing whilst we village traders are putting our lives at risk?"

"As the village midwife, I will invent an epidemic to back up the effects of your poisoned meat, and my patients will surely go along with the ruse." Lady Malla gave a curt nod. "Nothing like a nasty disease to put the fear of God into people. Joffrey's men might not make such regular visits to the village."

"At present Joffrey seems content to enjoy all the comforts Bayersby has to offer," said Ichtheus. "But once he has sucked the district dry, I believe he will move on to greener pastures."

Helled exhaled a breath that rattled her lips. "As a matter of interest, where do you suppose these 'greener pastures' might be?"

"I am not yet sure," replied Ichtheus. "In the meantime, let us all work together to find out."

CHAPTER ELEVEN

Unrest

Ichtheus bade the Committee of Law members farewell, and quietly left the cobbler's shop through the back door. In the yard, Braccus munched on a nosebag of oats supplied by Uther. Unhitching the donkey from a post, Ichtheus clambered onto his back. "Come on, old lad, 'tis time we headed for home." Braccus knew his way to Bayersby, and Ichtheus allowed the donkey his head. Needing time to think, he became oblivious to his surroundings.

Engrossed with his troubles, Ichtheus failed to see Braccus veer from the main road, choosing instead the less used pathway to Rigg Farm and past St Griswald's Church. The wily donkey harboured fond memories of carrots the shepherd's wife provided, and he wanted to sample more of the juicy treats. As he plodded along at a gentle pace, green meadows dotted with pale yellow cowslips and golden buttercups replaced Kilterton's cottages and smallholdings. A low range of hills appeared on the horizon, and lush fields gave way to rough moorland. Black-faced sheep grazed on patches of grass and, hearing the donkey approach, they lifted their heads to bleat at the unwanted interruption.

Brought back to reality, Ichtheus took stock of his surroundings and realised Braccus had chosen a roundabout route. "Hang it all," he muttered. "We have travelled too far along the track to turn back." He leaned forward in his saddle and fondled the donkey's ears. "Never mind, this is a good opportunity to visit the shepherd at Rigg Farm."

The pathway wound upwards, and Ichtheus dismounted to make the steep going easier for Braccus. "The last time we travelled this track, old lad, we had Oric with us." The haunting cry of a lone curlew added to Ichtheus' feelings of desolation.

On the left-hand side of the track, a stunted tree clung tenaciously to the face of a sandstone escarpment. At the top of the ridge, acres of scrubby heather stretched into hazy infinity. Despite the summer weather, a chilly wind whistled over the crags, and Ichtheus drew his cloak more closely about his thin shoulders. Roxdale Beck chattered along the valley bottom as it had done since the dawning of time and, drawing a weary hand across his eyes, Ichtheus wished the human condition was similarly intransient.

Situated in the lea of a hillside, Rigg Farm appeared rather more run down than Ichtheus remembered. Norbert and his family weathered dreadful conditions, especially during winter but, a consummate countryman, the shepherd usually nurtured his family, his flock of sheep, and his property.

Not long finished shearing, Norbert, aided by his eldest son, worked on winter-damaged stone walls close to the cottage. Rosalea and her younger son milked ewes inside a small enclosure abutted to the house. Rosalea's sun-bronzed face brightened at sight of Ichtheus. "I am that glad to see 'tis only you, Master Apothecary."

"Good gracious, I am not sure if I am flattered or offended," laughed Ichtheus.

Rosalea picked up her bucket of milk and walked over to where Ichtheus stood by the wall. "At first, I thought you might be another of them villains sent from Bayersby Manor to demand money and produce from us. Me and Norbert will have nowt left to sustain ourselves and our boys if Sir Edred's son carries on at his present rate." She sighed, and put down her bucket. "Visitors are few and far between in these parts, but them as do pass by tell me other folks in the district are suffering much the same as us." She stared at Ichtheus with troubled brown eyes. "I know not what is to become of us all, I truly do not."

"Take heart, Mistress. This very day I recalled the old Committee of Law members. We have a few ideas, but it may take a while to stop the ill-use of the local peasants and villeins."

"Thank God for that," said Norbert, joining the conversation. "Do you need me to do owt for the cause?"

"If you spot anything unusual, report it to me. If these rogues are to be stopped, the Committee of Law needs to be informed of what is going on – however insignificant the occurrence may seem."

"Not sure if this is important, but I was up at St Griswald's church t'other day, seeking a couple of sheep what strayed from my flock. I swear somebody was wandering around the old manse, but they disappeared when I called out."

Ichtheus narrowed his eyes. "Strange. Most former parishioners keep away from the church. To my knowledge, no-one has visited St Griswald's since Sir Edred's crazy priest departed. Since I am going past the churchyard, I will investigate."

Braccus missed out on his usual titbit, for the shepherd's wife had barely enough food to feed her family. But Braccus was having none of it. He dug his four little hooves into the ground and refused to budge.

Norbert grabbed the bridle and tugged. The donkey remained rooted to the spot. "You had best find some small morsel to pacify this beast, wife, otherwise I foresee our apothecary staying here for the night."

A small turnip taken from the shepherd's winter clamp did the trick and, after munching down his treat, Braccus set off without a qualm.

Ichtheus carried on along the desolate moorland pathway, mindful of the bogs that lay in wait for unwary riders. If the donkey missed his footing they would both perish and, sucked into the bottomless peaty depths, no-one would ever find them.

Harbouring no fond memories of St Griswald's church, Ichtheus recalled the time Esica Figg, moneylender and thief, had once used the place as a hideout. The fellow extorted money from local folk, and eventually had the temerity to challenge Sir Edred for his manor; not once, but twice. He failed on both counts, and Ichtheus felt no sorrow when the moneylender met his maker.

Father Chrispian, the last incumbent priest at St Griswald's, frightened his parishioners with fire and brimstone sermons to such an extent no-one dared return to the church. He accused Lady Malla of witchcraft and attempted to burn her at the stake. Sir Oswold had dashed to his wife's rescue and, in so doing, he sliced Father Chrispian with a broadsword.

In the general panic to release Lady Malla from the burning pyre, no-one gave the priest a second thought. Much to everyone's relief he disappeared, never to be seen again.

Now, according to Norbert, someone had been poking around the old church again. What if Sir Oswald's attempt to kill Father Chrispian had failed? If the fellow lived, where could he be hiding? Surely, he dare not return to the church. Loath to investigate but believing it to be his duty, Ichtheus tied Braccus to a gatepost, and entered the churchyard.

Gaps in St Griswald's roof suggested shingles had blown away during winter storms, some stolen perhaps. Ichtheus shook his head, wondering how many dwellings around the district had roof repairs implemented with second-hand wooden tiles.

Pushing open the great oak door at the front of the church, Ichtheus stepped inside. Little of value remained within the chilly, silent building. No doubt some folk had a few top-quality benches made from the missing pews. Bird droppings spattered the stone-flagged floor, and huge cobwebs festooned the rafters.

Gathering his courage, Ichtheus descended into the dark, fusty crypt. At the back of the subterranean room another flight of steps went up to another door, which allowed access to the graveyard at the back of the building. Dead leaves and earth sat in a pile at the bottom of the stairs. No sign of recent human habitation remained.

Glad to exit the church, Ichtheus wandered across the churchyard toward the manse. Weeds grew waist high, and dark green ivy clung to many of the gravestones.

A barrow outside the manse held tools, and a pile of stones sat in a neat pile on the uneven pathway. Clearly some enterprising individual was in the process of helping himself to free building materials, which could account for Norbert's sighting of someone in the vicinity.

Ichtheus contemplated setting a guard to catch the culprit but, thinking the idea pointless, he changed his mind. No-one would want to move into the manse and no new priest was in the offing. Let the local folk gain some good from the beleaguered church – they deserved some recompense in the wake of Father Chrispian's brutal regime. Duty done, Ichtheus unhitched Braccus, and continued his journey back to Bayersby Manor.

Before he entered the compound, sounds of drunken revelry reached Ichtheus. Once inside, a young stable boy with a bloody lip ran to grasp Braccus' bridle.

"What is going on here?" Ichtheus demanded.

Wide-eyed with fear, stable-boy Robert stared at Ichtheus. "More rough men arrived here shortly after you left." The boy fingered his bruised mouth and winced with pain. "I told the fellow what took Braccus' stall to find somewhere else to put his horse and he landed me with a fat lip. Sorry, Master Ichtheus, there ain't no other stalls left so I must tether Braccus in the open."

"Yes, do that, lad, then come inside and I shall treat your wound with salve of primrose."

A sight from Hell's kitchen confronted Ichtheus as he stormed into the house. Steam poured from cauldrons of food suspended over an open fire, one small boy rotated a spitted boar inside the inglenook fireplace. The room burned hotter than a smithy's forge and sweat-drenched servants ran hither and thither. Young female members of the household ferried heaped platters of stewed pigeon, vegetables, and jugged hare to the Great Hall. "What in the name of Christendom is happening here?" Ichtheus bellowed. "Have you all taken leave of your senses? Where has all this food come from? When I left this morning, precious little produce remained in the storerooms."

Mistress Foley, white faced and thin lipped, drew Ichtheus to one side. "Sir Ragnald's son, Joffrey, brought in another band of ruffians. I know not whence they came, but they carried enough supplies to feed an army. They are now in their cups and manhandling the maids. Lady Myferny begged Guwain to intervene, but the young fool is so drunk he is incapable of doing anything other than grin like a fairground fool."

The injured stable-boy's entry into the kitchen saved Ichtheus from a snap decision. Glad of an excuse to think things through, he took the boy's arm and led him to the apothecary's section of the kitchen. Jars of medicaments lay smashed on the stone floor, and shards of glass along with pieces of broken pottery gleamed amongst bunches of herbs dragged down from the rafters. Shocked to his core, Ichtheus cast around to find an intact jar of ointment. "Why would anyone create such havoc?" he asked the boy.

"Because these men are animals, Master Ichtheus. Bayersby's young workers outside fear for their lives."

"Do your parents live nearby?"

The boy nodded. "Aye, my folks have a cottage in Kilterton."

"Gather together all your friends, and creep away from the manor. Judging by the noise coming from the Great Hall, no-one will see you depart, nor will they miss you before tomorrow. The villagers in Kilterton will give shelter to the few youngsters whose parents live farther afield." Ichtheus gave the young fellow a gentle push. "May God go with you."

Bracing himself, Ichtheus addressed Mistress Foley. "I care not what Lady Myferny says, we must get her, along with her ladies and handmaidens, away from Bayersby as quickly as possible."

Mistress Foley tucked a few stray hairs back under her housekeeper's bonnet. "After those dreadful men arrived, Lady Myferny threatened to leave if Guwain refused to get rid of them. Since they are still here, Lady Myferny is, as we speak, in her quarters packing up her belongings. She plans to leave for Roxbrough at first light tomorrow." The housekeeper shook her head sadly, "And she is with child."

CHAPTER TWELVE

Exodus

Four conveyances left Bayersby Manor in the dawn of a damp, drizzly morning. One cart, driven by Dian with Mistress Foley seated beside her, carried foodstuff for the journey. A second cart with two maids in charge held clothing, and a few household items Lady Myferny could not live without. Ichtheus, with Braccus hitched to a cart full of medicinal supplies, brought up the rear.

At the head of the small cavalcade, a pair of sturdy horses, one behind the other, carried a tent-like litter. Lady Myferny and her two handmaidens lay inside the contraption.

"I would rather sit on this cart in the fresh air than inside that thing," muttered Mistress Foley. "Look how it sways from side to side. Poor Lady Myferny will be sick as a dog by the time we reach our destination."

Mistress Foley's words were barely out of her mouth when Wolfred and Malgwyn, two of Sir Edred's faithful retainers, called a halt. "Lady Myferny begs a rest," shouted Wolfred.

"We are suffocating inside this thing," cried Lady

Myferny, popping her head out between the drapes. She fanned herself with a pale hand. "Can we not tie back the curtains to allow more air to flow through?"

Wolfred and Malgwyn removed the tent flaps whilst Lady Myferny and her attendants walked a little way down the track to stretch their legs.

Ichtheus climbed down from his cart and wandered over to chat with Dian and Mistress Foley. "Leaving the manor proved easier than I anticipated," he said. "I expected Guwain to try to stop us."

"We left so early none of the revellers were awake." Mistress Foley rolled her eyes, "When they do surface, I suspect they will feel like death warmed over after the amount of food and drink they consumed last night."

Dian sucked in her breath. "I am so glad to be away from the manor, for Guwain would insist I clean up the mess."

"Why has Guwain been so unkind to you?" asked Mistress Foley.

"He is put out because I prefer to do menial tasks, rather than share his company." Dian's face reddened with anger. "And the way he speaks to his poor mother is a disgrace."

"You are both out of it now," soothed Ichtheus. "Though I dread to think what lies ahead. The road to Roxbrough passes through Dunburton and, by all accounts, the village is full of wayfarers and vagabonds. 'Tis a pity Lady Myferny chose Mistress Elfine's place at Roxbrough rather than her sister Demzel's home in Yaracumb. Had we gone in the latter direction we would not now be facing possible danger."

Mistress Foley wrinkled her nose. "I would not want to put up with the stink of humanity and the foetid air of a big city in summer. Not to mention the running sewer that is the Yaracumb River."

"Aye, and I would not relish time spent in Mistress Demzel's home." Ichtheus' expression spoke volumes. "She is a difficult woman."

"That is all well and good, Master Ichtheus, but where shall we stop tonight?" demanded Mistress Foley. "Lady Myferny will be too exhausted to travel further than Dunburton in one day."

Within sight of the village, Ichtheus indicated a lesser track that led to the Meeting of the Waters. "We shall take this detour and hope no-one spots us. There is a pleasant meadow a little further along the riverbank where we can set up camp." Ichtheus squinted up at the sky where patches of blue showed through the clouds. "At least the weather seems to be improving."

Roxdale Beck and Nidderdale Brook tumbled over a waterfall, joining together in a frothy torrent to become the River Roxnid. Faster flowing than the two smaller tributaries, the Roxnid raced along a deep valley toward the coast.

Bypassing the rushing water, Lady Myferny's group made their way downhill and followed the river bank until they came upon a flat grassy area. "This will do fine for an overnight stop," said Wolfred.

Ichtheus peered over a stone wall to observe an overgrown hay meadow. The grass, dotted with golden buttercups, sweet-smelling pink clover, and purple vetch had clearly not been mown for several seasons. "Methinks the fields hereabouts are part of the Dunburton Estate. What a waste! Since the former lord of the manor is dead, I wonder why no beneficiary has claimed the land?"

Dian and Lady Myferny's maids busied themselves preparing an evening meal, whilst Wolfred and Malgwyn detached the litter and made a comfortable sleeping place for the three ladies.

Utensils used for supper were cleared away, and the fire damped down for the night. Worn out after suffering months of Guwain's tyrannical behaviour and constantly on edge because of Joffrey's secretive, malevolent presence, the folk from Bayersby fell asleep almost as soon as they lay down.

A vivid sunset infused the valley with lurid pink light, reminding Dian of an ancient saying. 'Red sky at night sailors' delight. Red sky in the morning, sailors' warning.' She prayed the last line would not eventuate.

-oOo-

Lady Myferny's sudden departure from Bayersby Manor provided Joffrey with the perfect opportunity to put his plan into action. He meandered into the stables where Sir Edred's prize war horse, Balthazar, stood at the end of the stalls. Throwing a saddle on the animal's broad back and a bit between his teeth, Joffrey mounted and meandered out of the Bayersby compound. Haste was unnecessary, for Lady Myferny's heavy litter would slow the party down.

Joffrey followed hoofprints on the rain-dampened track until the thoroughfare divided into two. Sliding down from Balthazar's back, he scrutinised the terrain. Scuffed earth indicated the Bayersby party had chosen the left fork. The righthand track remained pristine, suggesting no person had walked upon it since heavy rain had washed the ground smooth. Not knowing how close he might be to Lady Myferny's entourage, Joffrey tethered the horse to a tree and continued through the gathering dusk on foot.

Approaching the Meeting of the Waters, Joffrey kept to the edge of the track where shrubbery afforded him cover. Convinced Lady Myferny's party would soon stop for the night, he remained extra vigilant. Sure enough, he spotted the Bayersby folk's encampment south of the waterfall. Seizing Dian would be easier than he anticipated. His heart skipped a beat. Once he held her prisoner, his future would be assured.

CHAPTER THIRTEEN

Skelgut Barber

Entering Lockton Castle, Archie Pender wiped sweat from his brow on the sleeve of his tunic. "Foof! 'Tis a long hike up the mountain from Skelgut. The older I get, the harder the journey becomes."

Kitchen maid, Faylinn, hastily placed a pot of cool water on the table in front of the red-faced visitor. "You will do yourself a mischief one of these days. I cannot understand why you choose to not ride your donkey up the hill, Master Pender?" Faylinn waited for the old man to slake his thirst, before questioning him further. "What brings you here in such a tearing hurry?"

"I bring good news for Mistress Fentwhistle," cried Archie. "Repairs to Langend Cottage are complete and she can move back home any time she wishes."

Lornika, eating her breakfast at the kitchen table, heard Archie's comment. Less than pleased, she brandished her spoon. "Lord Lockton relies upon me for valuable advice, I doubt he will want me to leave the castle." She directed warning glances at Faylinn and Archie. "Kindly keep the information to yourselves, Lord Lockton does not need to know my cottage is habitable again. Once he finds out, he will feel obliged to let me go."

"Your attitude is less than honest," snapped Archie. "I have come all this way to impart information, and that is exactly what I intend to do."

Upon receipt of Archie's news, relief flooded every part of Oric's being. Kind hearted to a fault, he refused to cast Mistress Fentwhistle out without a home to go to but, now her cottage was repaired, he could barely wait to get rid of the woman. No more listening to her sermons on how medicaments should be concocted. No more criticism on how the estate and its people needed to be managed. The interfering busybody no longer remained his responsibility.

"Faylinn, Genevieve – kindly assist Mistress Fentwhistle to pack her belongings, she is about to return home."

-oOo-

After Sir Edred's demise, Amery Trundle's exit from Dunburton remained trouble-free until two masked men ran out of the woods and knocked him off his driver's seat. The robbers left Amery sitting in a ditch with a bloody nose, and made off with the pony and trap and all his possessions. With only the clothes on his back and the silver sewn into the hem of his tunic, Amery trudged across the countryside. Along the way, he spent some of his money on a second-hand cart and an elderly mule.

Arriving in the city of Yaracumb, Amery paid through the nose for cramped, dismal lodgings, and soon decided life in the filthy, bustling city was not to his taste. Before his money ran out, he moved on. Several days later, tired and dispirited, he drove into Skelgut.

Back in her cottage, Lornika Fentwhistle scraped a meagre living. Desiring a more comfortable lifestyle, she sought another way of making money. She cleared out a lean-to on the side of Langend Cottage and tacked a 'room to let' sign on the gibbet-like name post beside her front gate.

At the end of Skelgut high street, Amery Trundle spotted Lornika's sign. Hitching his donkey and cart to the gatepost, he trotted up the path and knocked on the cottage door.

Lornika scrutinised the fat, pink little man on her doorstep. "Yes?"

Amery inclined his head and affected an ingratiating smile. "I hoped the room to let might still be available."

After haggling the price, Lornika agreed to rent Amery the lean-to.

Eager to replenish his coffers, Amery swiftly made his new accommodation into a consulting room. He set up a red and white striped pole advertising his trade as a barber/surgeon and made a poster to say he would also bleed the sick. For two days he scoured Firbrook Forest for medicinal herbs.

Curious about the new face in their village, people flocked to see the medicine man. Lies tripped from Amery's tongue and, coupled with his apparent expertise concerning every ailment known to man, he swiftly parted folk from their hard-earned money.

Taking advantage of the situation, Lornika lured many of Amery's patients into her cottage. Once ensnared, she gleefully charged her victims to tell their fortunes. She did not, however, appreciate the appalling stink drifting from Amery's quarters. Curious to ascertain the cause, she stamped into the lean-to.

Amery sat hunched over a trestle table littered with all manner of unrecognisable substances. A dozen or more live snails slithered around the inside of a covered glass bowl, hopelessly seeking to escape. In the middle of the room, a cooking pot sat on a bed of hot embers belching foul-smelling smoke from beneath an ill-fitting lid.

"Lawks, man," Lornika exclaimed, pinching her nostrils together between her thumb and forefinger. "What in God's name are you concocting?"

A fleeting memory of Sir Edred's horrible death popped into Amery's mind, and he suffered a momentary surge of guilt. Unlike the henbane he used to kill his patient, his new potion should prove an effective cure-all. Laying a podgy hand over his heart, Amery emitted a self-satisfied sigh. "Ah, Mistress Fentwhistle. You are smelling the result of my latest and most brilliant concoction. When I have completed my experiment, I believe this potion will cure almost all painful humours of the body."

"That's as may be, but the stink is evil enough to kill a cat." Always with an ear for a new recipe to add to her own collection, Lornika added guilelessly, "What ingredients have you used?"

Moving across to the pot, Amery lifted the lid. Smoke belched out, making the stench in the room worse. He controlled the urge to gag, and hastily replaced the lid. "I have an owl, plucked, disembowelled, and cooking in a new pot with a liberal sprinkling of salt. Judging by the aroma, the carcass is sufficiently charred to move on to the next step." A secretive smile played around Amery's lips. "You understand I cannot divulge any other ingredients used in my secret recipe."

Lornika covered her mouth and nose and made a beeline for the door. "For the sake of my cat – at least try to lessen the smell."

"Yes indeed, dear lady, I shall do my best." Amery waved his hand in dismissal. He had a recipe requiring parts of a cat, all he needed to do was catch the horrible creature.

Another market day dawned in Skelgut, and Oric made his usual pilgrimage to the village. He emptied Otty's panniers on to a table set up by the market committee. On his left, a woman displayed haberdashery, to his right a smallholder sold goat's cheese and vegetables. Further along the street, a fishmonger spruiked his wares. Enjoying a cool breeze blowing from the lake, Oric sat back to await customers. None came. One or two folks purchased from other stalls, but scurried past Oric's display of medicaments with downcast eyes.

Come midday, Oric gave up in disgust. He packed up his wares, and led Otty along the street to Archie Pender's cottage. The old man answered Oric's knock. "Put your donkey in the yard, and come inside."

"Not a penny piece have I made today," moaned Oric, sinking down on to a three-legged stool. "Have I done something to upset folks?"

Archie drew two pots of ale from a small barrel and passed one over to Oric. "Ain't nothing you have done, lad. 'Tis the fault of yon new barber what's set up in Lornika's lean-to." Archie cast his eyes down and shuffled his feet on the packed-dirt floor. "I been meaning to come up to the castle and tell you, but I felt off colour after trying out one of the fellow's potions for my sciatica."

"Why did you not come and see me?" Oric demanded.

"Because I ain't getting any younger and 'tis a long haul up your hill."

"Why not ride up on your donkey?"

"Last time I came to see you, the stupid beast took fright at a flapping raven. He bucked and tossed, and then he ran the rest of the way up with me clinging to the stupid beggar's neck. I tell you, Master Oric, I thought we might plunge over the edge into the valley and die." Archie clenched his hands to stop the tremours. "When this new fellow opened up, I took what I thought was an easy option."

"And has your pain eased?"

"Oh, aye, the pain went, because I remained comatose for Heaven knows how long. I only just managed to lift my head from the pillow this morning." Archie knuckled his eyes. "What day is it?"

Oric stared at the old man in consternation. "'Tis market day. For Heaven's sake, man, what medication did you take to knock you out for so long?"

Archie shrugged and thrust out his bottom lip. "Master Trundle said it was man dragon, or some such. To tell the truth, I never took much notice of what he said. I was in that much pain, I swigged the potion straight from the bottle. I ain't got no memory of what happened after that, save I had some mighty colourful nightmares."

"The medicament is most likely mandragora. It can be deadly poisonous if not handled correctly. Do you have any of the tincture left?"

"Aye, I think so." Archie scrabbled through items on top of a chest, and came up with a near-empty bottle.

Oric pulled out the stopper and sniffed. Lifting the bottle to the light, he inspected the contents. "You are lucky to still be alive after the quantity you supped. Drink plenty of water to flush the toxins from your system."

"I ain't the only one what suffered after taking one of Master Trundle's concoctions. The blacksmith's son Ruben was sick as a dog after paying the fellow a visit. As for Master Plunket, he is never away from Langend Cottage these days. In view of what you say, I am surprised he ain't dead."

"Plunket is a hypochondriac with the constitution of an ox," growled Oric. "No doubt Trundle is coining money from all manner of gullible folk. Methinks 'tis time I had a word with the gentleman."

A queue of people gathered in Lornika's front garden, many of whom Oric had treated in the past. Embarrassed at sight of the young apothecary, they averted their eyes.

"Clear off home, all of you," Oric shouted, jumping down from Otty's back. "This charlatan is more likely to kill you than to effect a cure. By all accounts he has no knowledge of medicine whatsoever. In future, when you feel ill, send for me."

Barda, the Firbrook Forester, dragged his pregnant wife away from the queue. "See, I told you we were making a mistake seeing this man."

Other would-be patients hung their heads, and scurried home.

Hearing the disturbance outside, Amery strode from his room to investigate. In his hand he held a gruesome wooden gadget with a gory tooth attached.

Horrified, Oric shoved Amery aside and ran into the lean-to. Desdemona Whittle lay across the table on her back, blood dripping from her open mouth. "Help me," she gargled, "I am bleeding to death."

Oric raced outside to gather medical supplies from his panniers, and returned to aid the lady. Amery stood over Desdemona, brandishing an iron implement incandescent with heat.

"What are you doing now?" cried Oric, knocking Amery's hand with the implement away. "Are you trying to maim this poor woman for life. Get out of my way whilst I properly attend to her."

Intimidated by the stranger's sheer size, Amery jumped

back, and dropped his iron implement back into the fire. "I know not who you think you are, but I sincerely hope you know what you are about."

Rolling up a small wad of clean, cotton material, Oric eased it into the gaping socket left behind after the tooth extraction. When the bleeding slowed, he helped Desdemona to sit up. She tried to speak but Oric stilled her with a gentle finger to her swollen lips. "Hush, you can talk to me when you feel better." He handed over a small package. "Tomorrow morning, remove the cotton wad from your mouth, rinse your gums with clean water, and rub the sore area with this powdered nutmeg. I have included a few sage leaves to place on the wound afterwards, they will help protect you against infection."

Amery waited until the woman left, then he turned his fury on Oric. "You wretched upstart! How dare you interfere with my patient! I have medical expertise to deal with all types of ailments. If you intervene in any of my treatments again, I shall have you flogged by the lord of the castle."

"You may have trouble with that idea," said Oric tightly, eyeing the barber with a look that would stun a maddened bull.

Amery wobbled his head from side to side. "Indeed! And why, pray, would that be?"

Oric wanted to hit the cocky little man, instead he drew a deep, calming breath. "Because *I* am Lord Lockton and the castle you see on yonder mountainside belongs to me, as does all the land surrounding it. I also own the lake and the forest hereabouts. Most of the dwellings in the district are rented by my tenant farmers and villeins. The same goes for the shops and cottages you see on the high street. For your information, I trained with a master apothecary and have my papers to prove it. If any of my people become ill,

I will take care of them." Getting a grip on his temper, Oric continued in an icy tone. "In future, *you* will stick to cutting hair and beards. If I hear otherwise, I will have you flogged and drummed from the district. Do I make myself clear?"

His anger spent, Oric rubbed his face. The adolescent fuzz on his chin had grown into coarse, golden whiskers – but not yet a full beard. Sight of barber Amery Trundle negated any desire for a shave.

Amery gathered up his left-over herbs and potions and threw them onto the fire. The already noxious smell grew worse and, holding his breath, Oric hastened out of the lean-to. Lornika passed Oric on the pathway. She grabbed up a bucket of water, stormed into Amery's room, and threw the contents onto the fire. Smoke turned into steam and Lornika threw the bucket on the ground. "If I get so much as a whiff of anything like that again – out you go!"

"Did you hear what that jumped-up fellow from the castle said?" Amery wobbled his head from side to side and effected a poor imitation of Oric. "No more practicing medicine. Do I make myself clear?" He fanned his red face with a battered straw hat. "Damn the fellow to hell! Now I must abandon my medical abilities and rely on barbering skills alone to earn a crust."

-oOo-

St Griswald's, a short distance from Bayersby Manor, ideally suited Joffrey's purpose. Local folk kept away, believing the church to be haunted. Taking full advantage of the isolated situation, Joffrey transported tools to stop up gaps in the walls and padlocks to secure both doors into the crypt. His only moment of unease occurred when the Rigg Farm shepherd shambled by. With no time to hide his tools, Joffrey raced to hide behind a large gravestone.

Learning his lesson, Joffrey gathered up his tools and placed them inside the church. Just as well, for a short time later, the Bayersby apothecary arrived. The old man poked around and then left. Much to Joffrey's relief, no-one else ventured close to the church and he finished the job in hand without interruption.

CHAPTER FOURTEEN

Dian Disappears

Too cramped to remain under the cart with her friends, Dian wandered away from the main party. She climbed over a stone wall and lay on her back amongst sweet-smelling clover. She longed for Oric's company, but to take up with a lord was unthinkable. Her tears blurred the silver half-moon that climbed the dark velvet sky.

A cold blade pressed against Dian's throat, jerking her back to reality. "If you wish to stay alive, keep your mouth shut!" Someone grasped a handful of her hair and yanked her onto her hands and knees. "Crawl until I tell you to stop. Make one sound, and my dagger goes straight into your heart."

At the edge of the meadow, the man anchored a sheet of parchment on top of the paddock wall with a stone. Remaining behind Dian, he hauled her to her feet and manhandled her along the track until they came to a fork. A bright shaft of moonlight illuminated a horse, cropping grass under a tree.

Dian recognised the distinctive animal immediately.

"That is Sir Edred's war horse!" she cried, "What is he doing here?"

"Now Sir Edred is dead, the horse belongs to me. Give me your foot, I will boost you on to his back."

For a terrible moment, Dian thought Guwain might be her captor. Looking down, she gasped. "Joffrey! What are you doing?"

"Taking you hostage, missy." Joffrey unhitched the horse and mounted up behind Dian.

"Why would you do such a thing? I am naught but a common serving wench."

"You are anything but common, dear girl, you are Oric's Achilles' heel." Joffrey's hot breath fanned the nape of Dian's neck as he placed a strip of cloth over her eyes and tied it firmly at the back of her head. Holding her tightly against his chest, he kicked the horse into motion.

"Where are you are taking me?" cried Dian, clinging to Balthazar's mane.

"To a secure hiding place where no-one will find you. Once Oric does as he is told, I shall move you to a different location."

"Do not imagine Lord Lockton will care about me. Our friendship is over."

Joffrey's laughter chilled Dian to the bone. "How wrong you are, dear girl!"

Night wore on and they stopped only to eat dry biscuits and answer calls of nature. Determined not to let Joffrey sense her fear, Dian refused to speak.

Deeming the distance between himself and Lady Myferny's party sufficient, Joffrey slowed his pace. Balthazar was stronger than most horses, but a long ride lay ahead, and it would not do to wind the animal.

"How much longer before we reach your destination?" Dian asked, breaking her silence for the first time in hours.

"Have patience, we shall soon be there."

-oOo-

Morning dawned bright and clear with no sign of the rain from the day before. Accompanied by her two ladies-in-waiting, Lady Myferny left the litter and fluttered down to the nearby stream to wash.

The maids-of-work set out a breakfast of smoked eel and oat cakes, whilst Wolfred and Malgwyn reattached the litter to the horses.

"Where is Dian?" asked Ichtheus.

"She took herself off to the meadow," replied one of the maids. "We ain't seen her since last night. No doubt she fell asleep in the grass and ain't woken up yet."

"Well go and seek her," snapped Ichtheus. Keen to get on his way, he did not want to be held up by a lag-along girl.

Giggling, the two maids climbed the stone wall and gambolled off into the meadow. A short while later they returned, all sign of merriment gone. One of the girls held out a red ribbon. "We found this hanging off a gate at the far end of the field. It belongs to Dian, but she ain't nowhere to be seen."

The second maid brandished a piece of parchment. "This was on top of the wall by the gate, but I ain't got no idea what the writing is about 'cos I never learned to read."

-oOo-

An owl hooted as Joffrey helped Dian down from Balthazar's back. She reached up to pull off her blindfold, but Joffrey smacked her hand away. "Keep your eyes covered until we move indoors. The less you know of your whereabouts the happier I shall be. Now get moving." He shoved Dian roughly, and she stumbled down a flight of steps. Assailed by a foetid, damp smell, she asked once again if she could remove her blindfold.

"Indeed, you can." Joffrey untied Dian's wrists, and she pulled off the cloth that covered her eyes.

Near darkness greeted her, and she rubbed her eyes. "I may as well put the blindfold back, for I can see nothing."

"Be patient. A tinder box and candles lie at the bottom of the stairs. We shall soon have light." A few moments later, a flame sputtered into life to reveal a cramped, windowless room. Opposite to the flight of stone steps, stood another iron-bound door with a padlock clasped to the latch.

"Where does the other door lead?" asked Dian.

Joffrey smirked. "None of your business! This abode might not be up to your usual standards but make yourself comfortable. You are going nowhere until I get what I want."

The soulless light in Joffrey's tawny eyes sent shivers down Dian's spine.

"Be economical with the candles, girlie, for there are not many. A woman will bring enough water and food to keep body and soul together until I return." Taking the stairs two at a time, Joffrey left the building and slammed the door. Dian heard a heavy lock click into place.

Exhausted, she plopped down onto a heap of damp straw and a large brown rat scuttled across her legs. Jumping to her feet, Dian ran up the stairs and beat upon the door. "Let me out!" she screamed over and over, but no-one came to her aid.

Curled into a ball at the top of the stairs, Dian finally fell asleep.

A key clicked in the door lock, jerking Dian awake. In the windowless room, she had no idea if it was night or day. The door creaked open and a shaft of brilliant sunlight blinded her. Afraid, Dian ran down the steps, but there was nowhere to hide.

"So, who do we have here?" said an old woman with a lantern. She closed the door, shutting out the daylight. Thin and frail-looking, the woman came close to Dian and held up her lamp. "My word, you are a beauty. I wager some man is going to pay a high price to save your lovely neck. And I have been promised a fine reward, so do not think to escape."

"Let me go," yelled Dian, diving at the old crone.

Well versed in the art of self-defence and survival, the woman side-stepped. She flipped Dian face down on the ground and knelt upon her back. Producing a length of horsehair rope, she tied Dian's hands behind her back.

"Oh, dearie me. I hoped you would be more amenable. You will now remain tethered until I decide to release you. Eating might cause you a problem, but I will cut up your food. You can pick it off the platter with your teeth."

Dian scrambled to her feet, determined to put a brave face on things. "How long am I to be kept here?" she demanded.

"I have no idea. But, in the meantime, let us try to be friends. I have no axe to grind with you, but your behaviour will dictate the treatment you get from me. My name is Doretta, what is yours?"

"None of your business!"

Doretta shrugged her thin shoulders. "Have it your own way." She waggled a grubby finger and smiled, revealing toothless gums. "Ain't no point yelling for help, no-one comes near here. And, in the unlikely event of you getting the door open, my vicious dogs have free rein of the walled area outside. Be aware the brutes are trained to go for the throat if I am not around to stop them." She placed her lantern on one of the steps. "Now eat your food like a good girl, we do not want you fading away." Muttering softly to herself she climbed the stairs, stepped outside, and slammed the door shut.

Once again the lock clicked into place. Laid on her side in the straw, Dian sobbed until she had no tears left. Sniffling, and starving hungry, she sought out the platter of food. Chunks of bread and cheese filled her empty belly, and she tipped milk from a clay pot into the empty dish with her chin. Lowering her face to the platter, cat-like, she lapped up the liquid.

CHAPTER FIFTEEN

Troubling Occurrences

One look at Ichtheus' worried face, and Lady Myferny knew instantly something was terribly wrong.

"Whatever ails you, Master Ichtheus? We have known each other too long to beat about the bush."

"Aye, my lady, we have, and there is no way I can soften the blow. Dian has been seized by some unknown person and is being held captive."

Lady Myferny's hand flew to her breast. "Dear Lord! When and by whom?"

"I am not exactly sure, my lady, sometime during the night is my guess. The two maids found a parchment anchored to the wall in yonder field. The note states I must ride to Lockton Castle and inform Oric. Then we are to await further instructions."

"What can Oric have to do with Dian's assailants?"

"Um, ah…" Ichtheus cleared his throat. "Perhaps the fellow knows Oric loves her."

"Good gracious, I had no idea," said Lady Myferny. "You must make all haste to Lockton Castle. Unhitch your donkey and go!"

"But who will drive my cart to Roxbrough? There are too many necessary supplies aboard to abandon it."

"One of the maids can take your place. Meanwhile, I shall try to gather together whatever the rogue demands for Dian's release."

"The note does not demand payment, my lady. The writer threatens to kill Dian if anyone attempts to rescue her. We have no choice but to do as we are told for the time being."

All colour drained from Lady Myferny's face. "Of course, you are right, Ichtheus. Before you leave, take supplies to see you through the journey to Lockton Castle."

Ichtheus nodded his thanks and handed Lady Myferny into her litter. "I am greatly relieved that you have decided to continue your journey to Roxbrough. Bayersby Manor is no place for a lady at present."

Lady Myferny patted Ichtheus gently on the cheek. "Take care, dear friend. Keep me informed if you are able. Should you need my help in any way, please do not hesitate to send for me." Leaning out of the litter, she waved her hand for Wolfred and Malgwyn to move forward.

Ichtheus informed Mistress Foley of Dian's plight. "Lady Myferny is upset, for she is uncommonly fond of Dian. The poor soul may be glad of someone with whom to share her worries."

Numb with shock, Mistress Foley helped Ichtheus to load Braccus' panniers with food and a few medical supplies. "Since we know not who these rogues are, see you watch out for yourself and mind you do nothing silly…" Tears welled in her eyes and she brushed at them irritably.

"My word, Mistress Foley, I did not realise you cared," said Ichtheus with tongue in cheek. "I promise to be careful."

"You great lummox, 'tis not for you I shed tears, but for

poor little Dian. If I find out who took her, I will strangle the wretch with my bare hands."

Ichtheus did not doubt the housekeeper's words.

Mistress Foley climbed on to her cart and squinted down upon Ichtheus' upturned face. "And I meant what I said about you watching out for yourself."

For part of the journey to Lockton, Ichtheus rode Braccus, at other times he walked to give the donkey a rest. Five nerve-racking days passed. Every step of the way Ichtheus kept a hand on his dagger, never sure if anyone followed. Keeping a weather eye open for robbers' ambushes proved exhausting, and he muttered a prayer of thanks as he packed up after his final night's camp. Almost out of provisions, he looked forward to a decent meal and a comfortable bed at the castle.

Entering Firbrook Forest, Ichtheus took a wrong turn. Dense undergrowth soon hampered the donkey's passage, and Ichtheus dismounted once again to help the donkey negotiate bramble thickets and trees. In no time at all, he lost all sense of direction. The further he travelled, the gloomier the woods became. Sounds of babbling water momentarily lifted his spirits and, hoping the brook might lead back to the main track, Ichtheus followed the watercourse. Coming upon a grassy plateau, he stopped to allow Braccus to graze. The donkey gleefully munched on sweet grass whilst Ichtheus tried to get his bearings. Across the brook he spotted a strange-looking construction made from branches, twigs, and leaves. Removing his boots, he waded across the shallow water to take a closer look. In front of the shelter lay a pile of smouldering logs. "Hello," Ichtheus called, "is anyone there?" No-one answered. Ichtheus poked his head inside the dwelling to seek clues as to the identity of the occupant. Beside a makeshift bed lay a large wooden cross and a bible. Ichtheus raked his fingers through his beard. Surely no educated man of God would subject himself to such dismal quarters. *Perhaps the fellow is doing penance. If so, where is he?*

Ichtheus waded back across the brook, dried his feet on his cloak and put on his boots. "Come along, Braccus, let us be on our way or we will not see Lockton Castle this day."

Poor light indicated late afternoon and, driven by desperation, Ichtheus blundered on through the forest. "I could die in here if we fail to find our way out, Braccus." The donkey dropped his head to grab a mouthful of grass. "Ha! 'Tis all very well for you, there is water aplenty and greenery for you to eat. You would survive very nicely under such circumstances." Ichtheus harrumphed. "At this rate I may yet be forced to partake of a similar diet."

Braccus lifted his head and pricked his ears forward.

"Did you hear something, old lad?"

The donkey swivelled his ears again, and Ichtheus listened for a sound. Not far away a woman screamed.

"Oh, my giddy aunt! Dian!" Hustling Braccus along, Ichtheus sped toward the sound.

A small ivy-clad cottage stood in a clearing. Well-tended vegetables and herbs grew in a sizeable garden in front of the dwelling. Chickens scratched in an enclosed run, and an orchard of six or more fruit trees grew behind a wooden fence.

No sound came from within the cottage, and Ichtheus tentatively walked up the pathway. From behind the cottage door, blood oozed on to the step.

"What funny business is this?" he cried, banging on the cottage door. "Dian, are you in there?"

"There is no-one of that name here!" quavered a female voice from within. "Go away and leave me alone. If you are not gone within a heartbeat, I shall set my dogs on you."

"I mean you no harm, Mistress, please keep your dogs in check," said Ichtheus, in a disappointed tone.

"Then why do you threaten me time after time? And why have you killed my rooster and nailed him to the inside of my door? I told you I am no witch, nor I do not practice Satanic arts. I shall count to three and then out my dogs shall come. One, two…"

"Nay, Mistress, stay your hand," cried Ichtheus in a panic. "I am naught but a simple traveller who has lost his way in the woods. And I certainly did not kill your rooster."

The cottage door cracked open to reveal a female face surrounded by a halo of brown hair streaked liberally with grey. Two canine muzzles pushed in at knee height.

"Identify yourself, or I *will* turn my dogs loose."

"The Bayersby Apothecary at your service, madam," Ichtheus stated hastily. "You have no need to fear me."

Reassured, the woman fully opened her door. "My name is Cordelia Ramshorn." Tall and sturdy, but well past the first flush of youth, her brown eyes gleamed with intelligence.

"How long have these threats against your life been going on?"

"A few months. At first it was only little things – like my washing disappearing from the shrubbery after I put it out to dry. Then someone began stealing my vegetables and eggs. At first I took no notice, thinking some half-starved urchin from Skelgut was the culprit. Lord knows the children from that village endured a hard time under Sir Ragnald's jurisdiction." Cordelia shrugged. "I became afraid when the perpetrator made threats against my life."

"Have you seen this person's face?"

"Not really. He usually visits late at night. Today is the first time he has arrived during daylight hours. I got a quick glimpse of his back as he disappeared into the woods. He wore a black priest's habit with a hood pulled over his head, and he brandished a large dagger. He continually raves about witchcraft, and how he plans to wipe all practitioners of black magic from the face of the earth."

Ichtheus' heart beat a little faster. The woman's description reminded him of Father Chrispian, the deranged priest who once preached at St Griswald's church. "Why did you not loose your dogs upon him?"

"Because I was afraid yon maniac would inflict more damage with his dagger than they would do to him with their teeth."

"Trust me, dear lady, you need to take this man seriously."

"Oh, indeed I do. He killed my rooster, it may be my turn next. I know not how much longer I can withstand his onslaughts."

"How long have you lived here?"

"Several years." Cordelia's expression tightened. "My husband died, and my step-children turned me out of the family home. I came to Skelgut to seek a new dwelling and came across this empty cottage. My life has been simple but pleasant – until this fellow began threatening me."

"You must leave and not return home until the man is apprehended," said Ichtheus. "Oric, the new lord of Lockton, will accommodate you. He is my friend and I am on my way to visit him. Would you accompany me and guide me to my destination?"

Cordelia nodded, and ordered her dogs to sit. "Give me a moment to pack a few necessities."

The dogs eyed Ichtheus suspiciously, but made no move toward him. Cordelia soon reappeared with a small bundle. "My chickens have been well protected against predators in their strongly built run, but I must let them out for fear they will starve. My vegetables will have to take a chance on rain to keep them alive."

"Hurry, Mistress, for I have another agenda," urged

Ichtheus. "A young woman has been taken, and I need to inform Oric, Lord of Lockton, of the situation as soon as possible."

CHAPTER SIXTEEN

Difficult Decisions

Arriving at Lockton Castle, Ichtheus and Cordelia crossed the drawbridge. The closed portcullis barred entrance into the bailey, and Ichtheus clanged the wall-mounted bell.

Rory stepped forward and, holding a lantern close to the grill, he squinted at the late callers. "Be warned, I am armed with a sharp dagger, so no funny business!"

"For goodness sake, Rory, 'tis I, Ichtheus, the Bayersby Apothecary. I am accompanied by Mistress Cordelia Ramshorn. Open the gate and let us in."

Grumbling about the lateness of the hour, Rory sheathed his dagger and returned to the wheelhouse. Moments later the portcullis creaked open.

"Where is Oric?" Ichtheus demanded. "I must speak with him immediately."

"I dunno – I ain't his keeper. Have a wander about, the place is big, but not that big. You are bound to come across him eventually."

Irritated beyond measure, Ichtheus thrust Braccus' reins into Rory's hands. "Stable my donkey and give him a nosebag of oats." Indicating to Cordelia's two dogs, he added, "And take these animals to the kennels – make sure they are also well fed."

Muttering all the while, Rory disappeared into the stable block with the animals in tow.

Josh Cole sauntered out of his workshop to investigate the disturbance. Seeing the visitors, his face cracked into a wide smile. "That is never you, is it, Master Ichtheus?" He grinned mischievously. "Could not keep away from us, eh?" He nodded to Cordelia, thinking he had seen her somewhere before but he could not quite recall where.

Engulfed in a bear-like hug, Ichtheus struggled to free himself. "This is not a social visit, Josh, I am the bringer of bad news. Where is Oric?"

Josh darted a worried glace at Ichtheus, wondering what could be so serious for the old man to risk the long journey from Bayersby to Lockton, accompanied only by an elderly woman. "You will find Oric upstairs in the library. He spends most of his evenings in there reading and writing in his medical journal."

"Thank you, Josh, I will seek him out directly. In the meantime, please escort Mistress Ramshorn to the kitchen, and introduce her to Genevieve and Faylinn." Ichtheus patted Cordelia's arm. "I am sure the girls will take care of you and find you a place to sleep." Hastening through the Great Hall, Ichtheus climbed a short flight of stairs that gave access to the Library.

Totally engrossed in an open ledger on his vast desk, Oric failed to hear the apothecary enter the room.

"'Tis good to see you hard at work," said Ichtheus.

"Um… Yes, I hope this interruption is important." Oric glanced up. "Master Ichtheus!" He vaulted over his chair, and hugged the old man so tightly Ichtheus believed his ribs might crack.

"How wonderful to see you," cried Oric. "I have so much to tell you. How long are you here for? Have you had anything to eat? I must tell Ned and Joe you are here, Josh too."

Ichtheus held up his hand. "Wait, do not call anyone in yet. I bring disturbing news and wish to tell you first."

Oric's happy smile swiftly faded. "Sit down, get your breath back, you look exhausted."

Ignoring Oric's concern, Ichtheus came straight to the point. "Dian has disappeared."

A cold hand of fear gripped Oric's stomach. "Disappeared? What do you mean, disappeared? She cannot vanish into thin air! Did she accompany you to Lockton Castle and get lost along the way?" Oric stood at the top of the stairs and yelled for stable-boy Walter to saddle Jester. "I shall ride out straight away and begin searching the woods."

To stop Oric from running down the stairs, Ichtheus grabbed the hem of his tunic. "No, no. Hear me out. If you do that, Dian could die."

Oric stopped abruptly, his face whiter than chalk. "What did you say?"

Ichtheus related what little he knew, and handed over the parchment the maids had found anchored to the wall next to the field gate.

It took but a heartbeat for Oric to read the note. "By all that is holy, I cannot sit here waiting for news! Do you have any idea who has taken Dian?"

"Not yet, but please try to stay calm. There is little we can do until someone contacts us with further instructions. In the meantime, let us keep this information to ourselves. We do not want folk running around, causing more trouble. In my view, the fewer people who know about the situation the better chance Dian stands of survival. Now, I suggest you rescind your order to have Jester saddled and tell Walter that you have decided not to ride out after all."

The pain in Oric's chest was akin to a kick from a mule and he had trouble drawing a deep breath. "If any harm befalls Dian, I will kill the swine."

"I am sure you will, but now I need you to call everyone to the Great Hall. I have more bad news to impart."

Surely no crisis could be worse than Dian's abduction. Pulling himself together, Oric went in search of his friends.

At Oric's shout, Hamish limped into the library.

Thanks to Oric's skill in mending broken bones, the old Scot could walk again. "What d'ye want at this time o' night y' young rascal? I was about to go to m' bed."

"You cannot retire yet – Master Ichtheus is here, and he brings bad news. Find everyone and fetch them to the library."

Chastened, Hamish hastened away to round everyone up.

"I know you believe Dian's disappearance needs to be kept quiet, Master Ichtheus, but my supporters need to know what is happening," said Oric. "They have my best interests at heart and they are more of a help than a hindrance in all situations." Oric frowned. "All except for Rory, that is. Lord knows who he would back in times of trouble."

Ichtheus grimaced. "Make no mistake, lad, Rory has only one interest – the preservation of his own skin."

Hamish returned to the library, followed by Ned, Joe, Josh, and Bannulf. "I sent for Walter, Erik and Arnald, too," he said. "They are practicing their swordsmanship by the light of torches behind the chapel. They will join us directly – always supposing they have ne' killed one another."

Exhausted from worry and his lengthy journey, Ichtheus focused bleary eyes on the familiar people around the table. "So much has occurred since I last saw you all, I barely know where to begin." He sighed heavily, "I am sorry to tell you, Sir Edred is dead."

"Sir Edred dead!" cried Oric. "But he was at the peak of good health when I saw him last."

"He suffered a particularly painful attack of gout, and he took exception when I suggested he moderate his diet and stop drinking. A ne'er-do-well medicine-man named Freeman arrived at the manor around that time." Ichtheus lifted his hands, then let them slap down against his thighs. "Thenceforth, Sir Edred refused to take my advice, preferring to listen to the new fellow instead. Soon after, I was informed of our lord and master's death."

"But how did Sir Edred die?" demanded Oric.

"I believe Freeman's filthy potions were to blame. My suspicions were further aroused when, immediately after the tragedy, the charlatan disappeared without trace. Sir Edred's bones were barely cold in his grave when Guwain took over the estate. Since then, the situation at Bayersby has become intolerable."

Ned stared at Ichtheus in disbelief. "How so? Life at the manor was mostly always pleasant."

"Aye, that was the case when Sir Edred was alive," retorted Ichtheus. "But things have gone from bad to worse since two unwholesome characters, namely Leofrick and Cadwin, arrived at the manor. Then Sir Ragnald's son, Joffrey, joined them. He reckoned not to know them, but I suspect both men are in his employ." Ichtheus huffed and shook his head. "Master Guwain is in his cups most of the time, and he ill-uses the servants. Many of Sir Edred's old retainers have left the manor. Bayersby now overflows with itinerants from God knows where. Lady Myferny is with child, and I persuaded her to leave. She has gone to her sister's place in Roxbrough. Mistress Foley and most of the female staff accompanied her.

Sir Edred's two faithful retainers, Wolfred and Malgwyn, rode with them. We stopped to rest at Dunburton and, sometime during the night, Dian disappeared."

A babble of voices drowned anything else Ichtheus said.

"Be quiet!" yelled Josh, thumping his fist on the table. "Did you say my sister has disappeared? If so we need to find her immediately."

"I am with you, Josh," replied Oric, "but does anyone know where Dian is?"

Unable to give Oric any more information, Ichtheus allowed the young men a few moments to compose themselves before raising his next concern. "I am the harbinger of even more bad news."

"Dear God," cried Oric, squeezing the bridge of his nose between his thumb and forefinger. "Surely nothing could be worse than the information you have already imparted."

"Perhaps not, but disturbing nonetheless," said Ichtheus. "On my way here, I became disoriented in the forest. Just as well I did. Had I not lost my way, a certain lady may not be alive right now."

Oric quickly raised his eyes. "To whom do you refer?"

"Cordelia Ramshorn. Her cottage lies deep in Farnrock Forest."

"Now I recall who the lady is," said Josh. "I have seen her in Skelgut selling vegetables to the locals at very reasonable prices. She seems like a decent enough soul. Why should her life be in danger?"

"I believe she is being terrorised by a crazy priest. Mistress Ramshorn says the fellow accused her of witchcraft." Ichtheus raised his bushy eyebrows. "Sound familiar?"

"Horribly so," Oric groaned. "Please tell me you do not refer to the dreadful Father Chrispian that Sir Edred once employed?"

"I would swear to it, and I suspect the same fellow you say caused the fire in Lornika Fentwhistle's cottage. With that disaster in mind, I have invited Cordelia to stay at Lockton Castle, for she must not remain in her isolated situation with a maniac on the rampage."

Oric immediately nodded his consent. "The lady is welcome to stay with us for as long as she chooses."

-oOo-

Hours spent discussing Dian's rescue escalated into days but, with no leads to follow, all plans came to naught. Barely able to contain himself, Oric suggested he ride to the area where Dian was last seen. "At least I will feel as though I am doing something."

"Nay, lad, that would serve no purpose," said Ichtheus. "'Tis a hard, five-day ride to Dunburton, and I reckon the lass will be long gone from there." Casting around for ways to distract Oric, he suggested they attend Skelgut's market the following day.

Oric agreed to accompany the old man, hoping to unearth some small clue as to Dian's whereabouts. Many a traveller frequented the market, perhaps one of them might have heard something.

Braccus and Otty, their panniers loaded with medicinal remedies and produce from Josh's garden, made their way down the mountainside. Parzifal gambolled along, stopping here and there to sniff at clumps of grass, and to cock his leg. Not long into the journey, Braccus gripped the bit between his teeth and pulled away from Ichtheus' grasp. Hanging on to his bonnet with one hand, Ichtheus attempted to catch up with the runaway donkey.

Oric grinned for the first time since Ichtheus had imparted his bad news. "Oish, yon little beast ain't improved with age, has he? And there was I thinking you might have a better grip on him by now."

"Mind your manners, boy!" snapped Ichtheus. "Since you are so clever, you run after the dratted donkey."

Thinking everything a wonderful game, Parzifal took off after his young master, got entangled between his legs, and bowled him over.

Braccus ran out of energy, slowed his pace, and began cropping grass under an oak tree.

With the stoical Otty in tow, Ichtheus caught up with Oric and the other two wayward animals. "Ye gods," he exclaimed. "Nothing changes. 'Tis just like our misadventures when we attended Kilterton Market together. I swear you put a jinx on all animals, Oric."

Parzifal lathered Oric's face with a wet pink tongue, loving every moment of the new game. "I believe you are right, Master Ichtheus," said Oric scrambling to his feet and brushing dry twigs and grass from his breeches. He fondled Parzifal's whiskery ears, "But I would not exchange any one of them for all the animals in Christendom."

Somewhat dishevelled and out of breath, Oric and Ichtheus arrived in Skelgut.

"My word, things have changed!" puffed Ichtheus, viewing the village's busy thoroughfare. "Last time I saw this place it was near derelict, but look at it now!"

The main street, bathed in sunshine, hummed with people. Children played at the lake's edge whilst their parents strolled amongst the many stalls, set up by local and visiting traders. All manner of goods from cheese and fresh fish, to leather and all else in-between was on offer for sale or barter. On the opposite side of the street, potter Manluss displayed jugs and bowls outside his shop. In the premises next door, the candlemaker sold beeswax and tallow candles. Inside the forge, the blacksmith hammered red-hot horseshoes on his anvil. Further down the thoroughfare, smoke billowed from the baker's roof hole, indicating fresh bread would soon be ready for sale. Ichtheus beamed. "What a delight to see so many small businesses up and running."

"None of it my doing," replied Oric in a flat tone of voice. "All credit belongs to the country folk."

Ichtheus did not believe Oric for one moment but, seeing his protégée lapsing back into melancholy, he tried to jolly the lad along. "Let us set out your wares. I am keen to observe how your medicinal skills have improved since you left Bayersby Manor." Down the street, a red and white-striped barber's pole outside one of the cottages attracted Ichtheus' attention. "Unless, of course," he added, "the competition has become too great. Is yon barber-surgeon good at his job?"

Oric bared his teeth. "That pole belongs to one Amery Trundle. He ain't been here long, but he has already made his presence felt and, I might add, not in the best of ways."

"Is that so?" said Ichtheus, his interest aroused. "What is wrong with the fellow?"

"One poor woman, subjected to his lack of dentistry skill, will never be the same again. Trundle extracted the wrong tooth and, when her severe pain continued after the event, I was called to remove the offending molar. Lord knows, poor Mistress Whittle had few enough teeth to begin with. Now she must cut all her meals into tiny pieces to enable her to swallow her food. I have since ordered the barber to do nothing in future but cut hair and trim beards."

"Hmmm, I need a hair and beard trim," mused Ichtheus, twisting a straggly lock of white hair around his fingers. "I might pay the fellow a visit. Unlike a bad medical procedure, a bad haircut takes but a week or two to grow back again." He grinned wryly and added, "Pity the same cannot be said for teeth."

Since Amery Trundle no longer practiced medicine, customers and patients lined up in front of Oric's table. Every one of them sought advice or needed a potion of one sort or another. Busy though he was, Oric failed to push Dian's predicament to the back of his mind. Thoughts of her consumed him every day and kept him awake most nights.

Lornika Fentwhistle accosted Ichtheus the moment he stepped through her front gate. Liking the look of the old gentleman with the long white beard and flowing hair, she fluttered her eyelashes and sidled up to him. "How would you like me to tell your fortune?" she simpered, taking hold of his hand. "Just glancing at your palm tells me you have an interesting future."

Ichtheus disentangled himself from the woman's clutches. "No thank you, madam, I would prefer my future to remain a surprise. I am here for a haircut and nothing more. Kindly show me to the barber's premises."

Shoulders drooping with disappointment, Lornika led Ichtheus into the lean-to at the side of her cottage. Hoping to win the old man over, she made him comfortable on the barber's chair. "Wait here, my dear, Master Amery will be with you directly."

Lornika knew exactly where to find the missing barber. Whenever the sun shone, the bone-idle fellow snoozed away his time on a bench beside her herb garden. Cursing under her breath, Lornika kicked Amery's shins. "Get off your backside – a client awaits you indoors."

The barber blustered into his domain with hair-cutting tools at the ready. Setting his eyes upon Ichtheus, he dropped his implements and fled.

"What are you playing at?" cried Lornika, chasing after Amery. "Come back here at once. A gentleman wants his hair cutting and you need the money to pay your rent."

Intrigued by Master Amery's peculiar behaviour, Ichtheus hastened to the door in time to catch a fleeting glimpse of the plump barber moments before he disappeared into the forest behind Skelgut's main street. "Oh, my giddy aunt," yelled Ichtheus. "Stop that man! He is not Amery Trundle, he is Master Freeman and I believe he is responsible for the death of Sir Edred of Bayersby."

Oric organised a search party and, with Parzifal in the lead, they set off to look for the missing man. But Master Trundle, alias Master Freeman, had vanished.

Hot on Trundle's scent, Parzifal ran along, nose to the ground, until he came to a shallow river. At the water's edge, he halted abruptly.

"I do not believe this is happening again," fumed Oric. "The fellow who set light to Lornika's cottage played a similar trick, only he took to the lake to fool my dog." Thoroughly dispirited, Oric pulled Parzifal across to the river's opposite bank. "I suspect we are wasting our time, old lad, but we will follow the water course for a little while in the hope you can pick up Trundle's scent again. Hang it all, the fellow has to seek dry land eventually."

-oOo-

In the distance, a dog barked and, terrified of being outrun, Amery thanked providence for the river he stumbled into. Cold water filled his boots as he waded along, and he soon lost all sensation in his feet and lower legs. Deeming he had sloshed far enough along the riverbed to outwit any dog that might try to follow, he scrambled out of the water and up the muddy riverbank.

A priest-like character barred Amery's way. "Lord in heaven!" squeaked the barber. "You gave me a terrible fright. Who are you?"

The unsavoury-looking man smiled, exposing yellow, horse-like teeth. "I am Father Chrispian." He indicated a strange tangle of vegetation on a level grassy area beside the river. "My humble residence lies yonder."

Having no-where else to run and nothing but the clothes on his back, Amery accepted Father Chrispian's offer of accommodation. Now he sat outside the priest's abode, fuming over his desperate plight. The shack was more like an abandoned eagle's nest than a dwelling, and small animal's bones scattered around the fire circle added to the unpleasant atmosphere.

"Have you had sufficient rabbit stew?" asked Father Chrispian.

"Indeed, I have. And a splendid feast it was," Amery lied. "Tell me, how come you offer me shelter and succour when you have no idea who I am?"

"I enjoy your company, and I believe we may have much in common."

"You do?" Other than homelessness, Amery wondered what traits he could possibly share with the tall, unsavoury-looking fellow.

Father Chrispian's opaque eyes gleamed in the firelight. He believed the newcomer might prove helpful in the capture and burning of witches but, for the moment, he chose not to voice his thoughts. "Perhaps God brought us together. Let us kneel and give thanks for our newfound friendship."

Not a religious man, Amery hesitated. Glancing at the priest's ferocious expression, he changed his mind and knelt. Some considerable time later, the priest completed his devotions.

Both legs locked with pain, Amery crawled to a nearby tree and hauled himself upright. Ready to turn in for the night, he was less than pleased when Father Chrispian beckoned him over to the fire and ordered him to sit down.

"Judging by the way you keep looking over your shoulder and jumping at every sound, I suspect you need to lie low for a while." The priest smiled, exposing his ugly dental array again. "Am I correct?"

Defeated and utterly miserable, Amery nodded.

"What you and I need is a safe place to bide for a while. And I happen to know of a woman who abandoned her cottage recently. What say we move into her premises and look after her property until she returns?" When she did return, Father Chrispian had no intention of letting her escape again.

"I will think about it," said Amery tentatively.

Lightning, followed by a low rumble of thunder and some fat drops of rain, aided Amery to make up his mind. "Yes, very well, I accept your kind offer. When do we take over the cottage?"

"We shall move in at first light tomorrow morning," said Father Chrispian. "A decent roof over our heads will be most agreeable, not to mention the use of a well-stocked vegetable garden and many chickens."

CHAPTER SEVENTEEN

A Malevolent Note

Unlike the rest of the men at Bayersby Manor, Joffrey drank very little alcohol. Nor did he overindulge with rich food. His trim body, dark skin and hair, coupled with tawny, cat-like, eyes made him popular with the ladies, but he kept them all at a distance. When the time was right, he would choose a mate of noble descent befitting a man of his ambition.

Deeming it time to spin another thread in his web of evil, Joffrey slid a sheet of parchment on to the table. Using a quill pen, he wrote a few lines. Satisfied with his work, he shook ground ash on to the wet ink. Blowing away the residue of powder, he rolled up the page, secured it with a wax seal, and sent for Leofrick.

The ex-warrior sauntered into the Great Hall. "You sent for me?"

"Aye," Joffrey held out the sealed parchment. "I want you to ride to Dunburton. Gather together any wayfarer who owns a horse. Tell them they can look forward to a good life if they follow you."

"And where do you wish me to lead them?" asked Leofrick warily.

"To Skelgut."

"Dunburton is a day's ride from here," whined Leofrick. "Then I face a further five days in the saddle to reach that mangy little village. Why is it always me that must run your poxy errands?"

"Because you will do anything for money, and I am offering to pay you a handsome sum to get this parchment to Oric of Lockton. If you refuse, prepare to feel a dagger between your shoulder blades when you least expect it. The choice is yours, my friend."

"Then ride I must," mumbled Leofrick, "for the alternative holds no appeal." His employer was not known for making idle threats but, when he was in funds, he usually honoured promised payments.

A vein pulsed in Joffrey's forehead, and he pressed a finger upon it. Leofrick would do as he was told, but never at the expense of his own skin. "When you reach your destination, tell your men to lie low in the forest behind Skelgut. Cover your face and sneak into the village after dark. Grab some poor urchin and terrify him into delivering the parchment to Lockton Castle. Once your duty is discharged, return to the forest and stay with your men. If everything goes according to plan, Oric and his entire entourage will leave the castle. When they do, move your men in and keep an eye on the place until I arrive."

-oOo-

Almost beside himself with worry, Oric paced up and down the Great Hall. Never in his life had he felt so useless. With every day that passed, his concern for Dian deepened, and he was ready to accept any demand to see her returned safe and sound.

Sensing his master's distress, Parzifal placed his whiskery paws on Oric's shoulders and licked his chin. Oric buried his face in the dog's wiry coat. "Precious friend, what would I do without you?"

"Master Oric! Master Oric!" A young boy from the village who worked at the castle each day ran into the room with Ichtheus in hot pursuit. Out of breath and terrified, the boy stopped halfway along the room.

Ichtheus pushed the urchin forward. "Go on, lad, show Lord Lockton what you have, and tell him how you came by it."

The boy proffered a rolled parchment and Oric snatched it with quivering fingers. He spread the page out on his desk and read the content.

Dian is safe and will remain so, providing you obey these instructions to the letter.

Gather together your people and begone from Lockton Castle before next full moon.

If you want the girl to remain alive, never return to the castle or the district of Skelgut.

No signature adorned the bottom of the page.

Oric snatched his hand off the parchment, and it rolled up with a snap. He strode over to the boy and grabbed the front of his tunic. "Who paid you to deliver this note?"

Ichtheus' angry voice cut through Oric's anger and distress. "Leave go of the boy! He is naught but an unpaid messenger." He patted the distressed little fellow and encouraged him to explain how he came by the note.

The boy regarded Oric with huge, tear-filled eyes, and wiped his drippy nose along the length of his sleeve. "I' truth Master Oric, I would never do owt to harm you. I was on my way home from work when a fellow I ain't seen afore came at me out of nowhere. He put a knife to my throat and said if I failed to give you this note he would kill me. No money changed hands, honest, your lordship."

The boy sobbed, and Oric felt utter remorse. "I am sorry, lad, I should never have doubted you." He opened a drawer in his desk and pulled out a copper coin. "Buy yourself a sweetmeat, but please promise not to tell anyone of your ordeal for the time being."

The boy sniffled and nodded.

"Dry your eyes and run along home. Try not to worry about the man who threatened you, he will be long gone by now." Oric rubbed his chest and took several deep breaths to slow his racing heart. "What do you make of that, Master Ichtheus? Did you read the note?"

"I did, and I am about to add to your unrest. In case you have forgotten, the next full moon is tomorrow night. That gives us little time to pack up and leave the castle."

"You are not advocating we do as the note says, are you? I shall ride out and search for Dian. There cannot be too many places hereabouts in which to imprison her."

"You are not thinking logically, lad. The girl may well die if we fail to comply with the note's instructions. We must vacate the castle as instructed, but we will regroup elsewhere and plan a strategy for rescuing her."

Oric shook his head in denial. "Surely the fellow will not kill her. If he does, he has lost his bargaining tool."

"I am afraid the rogue has you over a barrel. He clearly knows you well, and he believes you will not put Dian's life in danger."

"I will kill the swine once I discover who he is."

Ichtheus gripped the edge of the table until his knuckles turned white. "I think Sir Ragnald's son might be the culprit. Who else would employ such drastic measures to secure tenure of Lockton Castle?"

"Surely not! Skelgut's villagers will be less than helpful if they think Joffrey plans to take over the district again. They hated Sir Ragnald's guts, I doubt they will accept his son gladly." Oric held out his hands, palms up. "And, if I leave, folk will think I have abandoned them. What will I tell them, and where will I go?"

"As I see it, you have no choice. As to where we go, returning to Bayersby Manor might be our best option." Ichtheus sniffed, "Your presence might be just what Guwain needs to bring him to his senses. At the same time, we can formulate a plan to save Dian and Lockton Castle."

Temporarily defeated, Oric called his friends together in the Great Hall. No-one spared a thought for Cordelia, working in the vegetable garden beyond the castle walls.

"I am in receipt of another note," Oric announced. It states that we must vacate Lockton Castle before the next full moon if Dian is to remain alive."

"But why?" demanded Josh. "What does Lockton Castle have to do with Dian's abduction?"

"Master Ichtheus suspects Sir Ragnald's son, Joffrey. We believe he is the only person who would go to such lengths to seize the castle. In the hope of saving Dian's life, I have decided to return to Bayersby Manor. The situation under Guwain's jurisdiction is deteriorating day by day and, whilst we work out a solution for Dian's predicament, we will also try to put things right at the manor for Lady Myferny's sake. Pack your belongings and prepare to leave Lockton Castle immediately."

"I will no' go with you," said Hamish. "M' leg will no' stand the distance on foot or on horseback."

"Have you anywhere other than the castle to stay?" asked Oric.

"Aye, sir, Master Pender will gi' me a bed in his Skelgut cottage."

Rory hawked and spat on the hearth. "I been here all my life, and I ain't about to leave the district now. I will stay put at the castle. It will be interesting to see what happens after you all depart."

-oOo-

About to climb on to his cart, Ichtheus caught sight of Cordelia standing by the portcullis with her dogs. "Oh, my giddy aunt. I forgot to tell yon poor lady of our plans! What must she be thinking?"

Mounted upon Jester, Oric fought to stop the animal taking off. "Tell the lady to pack her belongings. She can travel with us to Bayersby on Faylinn and Genevieve's cart."

"Cordelia might prefer to travel with me," said Ichtheus. "We have much in common, and we can use the travelling time to discuss growing and concocting herbs into potions."

Riding through Skelgut, Oric stopped to talk to Archie Pender. He took the old man into his confidence and explained about Dian's disappearance.

Archie listened to Oric's story with growing distress. "I will gladly give Hamish a bed," he promised, "but the villagers ain't going to be happy. They will think you have abandoned them."

"Please tell them I am sorry, and that my departure is due to circumstances beyond my control, but please do not make my true reason for leaving common knowledge. If word gets out, Dian's life may be jeopardised."

"Your secret is safe with me, Master Oric. But I tell you this – if Joffrey is planning to take over the district in your absence, he can look forward to a bumpy ride. Folks hereabouts trust you, and they ain't going to take kindly to a new master, least of all Sir Ragnald's son. Archie squeezed Oric's hand tightly. "I will pray for your little lady and I hope she is safe and sound wherever she might be."

CHAPTER EIGHTEEN

Return to Bayersby

"With so many of us, plus Parzifal and Cordelia's two dogs, potential robbers may think twice before they accost us." In a lather to obey the instructions laid down on the parchment, Oric dreaded any delay, no matter the reason.

"I hope you are right," replied Ichtheus, securing his bonnet flaps under his chin. "Trouble-free, the journey from Lockton to Bayersby is long enough. Plus, our reason for leaving is not conducive to good spirits."

Jester and the other animals behaved admirably, perhaps sensing the urgency of the situation. No major incident occurred along the way, though Oric set a gruelling pace. Exhausted, everyone breathed a sigh of relief when Bayersby Manor came into view.

From a distance everything looked the same as ever but, upon closer inspection, the rundown condition of the Bayersby estate shocked Oric to his core. Farm equipment lay abandoned in the fields, and hay paddocks which should have been mown long since, ran riot with waist-deep grass. Scarlet poppies, white oxeye daises displaying bright yellow centres, and purple lady-finger vetch grew in profusion. Where summer crops would normally thrive, weeds choked last year's deep furrows. The time of year produced many wind-born seeds, ensuring a bigger and better dandelion crop next season.

Oric swivelled around in his saddle, trying to take in the extent of the neglect. Jester swung his head back and latched his teeth on to Oric's boot. Under normal circumstances Oric would have laughed. As it was, he whacked Jester's flank. "Not now, stupid animal. I have enough to worry about without you adding to my difficulties."

"How on earth has this state of affairs taken place in such a short time?" Oric demanded. "Has nothing been achieved since Sir Edred died?" He stood up in his stirrups to look further afield. "I can see no cattle, what has happened to the Bayersby herd? Few sheep were in evidence as we crossed the moor, either." Jester snickered and took a swift step forward. Oric's knees buckled and he sat down hard, his backside meeting the saddle with a bump.

"I am sad to report that most of the livestock has been marketed to raise cash. A few were slaughtered to feed Master Guwain's guests." Ichtheus leaned across the gap between their two mounts and squeezed Oric's arm. "This state of affairs is not such a shock for me, for I witnessed the downfall of the estate first-hand."

"Thank God you persuaded Lady Myferny and her handmaidens to leave. I dread to think how she would cope – especially since she is with child." Gathering himself together, Oric led his party into the manor compound.

A few chickens scratched about for insects. Two scrawny pigs snuffled in the earth wherever they chose. Dirty pails lay next to the well along with unwashed pots and platters. Flies buzzed in the late afternoon sunshine, laying clusters of maggot-bearing eggs wherever they found a morsel of decaying food or animal dropping.

Only one undernourished stable boy came forward to assist the new arrivals. Oric took pity on the lad, doubting he had strength to cope with the new influx of animals. "Eric, Arnald, give this young fellow a hand to stable our mounts. Bannulf, Ned and Joe, please unload the carts. Josh, check out the compound and buildings."

Eric came out of the stables at a gallop. "Lord knows when the stalls were last mucked out, the place stinks," he gasped. "We face much work to get this place shipshape again. And there is precious little fodder. Shall I turn our horses and donkeys out into the meadow to eat their fill?"

"Aye, do that, Eric, but make sure the gates are all intact."

Faylinn and Genevieve ventured into the kitchen to check out the pantry. "Ain't much food in here," Faylinn stated. "We have enough supplies of our own to last a few days, though goodness knows what we will do for food once they run out."

After a brief inspection outdoors, Josh scraped dirt from his boots by the door. "I think I can save some vegetables in the kitchen garden. A good watering will perk them up – always assuming the well ain't run dry. Most outbuildings are in reasonable repair, all they need is a good clean." He wrinkled his nose, "Especially the dairy, the place reeks. 'Tis a wonder no-one has fallen ill."

A few unkempt servants scuttled about the house, none of them familiar to Oric or his associates. They grumbled, showing resentment at the newcomers' intrusion into their lives.

Noise spilled from the Great Hall, and Oric scowled. "I do believe we are about to ruin the new Lord of Bayersby's jollifications. Are you ready for the fray, Master Ichtheus?"

Ichtheus nodded and held out his arm. "After you, your lordship."

Parzifal growled the moment he entered the Great Hall. "Catch a whiff of your old friend, Guwain, did you?" murmured Oric, grabbing hold of the dog's collar.

An amiable dog, Parzifal harboured only two pet hates. Father Chrispian and Guwain. Both had ill-treated him in the past, and he had not forgotten the kicks doled out to him.

Oric eyed pale squares of clean wall where tapestries had once hung. "I suppose they have been sold along with Sir Edred's livestock."

"Aye, a few," replied Ichtheus, "But Lady Myferny took some away with her."

The more Oric saw, the more he was reminded of the scenario he faced when he first inherited Lockton Castle.

Guwain lolled in a high-backed chair at the head of a long table. Next to his elbow stood a carafe of wine. Red faced, hair awry, tunic stained, he looked like a character from some ludicrous tragedy. Food spilled from platters indicated that the manor's rowdy guests had dined well, unlike the underfed Bayersby serfs.

Several men seated along each side of the table bellowed bawdy songs and clashed pots of ale together, the contents slopping down the drinker's fronts. The combined stench of unwashed bodies, sputtering tallow candles, and vomit caused Oric to gag.

Breaking free of his master's grasp, Parzifal ran at Guwain. He yowled and snapped at the youth's legs.

"'Od's blood!" screamed Guwain. "Get this monster away from me." He swung his legs up over the arm of his chair, leaving an expanse of plump backside unprotected.

Parzifal immediately latched on to Guwain's breeches, ripping off a chunk of material.

Oric ignored the dog, allowing him to shake the torn cloth like a terrier with a rat. "So much for your inheritance," he yelled at Guwain. "Are you not ashamed of yourself? You have turned your father's wealthy estate into a cesspit. Thank God Sir Edred is not here to witness the damage you have done."

Guwain staggered to his feet, knocking over the carafe of wine. Crimson liquid ran over the edge of the table and puddled amongst the dross on the rush-covered floor. "You upstart! How dare you speak to me thus! Get a grip of yon dog – unless you wish to see his throat slit." Making a grab for the dagger in his boot cuff, Guwain lost his balance and fell back into the chair.

Oric slapped his palms on to the table and leaned in close to Guwain. "I dare because I am no longer your subordinate – in fact, my rank is vastly superior to yours. If you care for Bayersby Manor's future, I suggest you shut your mouth and pay attention to what I am about to say."

Guwain ran sticky fingers through his hair and glared back at Oric. "Clear off! This is my manor to do with as I see fit."

"Fit? You ain't fit to clean the stables! Carry on at this rate and there will be no Bayersby Manor to do anything with. I hear Sir Ragnald's son, Joffrey, visits you regularly which, no doubt, explains the trouble you are in."

Guwain pushed back into his chair, looking not a little afraid. "Joffrey comes and goes as he pleases. These men are his friends, not mine."

"Have you no backbone, man? Get rid of the parasites!"

"I dare not," bleated Guwain. "I have few serfs left to protect me. Even my mother has deserted me along with her sour old housekeeper and handmaidens. Wolfred and Malgwyn, craven cowards both, took the opportunity to leave at the same time."

"Wolfred and Malgwyn are far from cowardly, they accompanied your mother to keep her safe. They will be back as soon as she is delivered into her sister's hands at Roxbrough. In the meantime, I intend to set this place to rights."

Oric summoned Bannulf, his two squires, Ned, Joe, and Josh to the Great Hall.

Given the choice to leave or face a fight, Joffrey's cohorts shambled out of the manor.

Throughout the evacuation, Guwain sulked his chair.

"Master Ichtheus tells me the former Committee of Law has been reinstated in Kilterton," said Oric, addressing the petulant young lord once again. "Those few good people will look to the care of the villagers and your tenant farmers. Meanwhile, I will attempt to set Bayersby on a profitable path once again."

Guwain threw a tantrum. "I will not allow you to interfere in my business," he yelled, beating his fists upon the chair's arms. "When Joffrey returns, he will see to anything that needs to be done."

Parzifal reared up onto the table, drool hanging from his jaws. Terrified of the dog, Guwain swiftly sat down again.

"Go to bed and stay there until the effects of the liquor you have imbibed wears off!" roared Oric, dragging Parzifal back on to the floor. "Like it or lump it, you will arise to a whole new regime tomorrow."

Rid of Guwain's surly presence, Oric and his friends began the horrible task of clearing several months' worth of accumulated filth from the Great Hall. The job done, everyone but Oric and Ichtheus retired to bed.

"Will you sup a pot of ale with me, Master Ichtheus?"

"Aye lad, I will, for I doubt sleep will come easily to me this night." Ichtheus took a long pull of his ale and wiped his moustache. "You dealt Guwain's ego a well-deserved blow, but once he sobers up, watch out. He will likely make a deal of trouble for us all."

"Oh, I am ready for him, Master Ichtheus. He caused Dian immeasurable unhappiness when I could do little to protect her. I will *never* forgive him for that. He also gave me a run around when he deemed me his subordinate. Now the boot is on the other foot, I plan to kick his lazy backside hard and as often as possible. More importantly, what do you reckon my next move should be regarding Dian's current situation?"

"I think the time has come to make some in-depth enquiries about Master Joffrey's recent activities."

CHAPTER NINETEEN

Joffrey Returns to Lockton Castle

Joffrey hung about St Griswald's church, occasionally sneaking to Bayersby Manor after dark to make sure Oric and his friends remained in residence. They showed no sign of departure.

Seeking out Doretta in St Griswald's manse, Joffrey gave her his final instructions. "Give me a few days head start, then pack up here and bring the girl to Lockton Castle. Cadwin will act as your escort." Joffrey enjoyed a moment of smug satisfaction. Soon he would leave for Lockton Castle, proving it possible to take over a district without the aid of an army or the spillage of blood.

-oOo-

"How much longer am I to be kept in this stinking dungeon?" cried Dian. "I have not seen the light of day since I was first thrown in here, and I have totally lost track of time. Joffrey is inhuman, treating me in this way."

Doretta emitted a sharp, derogatory snort. "Cease grumbling, girl. Have I not untied your hands? Are you not well fed and sheltered, do you not have constant light – albeit from a candle? If you ask me, you are naught but a spoilt brat. Anyways – I am told your gentleman friend has complied with the master's instructions, so your days here may be numbered."

A flutter of hope blossomed in Dian's heart, but common sense prevailed. "I have told you time and again, I have no gentleman friend. Why should anyone care what happens to me? I am naught but a simple maid of work."

"Oh, is that right?" cackled the old woman, releasing Dian's hands from her bonds. She thrust a plate of food at Dian. "Eat your dinner and shut up." She stomped back upstairs, and Dian listened to the familiar sound of the lock clicking into place.

Dian's gaze bounced from wall to wall then back to the door. Listening to the old woman's baying dogs had put paid to any idea of escape. Dian shuddered at the thought of being torn limb from limb if she set foot outside – always assuming she could break free. She searched again for a peephole to the outside world. No crack nor cranny allowed light into the dank room.

Utterly defeated, Dian ate her dinner. Afterwards, she splashed her face and hands with cold water and lay down to sleep. For the first time since her incarceration, she enjoyed happy dreams, walking with Oric through sun-dappled meadows.

The dungeon door creaked open, awakening Dian with a start. She had no idea how long she had slept, or what the time might be. A man stood by her bed and shook her roughly by the shoulder. "Wake up, girlie, 'tis time to move you on."

Cadwin held a lantern above his head, and Dian shuddered under the man's glassy green stare. "So, Joffrey sends you to do his dirty work, now, does he? Where are we going?"

"You will find out soon enough. Master Joffrey instructed me to make sure you arrive at your destination safely, but he said I could restrain you if you become difficult." The man pointed toward the stairs. "After you, m'lady. We can make this journey easy or we can make it difficult, the choice is yours."

Dian chose to do as she was bid – for the time being.

Cadwin manacled Dian's wrists together with a hefty chain, secured a blindfold over her eyes, and pushed her upstairs.

"Is this blindfold really necessary? Any chance of informing anyone of my whereabouts is highly unlikely, is it not? And what has happened to the old woman? I do not relish spending time alone with the likes of you."

A stinging slap to the back of her head took Dian's breath away and she stumbled, grazing her hands and knees on the stone steps. "You can expect more of the same if you give me any more cheek, girlie. Master Joffrey insists you be blindfolded in case he ever needs to use this place again. The fewer folk who know of the location the better."

Outside her prison, a cool breeze fanned Dian's face and she filled her lungs with clean fresh air. It felt good to be outdoors even though she could see nothing.

A fruity cackle indicated the old crone stood somewhere nearby. Dian's heart beat faster as she felt dogs sniffing and slavering at her heels.

"Best get a move on, dearie," said Doretta, "and, just in case you attempt to escape, I plan to remain with you and Cadwin all the way to our destination. Put one foot wrong and my dogs will have a piece of you."

Cadwin yanked Dian's arm, pulling her through the still dew-wet grass. "Your donkey awaits. Give me your foot and I will boost you onto his back. Once we get into the woods, I shall remove your blindfold." He sniggered, "After all, one tree looks much like the next and you will have no idea where we are."

-oOo-

Half-way to Lockton Castle, Joffrey's horse became lame and he was obliged to complete the rest of the journey on foot. Tired and irritable, he reached the mountain plateau several hours later than he had anticipated.

Sight of his old home stole Joffrey's breath away. Not a blade of grass grew out of place, a substantial herb and vegetable plot grew near the drawbridge, and the damaged battlements of his father's time at the castle had been repaired. Joffrey sniffed the air – even the moat smelled fresh and clean. He approached the small iron gate beside the portcullis, hoping it had been left unlocked.

Hearing someone tampering with the latch, Rory sauntered out of his gatehouse. "Wad'ya want?" he demanded, pushing his pasty face close to the grille. "We ain't expecting no callers."

"What are you doing here?" Joffrey retorted. "I expected to find the castle deserted."

"As an old retainer of Sir Ragnald's," grovelled Rory, "I always remain at my post."

"Very commendable, I am sure." Joffrey despised the greasy little man. "Let me in, or I shall deliver you a flogging."

Sir Ragnald's brat had not improved with age and, for the sake of peace, Rory planned to remain on the young man's good side, regardless of how much grovelling that might require. He shambled back inside his gatehouse and wound the handle to open the portcullis.

Joffrey cast his tawny eyes around the deserted bailey. "I sent a party on ahead, where are they all?"

"If you mean the fellow named Leofrick, he arrived with a bunch of scruffy followers a few days ago. He said to let them in under your orders. They ain't stopped drinking since they arrived. I wager they have downed most of the castle's stock of wine already."

Lack of funds prevented Joffrey from employing a decent group of supporters but, looking at the change in Lockton Castle's fortunes, he would not need the doubtful assistance of his current mob of drunken wastrels for long. "Get people up from the village to cook and clean," he ordered Rory. "And, whilst you are about it, organise a meeting with the serfs who work the land, I want to speak to them."

Rory rubbed his arms and avoided eye contact with Joffrey. "I doubt you will get anyone, sir. Ain't nobody wants to work here since Oric left."

"We shall see about that," said Joffrey, hurling his horse's reins at Rory. "When Leofrick sobers up, get him to inspect the horse's right, front leg. The beast has gone lame."

Everywhere Joffrey looked, indoors and out, he saw clean equipment and orderliness. In a few short moons, Oric had achieved everything Sir Ragnald had failed to do in years. Sir Ragnald had systematically ruined the estate and alienated the serfs, and he had started off with far more than Oric had inherited. Joffrey swallowed bile, experiencing a brooding resentment toward his father.

Despite Leofrick and the hirelings attempts to drink the castle dry, the buttery retained a good supply of liquor. Joffrey washed down cold roast meat from the pantry with a welcome pot of ale. Replete, he inspected a room at the top of the three-storey turret at the back of the castle. A spiral stairway provided the only access – unless the occupant chose to jump from the battlements, which encircled the tower. Situated away from the main living quarters, the accommodation contained little furniture. Joffrey made a mental note to have a bed brought up, plus a table and a chair or two. Making Dian reasonably comfortable was surely the best way to prolong her life. Not that Oric would ever know if she died, but Joffrey preferred to keep Dian in good health in case he ever made a challenge for the castle. Joffrey supposed she would need clothes, too, and he left the turret room to investigate the women's bower downstairs. No ladies had lived at the castle during his father's time and the room remained uncharted territory. One or two masculine items of clothing hung from a pole, indicating Oric may recently have slept there. No matter, Joffrey was after female paraphernalia. A carved chest drew his attention and, upon opening the lid, he discovered what he was looking for. He shook out the top item of clothing, enjoying a faint smell of lavender. The garment looked old and a trifle moth-eaten, but Dian would have all the time in the world to mend it along with everything else in the chest. Some quills and pieces of parchment lay in a wooden box on top of a small desk. Dian could have those, and the desk, though Joffrey doubted she could read or write. A truckle bed, pushed out of sight under a long table, would suffice for the girl to sleep on. Two small chairs completed the list. Finally, Joffrey found a well-stocked sewing box, which he felt sure Dian could make use of. Feeling pleased with himself, he lay down on the big bed in the sleeping alcove and fell asleep.

-oOo-

In the woods, the campfire settled down to a warm glow. Snores indicated that Cadwin and Doretta had fallen asleep, and Dian grabbed the opportunity to make her bid for freedom. She crept past Doretta's tethered dogs, but the dull rattle of the chains attached to her manacles caused the animals to bark. Awake in an instant, Cadwin seized hold of Dian and dragged her back to the campfire. He paid no mind to the rocks and hard ridges of earth, and Dian collected some nasty scrapes and bruises along the way.

Doretta eyed the raised purple weals on Dian's pale face and arms. "Stupid girl. Perhaps you will think twice before attempting another escape."

After three more miserable nights spent in the open, Cadwin and Doretta dragged their battered and bruised prisoner into Lockton Castle's bailey.

Rory recognised Dian immediately. "What happened to her?" he demanded. "I suggest you take her manacles off and get her cleaned up before you present her to Master Joffrey. He ain't going to be too pleased to see the state she is in."

"Her state ain't no fault of mine," replied Cadwin, quicker than a streak of lightning. He slanted a malevolent glance at Doretta, "Yon old crone failed to secure the donkey's belly strap. The saddle slipped to the side and the girl got dragged a fair way along the track before I caught up and released her."

Rory did not believe the weedy, green-eyed fellow who grasped Dian by the arm, but it was none of his business. As for the crone, she looked older than Methuselah and smelled worse than a barrel of rancid fish.

Disturbed by the loud voices, Joffrey jumped up from his bed and ran downstairs to investigate. He took in Dian's dishevelled state but ignored her bruises. Cadwin was not known for his gentle ways.

Offered no other option, Dian followed Joffrey up a spiral stairway, keeping the flickering light from his lantern in sight.

Opening the turret door with a flourish, Joffrey placed his lantern on the floor. "This, ladies, is to be your boudoir from now on."

In the dim light, Doretta noted the lack of contents. "But there ain't nowt to sit on and no bed to sleep in. At my time of life, I need a bit of comfort."

"I have selected some suitable items of furniture, Cadwin will bring them up directly. And you will find two lanterns along with a tinder box on the floor in the corner," said Joffrey, handing a large key to Doretta. "You may come and go as you please, however, I want you keep the young woman locked up. Bring water for her to wash and supply her with food. When you have done that each day, you will make yourself useful elsewhere about the castle." Turning to Dian he added, "This room and the turreted area above will be your domain for the rest of your life. Escape is impossible, for the castle is guarded night and day."

Dian tossed her head defiantly. "You waste your time with me, sir. No-one will pay money to have me released. Nor will anyone play the knight in shining armour and come to my rescue."

Joffrey's expression radiated smug superiority. "The last thing I want is money. Nor do I want anyone to carry you off. What I desire is long-term tenure of Lockton Castle and you are my security. Oric has been informed that you will remain alive, providing he keeps away." Joffrey put a finger under Dian's chin and tilted her face upward. "He cares for you enough to abandon his castle and he is unlikely to return if he thinks your life will be endangered." He removed his finger from Dian's chin, and narrowed his eyes. "I am no monster, and I would prefer your stay here to be comfortable. Behave yourself, accept what I offer, and your life will be reasonably pleasant. Put one foot wrong and I will see you suffer."

"Gor, what do you make of that?" exclaimed Doretta after Joffrey left the room. "Looks like I have fallen on me feet." She cackled, holding her sides. "Since I am a good deal older than you, looks like I might have a job for life." Attaching the key to a chain on her belt, she lit both lanterns, picked one of them up, and made for the door. "Best see if I can find us a bite to eat."

Left alone, Dian explored her new territory. She planned to escape and, with that idea in mind, she tried the latch on a small door opposite to the main entrance. To her surprise the door opened, revealing another flight of stone steps. Holding on to the rope guide along the wall with one hand and the second lantern in the other, she made her ascent. At the top of the stairs yet another door opened on to castellated battlements.

The night was dark, but soft moonlight illuminated a range of craggy mountains behind the castle. Dian battled tears of frustration – even if she managed to escape, negotiating the rough terrain without help would be nigh on impossible. She glanced down at the moat below. If she jumped, would the water be deep enough to break her fall? Wandering around to the other side of the turret, she peeped through the battlements. A group of men sat in the bailey, drinking and playing card games for copper coins. Disheartened, Dian returned to the room and sank to the floor with her back against the wall.

"By heck, talk about luxury," said Doretta, returning to the turret room with a platter of food. "You should see the well-stocked pantry downstairs! We ain't in no danger of going hungry." Without further ado, she stuffed her mouth full of soused herring and chomped upon it with her toothless gums. "Cadwin and Leofrick will be here directly with some stuff," she added, spraying Dian with bits of fish. "I reckon we can make ourselves a nice little nest in 'ere." She dropped one wrinkled eyelid in an expressive wink. "Master Joffrey don't want no aggravation with you trying to escape so I been instructed to sleep in the room with you."

The promised furniture arrived. The two men dumped everything in the centre of the room, and left the women to arrange it wherever it suited them.

Temporarily resigned to her lot, Dian set about putting the room to rights. As well as chairs, a table, and a desk, the men had delivered a truckle bed and a straw mattress. Dian was profoundly grateful for the latter, for the extra mattress would save her from sleeping cheek by jowl with the stinking Doretta.

-oOo-

Another summer day dawned warm and bright. Not one to lie abed, Joffrey arose early, breakfasted, and sauntered into the bailey to order Rory to saddle his horse.

"Are we going out today, your lordship?"

"No, *we* are not. You will remain here, but I will need your horse until my animal is rested."

"But I ain't got no horse, your worship, my mount is a mule."

"In that case I shall commandeer Leofrick's horse – he can ride your mule."

Returning to the castle, Joffrey descended to the men's quarters below the kitchen and kicked his two henchmen awake. "Assemble your associates, we are riding to Skelgut."

Joffrey passed along Skelgut's wide street, barely able to believe his eyes. Every building appeared to be inhabited by a family or tradesperson, and people bustled about their business in the early morning sunshine. Smoke from the hole in the bakehouse roof mingled with the smell of freshly baked bread. Further along the thoroughfare a house beside the lake sported a barber's pole.

A group of women with leather pails drew water from the lake for their morning chores. Ripples, made by a small boat, glinted in the hot sunshine as they slapped on to the stony shoreline. Within moments, the boatman pulled in a wriggling, silver fish.

Tired of looking like a vagabond, Joffrey informed Cadwin and Leofrick he was about to have a shave and haircut. "Whilst I am at the barber's, you two call everyone together for a public meeting."

Lornika Fentwhistle was not pleased to see Joffrey back in Skelgut with a band of disreputable ruffians in tow. Too late to escape, she watched the swarthy young man swagger along her garden path to her front door.

"Ah, Mistress Fentwhistle, I see you remain in your same cottage." Joffrey nodded at the barber's pole beside her gate. "Do not tell me you have added 'barber' to your range of dubious skills."

"No, I have not!" Lornika bristled. "Yon pole belongs to a ne'er-do-well fellow who is now conspicuous by his absence. Master Ichtheus of Bayersby was here recently and, after a mere glimpse of the old man, the barber took off into the woods like a ferret after a rabbit. I ain't seen hide nor hair of him since."

"Is that right," murmured Joffrey. "Since the fellow was working out of your lean-to, no doubt you will remember his name?"

"Remember his name?" screeched Lornika, "'Tis branded upon my brain, for the slimy toad left owing me rent money."

Joffrey eased his backside in the saddle, resisting an urge to kick the woman. "I am sorry to hear that – but tell me his name."

"Amery Trundle, for his sins."

Now Joffrey understood why the barber had made a run for it after spotting Ichtheus. The fellow had killed Sir Edred, and Ichtheus would be aware of the felony. Not only was Trundle wanted for Sir Edred's murder, he had killed people in Roxbrough with his filthy potions. Concerned the fellow might make more trouble, Joffrey decided to finish him off once and for all.

"Do you have any idea where this Trundle fellow has gone?" Joffrey asked with feigned innocence.

Lornika stared at Joffrey as if he was not quite all there. "If I knew that, I would have my rent money, would I not?" She leaned back to get a better view of Joffrey's face. "All of that aside, what are you doing back in Skelgut? I never thought you would have the nerve to return after Sir Ragnald's defeat."

Now it was Joffrey's turn to bristle. "How did you hear about that?"

"Oh, 'tis common knowledge. Oric's people soon spread the word after he moved into his ancestral home. I should watch out if I were you. He will be none too pleased when he hears you have returned. By the by – why *are* you here?"

"Oric will not be returning to Lockton Castle," Joffrey sneered. "Come along to my public meeting and you will discover what your future holds in store. Now I am returned to the district, folk need to know exactly where they stand."

CHAPTER TWENTY

Guwain Disappears

Josh dug vegetables from the Bayersby kitchen garden and handed them to Faylinn to put in her basket. "You know Oric is in torment over Dian's disappearance. On top of all that, he is coping with the mess Guwain has got himself into."

"He looks so gaunt," replied Faylinn. "His loss of weight worries me."

"Lord knows why Dian had to climb on her high horse and cut off their friendship. I reckon Oric wanted to wed her. Anyone with eyes in his head can see they love each other."

"Aye, everyone but Oric and Dian, it seems. But I know how she feels. She is from lowly stock and Oric is a Lord. Society frowns upon such involvements."

Josh handed Faylinn a soil-encrusted bunch of carrots. "Thank goodness that don't apply to us, then."

Faylinn blushed. "Did you just ask me to wed you?"

"Aye, maybe I did." Josh adored the plump little lass, and he had been trying to pluck up the courage to ask the question. "You will marry me, will you not?"

"I might think about it, but you had better come up with a more romantic way of asking."

"Oh… Women!" Josh checked to make sure no-one was watching and dropped to one knee in the dirt. Taking hold of her hand he said, "Dear Miss Faylinn, would you please do me the honour of becoming my wife?" To seal the deal, he planted a kiss on her palm.

Faylinn burst into giggles. "Oh dearie me, just look at you. My hands are dirty from the carrots and now you have mud all over your face."

"Come here, wench, and I will share some of it." Josh kissed her soundly on the lips and rubbed his dirty face on her neckerchief. "Now you will have to say yes, for no-one else would propose to such a grubby creature."

"Yes, oh, yes," cried Faylinn, kissing Josh back. "I will marry you, but first we must ask Oric's permission, for he is our lord and master."

-oOo-

Oric and Bannulf sat at the table in the Great Hall, organising a chart of work. Guwain sat slightly apart from the two men, a truculent expression upon his face.

"The only way to pull this place back together is by employing drastically frugal means," said Oric. He pierced Guwain with an icy-blue stare. "And when I say frugal, I mean no more partying, no more liquor, no more fancy clothes, and definitely no more jousting. I plan on selling all the horses not used for work – they will bring in a pretty penny, for they are all thoroughbreds."

"You will do no such thing," spluttered Guwain. "They were my father's animals. If you sell them, what shall I ride?"

"Try riding a mule! Furthermore, you can roll up your sleeves alongside the rest of us and engage in some good, hard work. Lord knows there is plenty to do."

"How dare you suggest I sully my hands with menial tasks?" Red faced with temper, Guwain rose unsteadily to his feet. "This is my manor and I refuse to lower my station in life!"

Oric wiped his hand back and forth across his forehead. "I cannot force you to work. However, unless everyone pitches in to fix the mess you have made, your 'station in life' will be on the street begging for a daily crust."

"You lie! My father was a rich man. Do not dare to usurp my position as Lord of this manor."

"I am afraid your magic pot of gold is empty. As for usurping your position, that is not my intention. It is high time you showed yourself to be worthy of your position. All I wish to do is retrieve whatever I can for Lady Myferny's sake."

"What if I do not give you permission to meddle in my affairs?"

Oric's bark of laughter held no humour. "As far as I can see, you have no choice. You have alienated your former serfs, and the mongrels you befriended have run away with their tails between their legs. The sooner you come to terms with your self-inflicted lot, the better we shall all rub along." Having said his piece, Oric turned his back to Guwain and continued his conversation with Bannulf.

The big warrior nodded his agreement, and suggested Sir Oswold be invited to Bayersby Manor to oversee proceedings for a while. "As an old friend of Sir Edred's, he can keep a record for Lady Myferny. At least that way our backs will be covered should Master Guwain accuse us of doing anything untoward."

The furious slam of the Great Hall door announced the departure of the young lord.

The next morning Oric awoke to a frantic knocking on his chamber door. It opened shortly thereafter to admit Bannulf, with a bowl of gruel in his hand. "Sir, I know not if you will be pleased or angry, but I am here to report that Guwain has gone. And he has taken two of Sir Edred's best horses with him."

Oric rubbed sleep from his eyes and swung his legs out of bed. "Frankly, Bannulf, I do not give a fig for Guwain's disappearance, but I am less than pleased to hear of the missing horses. That said, I have no intention of sending a search party after the lad. If it were not for Lady Myferny's love for her son, I would pray the little rat never showed his face around these parts again." A nasty thought entered Oric's head and he voiced his opinion. "Suppose Guwain returns to Bayersby with reinforcements? Rather than risk losing the manor to a bunch of thieves and wastrels, we had best look to our laurels and form a small defence force. Bannulf, will you organise some training for the young males of the manor? Erik and Arnald are well versed in swordplay – get them involved. And, whilst I am thinking of it, I may need to sharpen up my skills in that department, too. Who knows when I may be called upon to defend myself?"

"Aye, your lordship, a wise decision." Bannulf saluted and strode off like a man with a purpose.

Bone weary after another near sleepless night, Oric forced down his breakfast and donned a clean tunic and hose. No new instructions regarding Dian's fate had eventuated and, in a melancholy mood, Oric was not pleased when Josh popped his head around the door jamb. No doubt the lad had encountered more problems of one sort or another.

"Er... Could you spare us a moment or two? Faylinn

and I have something we would like to ask of you."

Judging by the beams on the faces of the two rosy-faced youngsters, the news was good for a change. "Come along in – take a seat. How can I help you?"

Josh twisted his cap around in his hands. "Well it is like this, you see… Erm… We, er… That is Faylinn and me…"

"We want to get married," said Faylinn, coming to Josh's rescue. "I know this might not be the best time to ask but, if Father Fransiscus is agreeable, we would like to hold a small ceremony on the steps of the priory later this year. Maybe have a gathering at the Kilterton Inn afterwards. We are here to seek your permission."

Oric was on his feet in an instant, hugging first Faylinn, then Josh. "My dear friends, this is wonderful news. Of course, you have my permission. You are both of marriageable age and a wedding is just what we all need to cheer us up. If I can help with the arrangements, please let me know."

The serfs who had left Bayersby after Sir Edred's death returned, and the extra pairs of hands worked wonders in the fields. There would be no grain crops, for Guwain's steward and bailiff were not amongst the returned members of the household, but Ned and Joe volunteered to cover the positions. Too late in the year to plant crops for use in winter, they made sure the fields were ploughed ready for next year's springtime seed sewing. Meanwhile, they helped Josh in the castle's large kitchen gardens. The boys produced fruit and vegetables, Faylinn and Genevieve preserved those that were not eaten straight away. Guwain and his hangers-on had gobbled up all of Mistress Foley's carefully salted and honeyed foods with no thought for the winter ahead, and Genevieve set a young kitchen lad to scour out the large, empty, earthen-ware crocks ready to receive new contents.

Ichtheus kept himself busy concocting medicaments and treating peoples' ailments. Missing Oric's input, he wandered into the library to enquire how his former pupil was coping with Bayersby Manor's everyday affairs.

Oric raised weary eyes from his desk and managed a wan smile. "I' faith, Master Ichtheus, the problems Guwain created in his short time as Lord of Bayersby are a challenge I would rather not have to face at present. But, for the sake of Lady Myferny and her expected child, I cannot abandon the estate. Money is needed to replenish the cattle Guwain so recklessly lost, and I am contemplating the idea of selling off Sir Edred's remaining destriers at Kilterton's next horse fair."

"Good idea," said Ichtheus. "But I know Guwain's situation is the least of your problems. I cannot bear to see you tearing yourself apart day after day."

"Yes, Dian is my major cause for concern. I cannot sleep for agonising over her welfare, and I have no idea what to do next."

"If it is any help, I have spoken to the Committee of Law. We resolved many problems together in the past. Perhaps we can unearth some clue as to Dian's whereabouts. What say we meet with them when we visit Kilterton for the horse fair. Perhaps we can kill two birds with one stone, so to speak."

Oric shuddered. "I would rather not use the word 'kill' in this instance, Master Ichtheus, the very word terrifies me."

-oOo-

Shades of purple and indigo tinged the sunrise, and thunder grumbled in the distance. Fearing a storm, Ichtheus scuttled back indoors to fetch wet weather gear. His cart, packed with medicaments to sell at the market, stood outside and he wanted to cover everything before the items aboard became soaked.

Ned, Josh, and Joe volunteered to take one of Sir Edred's destriers each. "We shall ride bareback," said Josh. "If the animals sell, we will not need to carry heavy saddles back to Bayersby."

Leading a fourth destrier alongside his own horse, Oric stroked Jester's glossy, muscular neck. "Take note, you black limb of Satan, if you misbehave I might sell you and keep the destrier." As the words left his mouth, Oric knew he would never part with Jester, for he had grown uncommonly fond of the big gelding despite his feisty ways.

Since his arrival at Bayersby, Oric had spent his days trying to put the manor to rights. The journey into Kilterton would afford him the luxury of discussing medical procedures with Master Ichtheus. After Dian, learning about herbal remedies remained Oric's greatest passion. "Would you mind if I ride alongside you on the cart?" he asked his mentor.

"Nay lad, I would be glad of your company."

Jester snorted as Oric hitched him to the rear of the cart. Ichtheus glanced back at the horse. "Why not leave yon grumpy beggar behind? He looks to be in a bad mood and we have not yet set off! You are welcome to make the return journey on my cart, too, so why bring the disagreeable fellow along?"

Oric grinned, showing a tiny spark of his old, cheeky wit. "Good of you to offer me a ride both ways, Master Ichtheus, but I may stay longer in the village than you would like. I know you have much work to do at Bayersby Manor, and I would not wish to cramp your style."

"Nice to see you have retained a modicum of humour, albeit cheeky," said Ichtheus, patting the cart's wooden seat. "Hop up beside me, I have some interesting information to share."

For a short while, Oric put his concern for Dian to the back of his mind whilst he engaged in the other topic close to his heart.

"Have you noticed how the parsley has self-seeded?" said Ichtheus. It is growing like weeds in the Bayersby vegetable plot."

Oric cupped an elbow with one hand and tapped his lips with a finger. "Did not an ancient physician and philosopher, prescribe parsley for the treatment of water retention?"

"Aye, that would be *Galen*," replied Ichtheus. "I read his work on the subject, for an old woman in Kilterton suffers from the condition. The medication lies in the cart, and I plan to deliver it to her today. According to the recipe, parsley boiled in wine is also good for chest and heart pain." Ichtheus slid a sideways glance at Oric. *Maybe a dose of such medicament might help to ease the lad's heartache.*

A streak of lightning followed by a huge clap of thunder stopped any further conversation. The horses bucked and whinnied. Oric jumped down and ran to unhitch them to prevent the cart from overturning. Rain raced toward the travellers as a solid wall of water, and everyone ran for shelter beneath a large beech tree. Thick overhead growth stopped the worst of the downpour, nevertheless, hefty drops of water penetrated the canopy and made the people beneath wet and uncomfortable.

The downpour ceased as fast as it began. Sunshine beat down, and steam rose up from the saturated ground. Hot and damp, the Bayersby folk continued their journey to Kilterton. Arriving in the village, they negotiated puddles left by the storm and went about their business. Ichtheus set out his medicines on the back of his cart, and Oric headed for the horse enclosure. As he groomed the animals ready for sale, he wondered what the day would bring.

CHAPTER TWENTY-ONE

Hanging Offence

Deep resentful silence descended upon the villagers as Joffrey and his men rode into Skelgut. Everyone stared at the arrogant young man, wishing he had not returned to the district.

"Where is Oric, Lord of Lockton," yelled forester Barda. "There is no place here for the likes of you, or your kind."

"Remove that man and take him to a place of execution!" yelled Joffrey. "I will brook no insubordination!"

Barda's wife screamed and fell to the ground.

"He has done nothing wrong save voice his opinion," cried wheelwright Brody. "If you wish to execute someone, you must first get permission from the lord of the castle, and Oric ain't here right now."

"Oric is no longer in charge of this district. I am here to take his place and, if you know what is good for you, you will do exactly as I tell you." He pointed his riding crop at Master Brody. "Since you did not realise the change of master, I will spare your life – but let this be your final warning. If you dare to contradict me again, you will join your friend at the end of a rope. Take the condemned man away and hang him from a tree."

Two of Joffrey's burly followers dragged Barda, kicking and screaming, to the nearest tall tree and disposed of him as instructed.

The victim struggled, made horrible gurgling sounds, and then became silent. Joffrey smiled. "Let that be a lesson to you all. Obey me and your lives will remain bearable. Cross me and you may expect a similar fate. Now, let us get down to business. He indicated Cadwin and Leofrick. These two gentlemen will act as my steward and reeve. You will pay your rents and taxes to them upon demand. You will also provide food for the castle. Unlike my father before me, I will not take everything from you – I want you to keep enough of what you grow to sustain your families. A well-fed workforce produces more wealth for the landowner. Lastly, I see the fields hereabout are filled with bountiful crops. August is almost upon us, let harvesting begin."

The branch from which Barda hung creaked as his lifeless body swayed in the breeze.

Joffrey's face twisted with disdain. "Sight of yon carcass is making me queasy. Someone cut it down and bury it. Does anyone know of a replacement forester hereabouts?"

A scruffy individual stepped forward. Sweeping lank black hair out of his eyes he said, "I know a bit... Before Dunburton was sacked and the lord killed, I used to labour for the local forester."

"Looks like you fell on your feet," sneered Joffrey. "Take the dead fellow's wife and children home. Since there is no longer a man of the house you can fill his boots. I expect you to manage the forest hereabouts. Fail, and you will meet your maker." Wheeling his horse around, Joffrey cantered away from the village with his men hot upon his heels.

The villagers' stunned silence erupted into an angry babble. The wheelwright's son Ruben bawled in terror, his mouth wide open, tears coursing down his face, snot running from his nose.

"For the love of all that's holy, stop that racket," yelled Jeremiah, clipping his son's ear. "You ain't helping matters, carrying on like that. Where is your mother?"

Annie stepped forward and stared at her husband with huge, fear-filled eyes. "I ain't surprised the boy is upset. That Joffrey is a monster."

Jeremiah slapped a hand over Annie's mouth, looking rapidly to the left and right. "Do not go making statements like that, unless you want to see us all dead," he whispered in his wife's ear. "And, if you cannot shut our boy up, take him home. I can barely think straight for the racket he is making."

Barda's wife lay in the dirt sobbing, her hands over her eyes. Her brood of children stood around, white faced, not knowing what to do.

The unkempt stranger dismounted and hauled the sobbing woman to her feet. "I am sorry for your loss, Mistress," he said. "Seems like we are both victims of fate, perhaps we can rub along together and be of help to each other. My name is Sedrich, what is yours?"

"Eliza."

"Well, Eliza, let us go home."

Shocked and afraid, people wandered back to their dwellings. The future looked bleak, and every person mourned the departure of Oric.

Desdemona Whittle sucked in her thin cheeks. "Fancy – yon woman loses one husband and picks up another man within the hour." She scowled and tapped her foot. "Here am I widowed this many a long year, and still no sign of a new husband."

Annie Brody rounded on the village gossip. "That surprises me not at all! What man in his right mind would want to take on a sour old crow like you? Have you no pity for yon poor young woman?"

"I agree with you, Mistress Brody," said Lornika Fentwhistle. "The old biddy's miserable face would sour a churn of milk."

"Who are you to call me miserable?" screeched Desdemona. "I ain't seen too many gentleman callers buzzing around your front door neither, unless you want to include that Amery Trundle fellow. But even he seems to have disappeared, and no wonder. Who would want to live with a red-haired wasp like you?"

Incensed, Lornika leaped at Desdemona, claws out. The raven on her shoulder flapped, squawking around the two women's heads as they fought each other tooth and nail.

Anger blazed within Hamish, and he cursed his lack of strength. Oric had been gone for only a short time and the villagers were already at each other's throats. Rather than see the women injure one another, he stepped in and dragged them apart. Archie pitched in to help. Grabbing hold of Lornika's red locks, Archie propelled her toward the lake. "Pray calm yourself, Mistress, you are doing no good to anyone, least of all to yourself."

Lornika smacked dirt from her clothes and settled the raven back upon her shoulder. "I will not forgive Mistress Whittle her outburst. She need not come to me for any more fortune telling, I can promise you that." Limping slightly, she returned to Langend Cottage and slammed the gate. Amery's red and white-striped pole teetered and fell over. Lornika picked it up and hurled it spear-like, into the bushes at the side of the road, then dusted off her hands.

"Och, what d' you make of that wee performance?" asked

Hamish, rubbing at a couple of neat puncture wounds in his wrist where Mistress Whittle had sunk in her only two teeth.

Archie's knees gave way and he sank down on the bench outside his cottage. "What I make of it is neither here nor there. I am an old man and near the end of my life, but I fear for the young folk of this village. Sir Ragnald may have ruined the estate during his time here, but his son is like his sire in looks alone. This young fellow will work the folk of Skelgut mercilessly, for he is avaricious and cruel. He will not squander the estate's assets as his father did. In fact, I believe Joffrey will become a rich fellow, and I foresee a miserable future for us all."

"Och, aye, you are right," mumbled Hamish, "but we have no choice other than to make the best o' things 'til Oric returns."

"Do you believe he will?"

"Aye, I do. The laddie has a strong sense of what is right, and he will want his family seat back, but no' at the expense of wee Dian's life. 'Tis my belief Oric will no' do anything about his stolen inheritance until he has her safe and secure. Once that happens all I will say is, watch out Joffrey."

"I hope you are right," replied Archie. Tired and depressed, he invited Hamish to share a pot of ale.

Sitting with his back to the street, Hamish supped his drink. The sun warmed his aching bones, and he sent up a silent prayer that Oric would soon come to everyone's rescue. About to begin another conversation, Archie's expression of dismay stilled the words on Hamish's lips. "What is wrong, old friend?"

"Did you see who just rode past the end of the street?"

"Hardly, I have m' back turned." Hamish swivelled around on the bench. The cause of Archie's upset was heading toward the steep track leading up to the castle. "Is tha' who I think it is?"

"Not sure, but I reckon yon newcomer is Guwain of Bayersby."

"Och, wonderful!" exclaimed Hamish. "That is all we need – another wee tyrant to bring turmoil upon the district."

Tired and angry after his long ride, Guwain urged his father's pedigree stallion up the hill toward Lockton Castle. Having had prior presence of mind, he had also picked out a fine broodmare. Once the horses were mated, their offspring would earn a pretty penny to pay for his keep.

Arriving on the plateau in front of the castle, Guwain's first reaction was much the same as Joffrey's. Clean, orderly and welcoming, the castle looked completely different from Sir Ragnald's years of tenancy. Guwain dismounted, strode across the draw-bridge and clanged the bell.

"Now, who is it?" bellowed Rory. "This place is getting busier than a thieves' market. I have done nowt but open and shut this blasted gate since Master Joffrey's arrival." Past caring who the newcomer might be, Rory wound up the portcullis without first checking the identity of the caller. Once the gate was fully open he stepped outside his gatehouse. "Oh, 'tis you is it?" he growled, squinting at Guwain. "I reckon Master Joffrey ain't going to be too pleased to see you."

"How dare you speak to me thus? Do you realise I could have you imprisoned for insubordination?"

"Yes, I am sure you could." Rory had heard it all before, but here he was, still winding the Lockton portcullis up and down, morning, noon, and night. He made a cursory bow. "Will I stable your lordship's horses? I am sure you are tired after your very long ride."

"Yes, do that." Guwain handed over the reins. "And whilst you are about it, have my presence announced to Master Joffrey."

Rory sighed, wishing he could be a fly on the wall when the two young bucks came face to face. Master Guwain had been a nuisance in Sir Ragnald's time at the castle, and Joffrey would not take kindly to the youth's arrival.

Looking more confident than he felt, Guwain stomped up the flight of stairs to the doorway, which gave access to the castle's living quarters. Daylight had faded, and oil lamps flickered in wall-mounted sconces. Gone were the stale smells of Sir Ragnald's day, replaced by a faint odour of lavender. No sound came from the Great Hall, and Guwain wondered if anyone was at home. He pushed open the vast oak door and stepped into the room.

Clean rushes covered the floor. Jars filled with dried copper-beech stood on either side of the inglenook fireplace. Few lamps burned, leaving the atmosphere gloomy.

Guwain almost lost control of his bladder when a strong arm encircled his neck, and a sharp dagger pierced the back of his doublet. "Identify yourself before I run you through."

"Stay your hand, sir, 'tis I, Guwain from Bayersby Manor. I am come to pay a social visit."

One of the lamps sent out a sudden spurt of flame, the popping noise it made disturbing the silence in the Great Hall. Guwain turned around slowly, his hands in the air. "See, I mean you no harm."

Joffrey's dour, unsmiling face put the fear of God into Guwain.

"Ain't you glad to see me?" Guwain thrust out his hand. "We enjoyed good times together when last I was here, did we not?"

Joffrey ignored Guwain's outstretched hand. "Glad is not the word that springs to mind. Why are you here?"

"Oric has returned to Bayersby Manor and I want rid of him. The fellow is insufferable. I would be willing to make over half of my inheritance if you return to the manor and help me to oust him."

Joffrey laughed uproariously. When his fit of hilarity finally subsided, he fixed Guwain with cold, narrowed eyes. "That is the funniest joke I have heard in a long while." He strutted around the Great Hall, his arms spread wide. "Do you truly believe I would give up this wondrous place in exchange for a share of your flea-pit manor?" He began to laugh again. "Oh, no, not on your life. My place is here, as Lord of Lockton." Joffrey paced back to Guwain and gave him a shove. "I suggest you return to Bayersby and sort out the mess you have made."

"But all my serfs have left the manor. I have no-one to back me." Guwain's voice rose to a petulant wail. "Oric is throwing his weight around and I am not allowed to have a say in anything. I cannot live like that. Maybe I could stay here, I promise to make myself useful."

Joffrey looked Guwain up and down. "What do you have to offer?"

"I bring a fine stallion and a broodmare; I am prepared to forgo monetary rewards for any offspring they produce. They will surely pay for my lodgings at the castle."

"Alas, I am unable offer you a room in the castle. But I will keep your horses in exchange for alternative accommodation and a sturdy mule." Joffrey put a finger to his cheek and stared at the vaulted roof in mock concentration. "I believe one or two cottages remain unoccupied in Skelgut, take your pick. You are a bright lad, you can grow vegetables to sustain yourself." Joffrey's eyes glittered with amusement, "Perhaps you will raise sufficient produce to sell at the markets for money."

Guwain's face reddened with anger. "You can keep your wretched cottages, your vegetables, and your poxy mule. I shall take my horses and repair to my rich uncle's establishment in Yarracumb. I will be more than welcome there."

Joffrey waved his hand dismissively, "Too late, my friend, the deal is done. I suggest you take up my generous offer before I have my men 'escort' you off the premises."

"You are naught but a thief, like your father before you," Guwain yelled, stamping his feet and shaking his fists in fury.

"I am no thief, I have simply accepted your horses in exchange for accommodation." Joffrey flashed an insincere smile, "You asked me for help, and I have obliged you. A cottage is available, but I cannot force you to move into it. The mule comes as a bonus – take him or leave him." He elbowed Guwain toward the door. "Since it is late, you may sleep in the stables, but be gone at first light."

-oOo-

Locked in her turret, sleep did not come easily to Dian. The conversation she had with Joffrey about his intention to incarcerate her indefinitely had plunged her into a deep depression. Her bed was lumpy and, on the other side of the room, Doretta snuffled and snored.

Picking up a lantern, Dian climbed the stairs to the open space above her turret room. Staring down into the bailey, she thought about jumping. The prospect of death, rather than spending the rest of her days with only Doretta for company, was tempting.

Movement below attracted Dian's attention. Barely able to believe her eyes, she wondered what Guwain might be doing at Lockton Castle. If he was here to stay, he would pester her mercilessly. Without Lady Myferny's protection, her already miserable life would become a living hell. Prepared to face a life or death situation rather than remain at Lockton Castle, Dian made up her mind to escape. Whatever method she chose, she would need to think things through carefully.

-oOo-

Guwain stood in the bailey, staring up at the wide arc of stars, trying to master his fury. *How dare that upstart treat me, a member of the landed gentry, in such a disgraceful fashion?*

The forced exchange of his horses for a mule, and accommodation he had no intention of taking up, stuck in Guwain's craw. But he saw no way of escaping with his animals, for he was vastly outnumbered by Joffrey's men. Defeated, he traced the castle's battlements until his eyes came to rest on the west tower, his old room when he had stayed at Lockton so many moons ago. A light flickered intermittently between the castellations, and Guwain wondered who might be domiciled there now. He squinted to get a better look. A female figure halted in one of the gaps and held a lantern out to illuminate the dark abyss below. It was none other than the maid, Dian.

Had the little minx deserted Bayersby Manor in favour of a better life with Joffrey? No doubt Oric knew nothing of the girl's whereabouts. What sweet revenge it would be to confront him with the information. Deciding to sleep on the idea, Guwain entered the stables and lay down in the hay.

The mule did not make a comfortable bed fellow, for the sway-backed creature kicked and farted. The final insult occurred when the mule relieved itself, splashing Guwain's face with warm urine. He slapped the animal on the muzzle and stomped outside in search of water to cleanse himself.

Come what may he was not going to ride anywhere on the unsavoury beast. Afraid to confront Joffrey again, he made up his mind to sneak away early, taking his horses with him.

Up before dawn, Guwain saddled his horse, and put a bridle on the mare. Leading both animals across the compound, he came to the gates. But the portcullis was locked. Too big to fit through the side gate, Guwain fretted over how he could get his horses out of the castle undetected.

"Good morning to you, young sir," said Rory, stretching and scratching his belly. "Master Joffrey warned me you might try to make off with his newly acquired horseflesh. He said to raise the alarm if you became difficult. What say we save both of us a flogging and pop Master Joffrey's horses back in their stall? If you wish, I will help you to saddle the mule that has been allotted to you." Rory yawned and rubbed the back of his neck. "By all that's holy, I will be glad to see the back of the beast, for he is a horrible creature. By the by, he answers to the name of Rattles because he is old and bony."

"I have no need of your emaciated mule," stated Guwain, holding tight to his horses' reins. "They are not Master Joffrey's horses, they are my horses, and I intend to ride out of here. Open the grille at once!"

"What kind of fool do you take me for?" A yellow glob of spittle shot from Rory's mouth and landed with a splat next to Guwain's foot. "My master has his heart set on building up a good stable, 'tis more than my life is worth to let you make off with those fine animals."

Defeated, Guwain trailed back to the stables to exchange his beautiful horses for the crabby mule. He had no intention of taking up residence in either of the hovels Joffrey had offered in Skelgut, nor could he face his uncle in Yarracumb mounted upon such a fleabag of an animal. Instead, he made up his mind to return to Bayersby Manor. Using his knowledge of Dian's whereabouts, he spitefully determined to cause as much trouble for Joffrey as he could muster.

CHAPTER TWENTY-TWO

Kilterton Horse Fair

The storm from earlier in the day had grumbled away into the distant hills. Birds in the trees shook their feathers free of raindrops and trilled melodiously amongst the branches of the gnarled horse-chestnut trees that lined each side of Kilterton's main thoroughfare. Market stall-holders set out a few paltry wares but, since Guwain had become master of the manor, the countryfolk had no money to spend and little produce to sell or barter.

Arriving in the village alongside Oric, Josh went in search of his parents. Eadbald and Frida Cole lived in a dirty tumbledown cottage at the far end of the street, and Josh was ashamed of them. However, he could not visit Kilterton without calling in to see how they fared.

Ned and Joe settled Sir Edred's four magnificent destriers into the horse-sale yard and, not wanting prospective buyers to think Jester was for sale, Oric hitched the gelding to a post outside Uther's boot shop. Depressed by the lack of potential customers, he resigned himself to a long, dreary morning.

Sir Oswold entered the horse enclosure as Oric was on the point of packing up for the morning. "Good to see you my young friend," boomed the one-armed knight, slapping Oric on the back. His eyes lit up at sight of the four animals on sale. He ran his hand down the fetlock of a big bay, lifting the animal's leg to inspect his hoof. "Do these animals belong to you?"

"Er… Yes and no," said Oric, drawing his eyebrows together into a deep frown. "I have taken it upon myself to sell Sir Edred's horses to raise funds. As you are aware, Guwain squandered almost everything in the manor's coffers during his short time as lord of the manor, and now he has disappeared." Oric waved his hand in disgust. "According to the kitchen serfs, he had developed a liking for highly spiced food, never mind a pound of ginger purchases a sheep, and the equivalent amount of mace buys half a cow. Mistress Foley was obliged to instruct the cooks to provide a completely different diet to the one enjoyed in Sir Edred's day." Some of the high colour subsided from Oric's cheeks, and he smiled wryly. "Not that Sir Edred stinted himself in the food or liquor department. Had he been more moderate in his habits he might still be alive and we would not now be facing so many problems."

"Where do you suppose Guwain has gone?" asked Sir Oswold. "Not that you care, I am guessing."

"Indeed, I do not!" retorted Oric. "But for the sake of his poor mother, I suppose I must eventually try to find him. He is, after all, the rightful Lord of Bayersby. Speaking for myself, I would prefer to see the return of the two horses he made off with." Anger coloured Oric's cheeks a deep pink. "The wretched youth took the best stallion and broodmare. I had planned on keeping them to rebuild Bayersby's stock of horses after selling all the others."

Sir Oswold sighed heavily. "Before you returned, I tried to advise the lad, but he would have none of it. He sold most of his father's cattle to raise money to satisfy his fancy tastes. Bayersby Manor became a popular stopping off place for traders of exotic goods."

"Traders stopped calling at the manor once money ran out. We can live without useless luxuries and fine destriers, but we cannot live without cattle and produce," said Oric. "If we are to survive next winter I must address the problem and raise funds quickly."

"Sir Edred would turn in his grave if he knew the trouble his son is causing," said Sir Oswold, wiping his brow with a large piece of linen cloth. "Since I came to market hoping to purchase a horse, I may be able to help you out to a lesser degree." The owner of his own smallholding, Sir Oswold had money enough to buy whatever he wanted. "My old destrier is too decrepit to ride these days and I recently retired him out to grass. My work-horse is just that, and he makes for an uncomfortable ride. I would like to purchase one of your animals."

Oric brought a big bay out of the enclosure and walked him up and down before Sir Oswold.

"It is commendable of you to shoulder Guwain's responsibilities," said the one-armed knight, "but who is looking after your affairs at Lockton Castle?"

"Thereby hangs another tale, and the reason Master Ichtheus has called a meeting with the Committee of Law. I will tell everyone what is happening when we get together in Uther's shop at noon. By the by, is Lady Malla with you?"

At mention of his wife, Sir Oswold thrust out his chest with pride. "Aye, she is somewhere about the village. Her midwifery keeps her busy, tending to mothers and babies. I shall go and seek her. We will meet you at Uther's place."

Leaving Ned and Joe to keep an eye on the horses, Oric wandered along the high street to chat to the other traders.

Aidie Kirtle, Kilterton's haberdasher, determined to put a good face on the situation, filled her table with ribbons and gewgaws. As with all the other traders, no-one approached her stand. "I am sorry for your lack of customers," said Oric, digging in his pouch for a handful of coins. His heart filled with love, he selected a rabbit-fur hood for Dian. "I will take a selection of your coloured ribbons, too." Thinking positively about the love of his life made him feel less depressed.

Tewdric Bascoomb stood beside his shop door looking glum, the sound of his wife's shrill voice clearly audible from within the premises. Oric made sympathetic eye contact with the small, bald man. "Do you suppose we could have a meeting of the Committee of Law without Helled?" he asked quietly. "She puts everyone in a bad mood and prolongs procedures."

Tewdric nodded. "I will try to dissuade her." The butcher rolled his eyes, "Not that Helled pays attention to anything I say. Nevertheless, I will tell her I am going to the meeting come what may. She will not leave our daughters alone in the shop for fear someone diddles them out of a copper or two."

"Good man," said Oric, patting Tewdric's arm. "I will see you at the cobbler's shop at noon."

One of very few stall holders, Ichtheus was the only trader doing any business. He handed out lotions and potions to his patients, but Oric noted that he took no money in exchange for medicine. "You ain't going to get fat on those returns, Master Ichtheus."

"I know, but what can I do? Folk are suffering, and I am not about to add to their woes. I told them they can pay when they are back on their feet."

"Have you kept a record of who owes what?"

Ichtheus looked sheepish. "No need for that, I will remember."

"Is that right?" said Oric, knowing Ichtheus would never chase his patients for payments. "I am going to the inn for a bite to eat, would you like me to get you a pie and bring it across for you?"

The queue in front of Ichtheus' stall dwindled, and he nodded. "I will pack up here and find a safe place to leave Braccus and my cart."

"Take the donkey over to the horse yard. Ned and Joe are standing guard over the Bayersby animals, I am sure they won't mind watching out for an extra beast, especially since I promised to send them something to eat," grinned Oric, revealing his strong white teeth.

Many people crammed into the inn and their angry chatter rattled the rafters. Few could afford to buy the landlord's ale. Smoke from a fire on the central hearth drifted up through the specially designed hole in the roof, but still the atmosphere remained thick and heavy. The people of Kilterton looked more down at heel than Oric had ever seen them. Something had to be done, and soon.

Ex-warrior Egglebart sat at a long trestle table in an alcove. Seeing Oric, he leaped to his feet and thrust out his hand. "Welcome back to Kilterton, though you will find the district less prosperous these days." Red hair awry, Egglebart looked much the same as always. Like Sir Oswold he owned his own smallholding and remained pretty much self-sufficient. Rather than pay rent, he paid taxes once a year to the manor.

Oric raked the room for sight of Egglebart's wife. "Is Etheldrida not with you?"

Egglebart snorted and ran his fingers through the mat of ginger whiskers on his chin. "Ha! Can you imagine me coming to the village without her? She now gives away her vegetables and home-made pies to poorer members of the community. I believe many families would starve without her help."

Oric visualised the generous, raven-haired woman and laid his hand on Egglebart's shoulder. "You are a lucky fellow to have such a wife. I look forward to seeing her when the Committee of Law assembles."

Across the room, Eadbald Cole sat at a greasy table with a pot of ale in front of him. Frida accompanied her husband and she, too, held a drink in her hand. Josh sat beside his parents, all three arguing.

Oric had little time for Josh and Dian's parents. Frida was a bad mother and Eadbald nought but a drunkard. His dubious skills as an odd job man would not be providing a lucrative income at present so Oric presumed Josh had paid for the couple's liquor. The Cole's altercation worsened and, feeling the need to support Josh, Oric left Egglebart to finish his ale in peace.

Eadbald confronted the newcomer with rheumy eyes. "Oh, 'ere he is, Jack the lad! P'raps he can throw a glimmer of light on the mystery."

"What mystery would that be?" demanded Oric, doing his best to remain polite.

"The disappearance of our Dian, that's what," screamed Frida. "She ain't been the same since she went to the manor as a ladies' maid. Got ideas way above her station, she has."

Oric grabbed hold of Eadbald's greasy neck cloth, his mind working overtime. "How do you know about Dian's disappearance? Have you abducted your own daughter to demand money? If any harm comes to the girl, I will tear you limb from limb!" Sickened by the stench of the drunken man, Oric let go of him abruptly. Eadbald lost his balance and fell to the floor.

"Get up you miserable cur. I will find your daughter, and not a penny piece will you receive from me."

"Nay, Oric, you have the wrong end of the stick," cried Josh. "My parents know nothing of Dian's disappearance. They are every bit as angry about it as you, but for a different reason. That is why we are arguing."

A vein in Oric's neck pulsed. "Then what *exactly* are you arguing about?"

Resentment pinched Frida's thin lips. "You come in here throwing your weight about when we are the injured party. Unless you can solve the mystery of our Dian's disappearance, clear off and mind your own business."

Eadbald staggered to his feet and lurched forward. Oric reached out and shook him by the shoulders. "I said – what were you arguing about?"

"We are being threatened!" squealed Eadbald. "A merchant eyed off our Dian long before she went to Bayersby Manor. He made an offer for her and said he would collect her next time he came through Kilterton. I accepted a pouch of copper coins from him as a pledge and promised to have Dian here by the time he returned. But that was a while ago and I thought the fellow must have forgotten. In the meantime, our Dian was whisked off by the Bayersby housekeeper. When the merchant showed his face again, he weren't too pleased to find the girl gone and demanded his money back. Said he would slit my throat if I failed to repay him or come up with the girl."

"Needless to say," Frida chipped in, "Eadbald ain't got no money so he went off in a hurry to fetch our Dian back from the manor. When he got there, he was told the girl had gone to Roxbrough with her mistress. I want our Josh to ride as fast as he can and fetch her back."

Oric glared at Eadbald. "You stupid man, Dian is no longer yours to sell. Lady Myferny purchased her long since. You cannot expect to claw her back and barter with her all over again."

"Well, I reckon our daughter ain't up to much," greased Eadbald. "I am doing Lady Myferny a favour, taking Dian off her hands. As a bonus, I offered my services as odd job man at the manor for a day or two. But now the wench has left the district and our Josh refuses to bring her back. To save me own skin, I am now obliged to ask around 'til I find someone else to fetch her."

A cold hand of fear squeezed Oric's stomach. Eadbald's interference could well get Dian killed. Ready to tear out his hair, he agonised over what to do. Perhaps some misdemeanour might be invented so husband and wife could be charged and put away until Dian was found. This was yet another problem he needed to put to the Committee of Law.

CHAPTER TWENTY-THREE

Committee of Law Meet Again

Ichtheus ticked off each Committee of Law member upon arrival at Uther's shop. Egglebart and Etheldrida from Rookery Farm, Sir Oswold and his wife Malla from Cowslip cottage, Tewdric the butcher, mercifully minus his wife Helled, Uther of course, and Norbert the Rigg Farm shepherd. The only person missing was Oric. "Has anyone seen the dratted boy?" Ichtheus demanded. "I have never encountered anyone with such a poor sense of time."

"Here I am, Master Ichtheus." Oric blew into the backroom along with Josh. "I am sorry to be late, but we got into an argument with Josh's parents."

"What is the matter with them now?" growled Ichtheus. "I suppose they are bleating about the absence of their children."

"Their children are doing very well," said Lady Malla. "I check on them regularly. They have never looked back since moving into Oric's moorland hut with Josh's younger brother."

Many moons ago Oric had saved Sir Edred's life during a battle with a moneylender named Figg. As a token of his regard, Sir Edred had rewarded his saviour with a plot of land on the edge of High Moor. Oric created an herb garden and built a hut in which to experiment with his medicaments in peace, away from the busy Bayersby kitchen. Before Oric removed to Lockton Castle, Josh had asked if his younger brother could take care of the place. Shortly afterwards, with Dian's help, the entire Cole brood deserted their parents' hovel and took up residence with their brother. Conditions in the hut were cramped but a good deal more savoury than Eadbald and Frida's filthy cottage. The children helped their brother to look after the garden and did odd jobs at Bayersby Manor. A diet of fresh vegetables, snared rabbits and fresh country air put roses in their cheeks and flesh on their bones.

Ichtheus knocked his dagger handle on the table to bring the meeting to order. "The floor is yours, Oric. Tell everyone what is going on."

"As you all know, conditions at Bayersby Manor became untenable under Guwain's mismanagement. Several days ago, Lady Myferny left, along with her female companions and her maids. She plans to remain with her sister in Roxbrough until after the child she is expecting is born. Hopefully, by then, the Bayersby estate will have returned to normal."

"Things are equally chaotic in Kilterton," interrupted Uther. "Folk are struggling to pay the tithes and rents Guwain demands. No-one has any money for new footwear, and repairs to old boots are few and far between. I know not how we shall all survive at this rate."

Concerned, Norbert scratched his woolly head. "I made a short detour to visit my friends at the tannery and found them packing up their tools. Meerig and Lanaval believe they will be better off working for a tanner in Yaracumb."

"We have seen a lot of folk pass our place heading east," said Egglebart looking glum. "They tell us the Lord of Uggleburston requires serfs, and many hopefuls are going from this area. At the current rate of departure, no-one will be left to work the Bayersby Estate. None of the runaways seem concerned over broken bonds with the Lord of Bayersby."

Etheldrida's black curls bobbed as she nodded her agreement. "The serfs think Guwain is on the road to ruin and they believe he will not bother to send his men to fetch them back."

"How Sir Edred sired such a miserable son is beyond my understanding," Sir Oswold growled. "I tried to keep an eye on the place, but Guwain made it abundantly clear my assistance is not welcome. He ordered me off his premises and I had no choice other than to leave him to his own devices."

"That is all very well, Oswold," interupted Lady Malla, "but we cannot stand by and see all that Sir Edred worked for fall apart. Surely someone can make Guwain understand that he will have no place to call home if he continues with his extravagant lifestyle."

"Guwain is no longer part of the problem," said Oric, managing to get a word in at last. "He disappeared a few days ago, taking with him one of his father's finest stallions and a broodmare. No doubt he believes he will make a fair living out of the animals, one way or another."

"Where has he gone?" Sir Oswold demanded.

"I know not, and I care even less," replied Oric. "What I do care about is Dian's whereabouts. She was spirited away by some unknown person on the way to Roxbrough with Lady Myferny."

A collective gasp whooshed around the room.

"How do you know she was taken?" Etheldrida loved Dian like a daughter and Oric's news was devastating.

"I received an anonymous note a few days ago." Oric fished around in his pouch and produced a roll of parchment. "Bear with me, and I shall read it out loud." He swallowed hard to dislodge a lump of emotion that threatened to block his throat.

"The maid, Dian, is held captive in safe but unpleasant quarters. To ensure her safety, gather together your people and begone from Lockton Castle before the next full moon. If you wish the girl to remain alive, never try to find her, and never, ever return to the Lockton district."

A rush of protests prevented Oric from adding his conclusions.

Ichtheus shouted for silence. "Let the lad continue, he has more to say."

Oric swallowed hard again. "I had planned to make secret enquiries but now I find myself in a difficult and worrying situation. Eadbald and Frida Cole say they have sold their daughter to a merchant and taken his money in advance. They are threatening to cause trouble if she is not returned to Kilterton before the merchant returns to claim his prize. The Coles demand that someone rides to Roxbrough to bring Dian back to Kilterton."

"That is outrageous," snorted Etheldrida, her large bosom heaving with indignation. "This business of selling one's children into service does not sit well with me."

Oric cracked his knuckles. "In this instance, the practice is illegal. Dian is no longer theirs to sell, and her parents' insistence that she be found could well serve as her death sentence. The Coles have no idea of the true circumstances and they must be stopped from making a fuss."

"Perhaps if we tell the Coles the truth it will silence them," suggested Lady Malla.

Ichtheus tapped a finger on his lip. "I fear the truth, in this instance, will only make matters worse. Eadbald is not the sharpest tool in the box. He would likely make matters worse by sharing the knowledge with all and sundry." Firmly compressing his features, Ichtheus continued. "Besides, Oric and I suspect Joffrey is the culprit, however, we have no proof."

"That little toad! I will have him hung, drawn and quartered before you can say dagger!" roared Egglebart.

Oric put a restraining hand on Egglebart's arm. "Settle down, my friend. Your reaction is much the same as mine – until I thought it through. We dare not challenge Joffrey until we know Dian is safe."

"Surely we cannot sit on our hands doing nothing," cried Egglebart. "What shall we do?"

"I am open to suggestions," said Oric. He felt the need to pace but there was insufficient room. Instead he clenched his jaw and gnawed his lip.

Level headed as ever, Sir Oswold said his piece. "Dian could be anywhere. Let us make discrete enquiries and when we have new information, we shall meet again and decide what to do for the best."

"If Dian dies, Joffrey will lose his bargaining tool," reasoned Lady Malla. "Therefore, I do not believe she is in immediate danger."

Oric felt sick. "That is all well and good, but how is poor Dian feeling? I do not believe she is being treated well, never mind what the parchment says."

"I understand your worries, Oric, but for the sake of all the people hereabouts we must also concentrate on returning Bayersby Manor to its former profitable status," said Sir Oswold. "When word gets around that you are managing the estate, many of Sir Edred's serfs will return."

"What if Guwain returns?" asked Etheldrida. "Will he not go back to his wicked ways and plunge the district into despair again?"

"Oh, Guwain will come home for sure," replied Ichtheus. "He will not give up his inheritance, and nor should he. What he needs is someone to push him in the right direction. That said, he will find himself without sympathetic supporters, when he does decide to show his face. Oric and his men drove the Dunburton hangers-on out of Bayersby. Cowards all, I doubt they will want another dose of the same medicine."

Oric raised weary blue eyes. "Do you have anyone in mind to do the pushing? You would be my first choice, Sir Oswold, but I cannot expect you to volunteer too much time. You have your own smallholding to run."

"What about Bannulf?" said Ichtheus. "He is strong, trustworthy, and he has a good grounding in running an estate. His steady temperament is infallible, and he is as stubborn as a mule. When Guwain reclaims his manor, he will find Bannulf a formidable mentor and taskmaster."

-oOo-

Guwain hitched his mule to a post, and stormed into the Kilterton Inn. "Where is Oric?" he bawled. "I was told I could find him in here."

"He was here around noon, but he left shortly thereafter." Bewildered, the landlord called for his wife. "Hey, Bridgett, do you know where Oric went?"

The innkeeper's wife was not keen on Guwain, and she resented his attitude. "Someone might have said he was meeting a few cronies at the cobbler's shop. Mind, I only think that is what I heard."

Guwain tore out of the inn and across the yard.

A stable boy chased after him with the mule in tow. "Hey, mister, you forgot your animal."

"A pox on the ornery beast," Guwain yelled back. "You keep him. I never want to set eyes on the abominable creature again."

The stable boy could barely believe his luck. To be given a valuable animal was both unexpected and delightful. He crept home with the mule in tow, hoping the young lord would not lay charges of theft at a later date.

Lightheaded from hunger, and exhausted from his embattled ride on the mule, Guwain could hardly wait to vent his spleen upon Oric. Once the insufferable Lord of Lockton knew where his precious lady-love was being held prisoner, he would ride off into the sunset like a latter-day Sir Galahad and rescue her. With luck he would engage Joffrey in the fight of his life and they would kill each other.

Heart thundering against his chest wall, Guwain banged Uther's shop door back against the wall. He strode into the cramped room and stood, legs spread wide, arms folded. "I have some important information to impart." Fixing his mean, piggy eyes on Oric, he added, "No doubt it will be of particular interest to you. Your precious lady-love is imprisoned in Lockton Castle under Joffrey's dubious care. If you want her, I suggest you go and rescue her. Now, clear off out of my district and leave me to run my own affairs." Turning on his heels he made for the door.

Sir Oswold grabbed Guwain's arm. "Not so fast, young man. You have some explaining to do. Not only that, you need to hear about the overseer we have organised to run your manor until we deem you fit enough to do it for yourself."

Guwain threw off Sir Oswold's hand, his petulant face turning an unpleasant shade of puce. "How dare you interfere in my affairs. One more word out of you, sirrah, and I shall have you flogged."

"Oh aye. You and whose army?" Sir Oswold roared.

"I have my own men, trained soldiers all. They will make minced meat out of you. At my command they will travel anywhere at any time."

Oric stood up so quickly, his chair overturned. "You devious little bastard," he bellowed, grabbing Guwain by the throat. "Your so-called soldiers have run away. Until you learn some common sense, Bannulf will oversee your manor. You will follow his orders. If you fail to do so, you will answer to me." Spittle flew from Oric's mouth and splattered onto Guwain's face. "Furthermore, if you wish to see the light of another day, you had best tell me everything you know about Dian." Disgusted, Oric flung Guwain against the wall.

Guwain slid down to the floor in a blubbering heap.

"Someone pick him up, for I will kill him if I have to lay hands on him again."

A stunned silence followed Oric's outburst as Committee of Law members assimilated what had been said. Gone was the boy Oric, here was the man. Not only an honorable man, but a mighty lord who understood exactly who he was.

CHAPTER TWENTY-FOUR

Out of the Skillet, into the Fire

Dian tossed and turned on her lumpy bed, listening to Doretta's snores. She dreaded another boring, pointless day spent locked in the turret room, but how could she escape? Doretta looked puny, but Dian knew otherwise. Only once had she tried to overpower the old woman and found herself face down in the dirt for her trouble. To affect a successful departure from Lockton Castle, more brutal methods needed to be applied. Dian could think of no other way than to knock Doretta senseless, but with what? The furniture in the tower room was too heavy to lift, she needed something lightweight but sturdy.

During the Yuletide holidays spent at Lockton Castle with Sir Edred and the Bayersby folk, Dian had seen one of Lady Myferny's companions using a spinning wheel. To work the apparatus comfortably the operator sat on a three-legged stool. Made from solid oak, the stool would provide the perfect weapon. Perhaps Joffrey could be persuaded to send the spinning wheel and the stool up to her room.

Doretta woke and swung her stick-like legs out of bed. Watching the woman don layers of clothing, Dian tentatively put forward the idea of an occupation. "I cannot spend the rest of my life twiddling my thumbs. Ladies do embroidery to entertain themselves, but I never learned." Dian lied, for most of Lady Myferny's garments bore evidence of Dian's skill with a needle.

Doretta backed away with raised hands. "Do not look at me, girl. The only needlework I know anything about is mending my own clothes. Can you not think of something more practical than fancy embroidery?"

Dian pretended to think for a while. "If I had a spinning wheel, I could turn raw wool into thread." Lies tripped glibly from Dian's tongue as she contrived to sound plausible. "Perhaps Joffrey would allow me a loom as well, then I could weave the thread I spin into cloth. Thus, I could make woollen garments for everyone."

Reaching for the key at her waist, Doretta made for the door. "I will speak with Master Joffrey next time I see him – if I remember."

Dian nodded her thanks. She did not hold out much hope, but at least she had made a start. Each time she heard the key turn in the lock of her turret room she braced herself. She expected a visit from Guwain any day, but when the door opened only Doretta entered the room.

Several days of idle boredom drifted by, and Dian began to think her pleas for a spinning wheel had fallen on deaf ears, always supposing Doretta had mentioned the request to Joffrey in the first place.

Late one afternoon, Dian climbed the stone stairway and strolled along the open area behind the battlements above her room. The sun dipped away behind nearby woods and she wondered if Oric watched the same sunset. She missed his company but resigned herself to a life spent without him. Even if she managed to escape, she dare not seek him out, for they had no future together. She returned to the turret room feeling more depressed than ever. Oric would not give her a second glance looking the way she did. Her once-glossy chestnut brown hair hung about her shoulders, lank and unkempt. Weight had dropped off her since her incarceration, for she could barely be bothered to eat. Second-hand clothes drooped in baggy loops about her body. Feeling thoroughly miserable, she lay on her bed and stared at the wall.

Sounds of a heavy item being bumped up the stairs dragged Dian from her stupor. Any diversion in the endless days of nothingness was welcome, and she jumped up expectantly. Someone hammered on the turret room door. Awakened from her afternoon slumber, Doretta fumbled for the heavy key she kept on a chain at her waist. Grumbling at the disturbance, she unlocked the door to reveal Rory, red faced and sweaty, with a spinning wheel slung across his back.

"By heck, miss, 'tis to be hoped you ain't going to order too much more of this heavy stuff, for I fear I shall expire before my time if I has to drag owt else up here." Rory dropped the spinning wheel on to the floor with a crash. "There you are, miss, and many hours of happy work I wish you." He left the room shaking his head. In his opinion, folk who actively sought work were daft.

"Wait!" cried Dian, seeing her plan falling by the wayside. "I appreciate the trouble you have taken, but I am unable to work comfortably without a small seat of some description."

"Lord save me, miss, I have but one pair of hands. The stool you seek is at the bottom of the stairs. Allow me time to catch my breath and I will fetch it up for you."

"Be off with you, Rory, I will fetch her *ladyship's* stool." Doretta cackled. "Save you one journey at least, y' lazy sap."

Dian hugged herself. The silly old woman was about to collect the instrument of her own destruction.

-oOo-

Dian woke with a start. Bright moonlight slanted through the tower-room window, illuminating the old woman asleep on her bed. Dressing swiftly and silently, Dian knotted a spare set of clothes into a shawl. If she was going to escape, it was now or never. She picked up the heavy stool and approached Doretta's sleeping place. Raising it in the air she let it drop, but not on to Doretta's head. How could she batter another human soul whilst they slept? She did not want to kill the woman, just to stun her long enough to make an escape. Better to wait until Doretta was awake, catch her by surprise, and then do the deed. Somehow, that seemed a less barbaric idea.

Doretta's snores ceased abruptly, and she sat bolt upright in bed. "What are you doing girl, prowling about like a cat after a rat? Surely you ain't contemplating work at this late hour. If you start that spinning wheel a-whirring, I will not get another wink of sleep."

The old woman was right – Dian felt like a cat in a cage, but the rat she was after lay right there in front of her. She lowered the stool to the ground, thankful that she still harboured a spark of decency.

Sleep eluded Dian for the rest of the night. Sitting by the window, she watched dawn poke misty fingers across the countryside. Daylight spread, and Joffrey appeared in the bailey. A horse with panniers attached waited patiently by the portcullis. More men brought horses from the stable and hitched them to carts. Joffrey mounted his horse and yelled for Rory to open the gate.

The noise awoke Doretta, and she joined Dian at the window. "Huh, I see his lordship is off and out to terrorise the local population again. Poor beggars are forced to give him whatever goods and money he demands," Doretta sniggered. "But who am I to complain? My life has improved markedly since Joffrey took over Lockton Castle." Throwing a shawl around her shoulders Doretta let herself out of the turret room. "Wait here, *m'lady*, I will return directly with your breakfast." She trundled off, locking the door behind her. *Wait there, m'lady! As if the fancy little madam has any other choice.* Doretta cackled at her own joke as she descended the spiral stairway.

The absence of Joffrey and his men would make Dian's escape less fraught and she decided today was the day. She dumped several hanks of wool she had spun over the past few days on to her bed, and took up a position behind the door with the stool in her hand. A little time passed before she heard the key click in the lock.

Doretta stepped into the room with a laden breakfast tray in her hands. Dian struck. The stool made glancing contact with the side of Doretta's head and landed heavily on her shoulder. The old woman dropped the tray, staggered forward, and fell face down on to the bed.

Quicker than a spider with a fly, Dian grabbed a hank of wool. She pulled the woman's wrists behind her back and lashed them together with the strong thread. Rolling her over she removed the door key from the chain at Doretta's waist. Anxious that she may have hit the old woman too hard, Dian checked her pulse. A steady heart beat throbbed under her fingers.

Eyes half closed, Doretta's mouth fell open and she began to snore. Assured that she had inflicted no lasting damage upon the old woman, Dian grabbed her spare clothes and raced for the door. On the way out, she inserted the key in the lock and turned it. Slowly, silently she tiptoed down the stairs. At the bottom she crept along the hallway. No-one was around to stop her. Aware that Doretta's horrible dogs might be prowling the bailey, she flattened herself against the castle walls. She need not have worried, for both animals were tethered behind the chapel out of everyone's way. Inching her way along, heart thundering in her breast, Dian came to the gatehouse. Beyond, the portcullis was firmly shut. Smothering a cry of anguish with her closed fist, she dropped to her knees. She had not properly thought out her plan. To come this far and then not be able to escape was almost more than she could bear. The very least she faced was a thrashing once Joffrey heard of her misdemeanour.

A gentle tap on the shoulder swiftly brought Dian's head up. Rory's face loomed above. "What do we have here?"

"I, I, er … Doretta allowed me out for a stroll, I tripped and fell." Dian scrambled to her feet and dusted herself down.

"I doubt you are telling me the truth, missy." Rory cocked his head to one side. "Joffrey informed everyone that you are to remain locked up, day and night, for as long as you live."

"Please, sir, take pity on me and let me out. When I return to Bayersby Manor I will sing your praises. You will be rewarded for your kindness if you let me go, I promise."

Rory looked Dian up and down, seeing only a beautiful young woman. For the first time in his life he felt empathy for another human being. What crime had she committed to deserve such a harsh sentence? Incarcerated for her entire life, denied a husband and children, did not seem right or fair. If he allowed the young woman to escape and, if she made it back to Bayersby, his reward might well be great. On the other hand, what excuse could he come up with to explain her disappearance to Master Joffrey?

Rory's mind worked overtime. Master Joffrey had ridden into Skelgut with his cronies, no doubt to cause more upset amongst the villagers. "Do not expect me back before nightfall," was his parting shot as he clattered out of the bailey with his men, horses and carts.

Grasping the back of Dian's kirtle, Rory ushered her into his wheel house. "You stop yourself in here, and do not make a sound." He sucked in a ragged breath, "Dear God, I know not why I am doing this – but I tell you what, girl, if we get caught we will both have cause to feel sorry for ourselves." With a glimmer of wry humour, he added, "That reward you speak of had better be good."

Flooded with a sense of relief, Dian hugged the smelly old gatekeeper.

"Goodness me," Rory huffed, turning pink with embarrassed delight. "I ain't never been squeezed by a young woman before." He gently pushed her away. "Enough of this nonsense. Tell me, what did you do to Doretta? I cannot imagine she let you go easily."

Dian grimaced. "I hit her with the three-legged stool and tied her hands behind her back with a length of wool I had spun." Holding up the door key, she added, "I left her locked in the turret."

"Dear Lord, she ain't dead, is she? Killing folk is a hanging offence! I want no truck with that kind of crime."

"Heavens no, Doretta is not dead, but she will have a mighty headache when she wakes."

"Must be your lucky day. There ain't nobody save me and a couple of stable boys in the castle at present. Doretta can holler all she likes, no-one will hear her. Give me the key to the turret room and I will dispose of it. Stay here 'til I make sure the stable boys are busy, then be prepared to make a speedy departure."

Moments later, Rory returned. "All clear." He unlocked the small gate in the portcullis and pushed Dian out. Following her to the end of the drawbridge, he threw the turret room key into the moat. "It will never be found in there." Rory's face crumpled with wheezy laughter. "Might be a while before yon old biddy gets rescued. And serve her right."

"But what will happen to you, Rory? Will Joffrey not punish you for allowing me to escape?"

"I ain't going to admit to anything! Worry not about me, I am well able to look out for myself. I just hope you can do the same. If you plan on returning to Bayersby Manor, you have a long road ahead of you."

Standing outside Lockton Castle, Dian took one last look back at the formidable structure. *Surely Joffrey lies. Oric cannot have given up his inheritance because of me.* Pushing such thoughts to the back of her mind, Dian began her journey down the mountain side. How different her two departures from the castle were. The first time she left with a broken heart. This time she was running for her life.

Skirting the village of Skelgut, Dian hastened into Farnrock Forest. She soon got lost. Darkness fell, and she climbed up into an oak tree. Clinging to a high branch, she hoped to remain safe from the wolves she could hear baying in the distance. Nearby rustles and creaks prevented sleep. Tears coursed down her cheeks, and she longed for her own safe bed at Bayersby Manor. She watched the moon 'rise and exhaustion eventually overtook her. Her heavy eyelids drooped, and she dozed.

Dian awoke to the sounds of the forest in full song. Early-morning sunshine sent shafts of pink light slanting through the trees, lifting her spirits. She climbed down from her overnight perch and stretched her cramped limbs. Rounding the enormous tree trunk, she was horrified to find that she was no longer alone.

"Well now, what do we have here?" said Amery Trundle to Father Chrispian. "We venture out to collect mushrooms for our breakfast and we find added treasure."

Father Chrispian clapped his hands and performed a strange, circular little dance. "What a pretty witchling," he chanted in a sing-song voice. In his mind's eye, the young woman sat atop a fiery pyre with her hands tied to a stake.

Shivers ran down Dian's spine. She recognised both men from old, and she knew neither one would think twice about killing her if her demise suited their purpose. The folk of Kilterton and Bayersby believed St Griswald's ex-priest to be dead, but here he was doing a horrible little dance and chanting mantras about burning witches. Master Freeman, wanted in connection with Sir Edred's death, looked only marginally less insane than Father Chrispian. To escape the confines of Lockton Castle and be confronted by two of the most dangerous men she knew seemed wholly unfair. Feeling sick with apprehension, she decided to brazen the situation out.

"Good morning," she said, ducking her head deferentially. "I am glad to find you both in good health. However, I am in a hurry so, if you will excuse me, I shall be on my way."

"You look exhausted, why not accompany us home and have some breakfast to set you up for your journey." Amery smiled and pointed to a pathway between the trees. "We share a nice little cottage a short way from here, do we not Father?"

Dian bobbed a curtsey. "Thank you for the kind invitation, Master Freeman, but I have already breakfasted," she lied. "If I wish to get to my destination in good time, I must be on my way."

Amery returned Dian's curtsey with a small bow. "Amery Trundle at your service, my dear. Come with me and I will supply you with comfortable lodgings."

"But you called yourself Freeman when you were at Bayersby Manor," exclaimed Dian. "Do you realise you are wanted for the murder of Sir Edred? Half the county is out looking for you."

Snakelike, Amery smiled. "And that is precisely why I used the alias. The name Freeman protected my identity, for I knew the folk of Bayersby would be after my hide following Sir Edred's demise."

"That makes no matter to me," said Dian, praying her apparent indifference might save her from being detained. She pushed past Amery and proceeded to walk away.

Amery shot out a plump, pink hand and fastened it in an iron-like grip on Dian's wrist. "Not so fast, young woman! My invitation is a command not a request. Your presence is sure to guarantee me safe passage should my whereabouts be discovered."

"Like she has any choice?" Father Chrispian tittered. He continued his macabre dance, his thin black hair streaming out around his shoulders. Every now and again he stopped to pinch Dian. "Ooh, this little beauty has plenty of succulent flesh on her bones. Rendering her down on my fiery pyre will take a long time."

"Pay the priest no mind," Amery whispered in Dian's ear. "I had my suspicions about Father Chrispian from our first encounter, now I am convinced the man is deranged. Stick close by me; together we shall keep a watchful eye on him."

To keep Dian safe, and to stop her from running away, Amery decided to lock her in a stoutly-built henrun at the back of the cottage. Keeping a tight hold on her, he lifted a padlock and key from a hook in the cottage door. He marched Dian down the yard and pushed her into her prison. He slid the bolt across and clamped it with the padlock. "Worry not, my dear," he crowed, pocketing the padlock key. "Father Chrispian cannot get at you in there."

Every now and again Amery sauntered out of the cottage to check his prisoner. He brought her food, and a bundle of dry grass and leaves to sleep on.

Father Chrispian also paid Dian one or two visits. He stood outside the enclosure eyeing her up and down, licking his lips but saying nothing. Dian's fear knew no bounds when he hammered a tall stake into the ground and surrounded it with fallen tree branches.

Dian sat down, making herself as small as possible. She had jumped out of the skillet into the fire and she had no idea what to do next. Hugging her knees, she tried not to cry.

CHAPTER TWENTY-FIVE

Another Long Journey

Outside Uther's shop, the Committee of Law members bade each other farewell, each promising to work hard at restoring Kilterton to the way it had been when Sir Edred was alive. Knowing at last where Dian was being held captive, Oric wanted to leave for Lockton Castle immediately.

Ichtheus dissuaded him. "It would be foolish to set off unprepared. Far more sensible to return to Bayersby Manor for one night, load up with provisions for the journey, and set off at first light tomorrow morning."

"Aye, Ichtheus is right," said Egglebart. "You ain't dealing with a fool. Joffrey will kill to retain his seat at Lockton. Everything you do from now on must be carefully thought out when your mind is alert. Best to let your fury abate and apply a dose of cold, hard logic."

Despite his eagerness to rescue Dian, Oric saw the sense in what his friends suggested. He stepped forward and embraced both Egglebart and Etheldrida. "You have supported me through thick and thin, and I love you both. Pray God I can secure a satisfactory ending to this terrible situation."

Etheldrida turned away before Oric could see her tears. She was more afraid for Dian than she had ever been for anyone else in her life.

Returned to Bayersby, Oric refused to retire to bed until he had packed everything he might need into Ichtheus' cart. He instructed squires, Erik and Arnald, to saddle Jester and to hitch Braccus to the cart before dawn.

Ichtheus glanced at the sky. "We may get more rain tonight, please wheel the cart into the stables to protect the dry goods."

"May I accompany you, Ichtheus? I long to return to my home," said Cordelia. "Surely the madman who sought to frighten me away from my cottage will be long gone."

Ichtheus nodded his agreement. "Aye, dear lady, I will enjoy your company. When we arrive in Skelgut I shall accompany you to your cottage to make sure all is well."

His mind busy with a jumble of thoughts, Oric struggled to sleep. As soon as the sky showed a glimmer of light he leaped from his bed, ready to begin the journey to Skelgut.

Not yet fully dawn, Guwain remained in his chamber but Josh, Ned, and Joe arose early to join Oric in the compound. "Ready when you are," they chorused.

"Nay, lads, you cannot come with me this time. Too many people entering Skelgut will surely draw unwanted attention. Once I find out how the land lies, I promise to send word if I need you."

Much against their better judgement, Ned and Joe agreed to remain at Bayersby Manor for the time being. They shook Oric warmly by the hand and wished him Godspeed.

"Much hard work and commitment lies ahead for the county folk in the Bayersby and Kilterton districts," said Bannulf, joining in the farewells. "But I am confident everyone will pull together – especially since Guwain's bully boys no longer hold sway. And I will have Ned and Joe to help me."

Bannulf embraced Oric. "May God go with you every step of the way."

"And you, Bannulf, I fear hard roads may lie ahead for us both."

"I suppose any attempt to deter you from this exercise will be a waste of my breath." Ichtheus slanted a sideways glance at Oric. "But you cannot stop me from accompanying you to Lockton Castle."

"You are welcome to come as far as Skelgut, Master Ichtheus, after that I go alone."

Cordelia clambered on to the cart beside Ichtheus. "I understand how you feel, Oric, but should you not take someone with you? Perhaps not Ichtheus, but certainly someone just as fit as yourself. Goodness knows what dangers you will face, and an extra pair of hands may make the difference between life or death."

Oric shook his head. "I secretly entered Lockton Castle once before, and I will do it again. Only this time I have the advantage of knowing the lay-out of the building."

Silent during the farewells, Josh stepped forward to say his piece. "Say what you like, Oric, Dian is my sister and I am coming with you regardless of what you say."

Recognising the stubborn look on Josh's face, Oric acquiesced. "Very well, you may come – but you must obey my orders without question once we reach our destination. Is that clear?"

Before Josh could answer, Faylinn tore across the compound and hurled herself into his arms. "Take care of yourself my brave hero. I do not want to lose you before I get the chance to wed you." She planted a kiss on his lips and pressed a lucky charm into his hand.

Blushing redder than a boiled beetroot, Josh pushed the rabbit's foot into his pouch. "Fear not my dear, I shall return."

"Now, are we ready to set off?" cried Oric. He seized Jester's reins from Eric's hand, and put his foot in the stirrup. Before he could swing his leg up and over the saddle, the horse took off with Parzifal in hot pursuit.

"There they go again," Ichtheus chuckled. "Why the daft lad persists in riding that animal is beyond me. As for Parzifal, I have lost count of how many times he has received a nip from Jester. I swear he would follow his beloved master into the jaws of Hell.

Oric clung to Jester's side as the horse trotted along the narrow pathway. Red faced and winded, he eventually managed to get into the saddle and slow Jester's pace. "Ye gods, you will be the death of me one of these days," he panted.

Jester merely snickered and looked angelic.

Joining the Roman Road, Oric manoeuvred the now calm gelding up beside Josh's horse. "I have made this journey so many times, I reckon I could do it blindfolded."

"Aye, and nearly always in unfortunate circumstances," Josh replied. "But this time is one of the worst. The sooner Dian is out of Joffrey's clutches the happier I shall be. Do you have a strategy yet?"

"No, not exactly. I shall talk to a few of our trusted friends in Skelgut to learn the lie of the land, maybe find out how many men Joffrey has at his beck and call. Once I know exactly where Dian is imprisoned, I will have a better idea of how best to rescue her."

The weather behaved in typical fashion for the time of year. Intermittent showers dripped through the forest's thick overhead canopy followed by sunshine, which barely penetrated the gloom. The travellers rode in miserable silence, stopping only at nightfall. After sharing a supper of dried herring and hard biscuits, they huddled together under Ichtheus' cart, swatting at biting, stinging insects, which appeared at dusk.

Late afternoon on the fourth day, Skelgut came into view. Rather than enter the village together and attract unwanted attention, everyone agreed to enter the village at intervals. Oric was first to go, and he plodded silently along the street with Jester in tow. Ordered to heel, Parzifal did as he was told for the first time in his life. Arriving at Archie Pender's cottage, Oric took the gelding into the back yard and tethered him to a fence post. He knocked on the cottage door and was greeted by a delighted Hamish. "Och, laddie, ye are a sight for sore eyes. Come away in. Archie and I wondered when ye would return."

A little while later, Ichtheus' cart scrunched along Archie's pathway, and Hamish hastened outside to help unhitch Braccus. Next to arrive, on foot, was Cordelia, followed shortly after by Josh.

Delighted to see his friends again Archie threw more logs on to the central hearth, and busied himself with a large pot of turnip and onion stew. "Sorry I have nothing more substantial to offer you, but all of us villagers are near destitute again because of Joffrey's high demands for money and produce." Archie squinted, "But unlike his father, he has an eye to the future. Joffrey ploughs much of his ill-gotten gains back into the estate. As a matter of fact, he made his latest collection not long before you arrived."

"Oh, my giddy aunt! Seems we had a narrow escape," exclaimed Ichtheus. "Do you know how many men Joffrey employs?"

Archie stirred the pot of stew vigorously, sending random spills of liquid to sing and sputter on the hot logs. "I ain't exactly sure. He usually brings a few fellows with him when he comes to the village, but I know not how many he leaves behind in the castle."

"If we are faced with a fight," mused Oric, "we will send for reinforcements from Bayersby and Kilterton. That said, I intend to avoid a confrontation with Joffrey until Dian is rescued. Once she is safe there will be no holds barred to remove him from Lockton Castle, alive or dead."

"Many of the villagers think you have deserted them," said Archie, handing out wooden bowls filled with stew. "Once they know the reason for your sudden departure, I believe a few of them might support your cause."

"I would like to think so," replied Oric, "but folk are fickle – we shall see…"

After supper, Oric left Archie's crowded cottage. He lay on his back on a grassy patch in the back yard, staring up at the night sky. Perhaps Dian was looking at the same stars. The thought that his dear love was so close, yet so far away, tore at his heart.

-oOo-

"I am telling you, summat is going on at Archie Pender's place."

Jeremiah Brody turned around in bed to face his wife. "Cease your prattle, woman. I am up from dawn 'til dusk keeping up with Master Joffrey's demands, and I need my sleep."

"Will you listen to me!" cried Annie, shaking her husband. "Mistress Fentwhistle and me was getting water at the lakeside on dusk, and we thought we saw Oric sneak around the back of Master Pender's cottage with a horse and that big shaggy dog of his." Annie gabbled on, too excited to hold her tongue. "We was curious, so we waited about a bit. It got a lot darker, then the moon came up and we could see along the street." Annie jabbed a sharp elbow into her husband's ribs. "What do y'suppose happened next, eh?"

Jeremiah groaned. "I ain't got no idea, but I am sure you are going to tell me."

"An old fellow with a donkey and cart came next, then followed a woman what looked suspiciously like the one what lives in that cottage in the woods. She had barely arrived at her destination when another fine-looking young fellow followed her. He was leading a horse an' all. But he never had no dog." Annie's eyes glittered in the candlelight. "And where do you suppose they all went?"

Jeremiah feigned interest. "Surely not Archie Pender's place, he ain't got room in his yard for a cart and all those animals."

"Right first time, husband. I know summat is going on, and I mean to find out exactly what, first thing in the morning." Holding her straggly hair away from the candle, she leaned out of bed and blew out the flame.

Lornika Fentwhistle paced up and down inside her cottage, talking to her cat. "Oric is back, leastways I think it was him." The cat arched his back and rubbed against Lornika's legs. "Took an instant dislike to the cocky young fellow when he first arrived, but now I give credit where credit is due. Our new Lord of Lockton turned the village around after the fiasco of Sir Ragnald's days. Then, for some reason best known to himself, he ups and leaves. I thought Joffrey was dead, but the black-hearted rascal returned before Oric's bed barely had time to cool." Lornika shivered. "I tell you, Mr Puss, if Master Joffrey wanted to scare us all witless, he surely succeeded with the hanging of forester

Barda." Seeking comfort, Lornika picked up the cat and settled him on her lap. "I hope Oric has returned to get rid of the tyrant." The cat purred and pumped his feet on Lornika's leg, prickling her skin with his claws.

The morrow saw Lornika Fentwhistle begin her infiltration of cottages. Her first call was on Mistress Brody. Together they made up a visiting list and set about informing everyone in the district of Oric's return.

Unaware of the latest development, Oric honed his axe and dagger on Archie's grindstone. "Would you please locate a grappling iron and length of rope?" he asked the old man.

Archie returned to the cottage with the required articles. "I purchased them from the blacksmith," he said, clattering the grappling iron on to the table. "He wanted to know why I would want such equipment. I might have raised his suspicions by saying I needed to climb on to my cottage roof. He asked why I did not use a ladder, which stumped me for an answer. Some of the villagers are behaving oddly an' all. I caught Mistress Fentwhistle coming out of Annie Brody's place. She positively yelped when I bid her good morning. Why would she do that, unless she is doing summat untoward?"

Oric paid scant attention to Archie's words, his mind working overtime. Under normal circumstances he would rally a group of followers, order Rory to open the portcullis, and march into his property to arrest Joffrey. But with Dian's life at stake, he needed to approach the castle secretly and carefully.

CHAPTER TWENTY-SIX

Rory's Legacy

Taking the bull by the horns, Ichtheus confronted Oric. "Going alone to Lockton Castle is nothing short of foolish."

"Maser Ichtheus, I am quite sure…"

Josh cut in. "You may as well save your breath for the task ahead, Oric. No matter what you say, I am coming with you. Dian's chances of survival will be greater if two of us make the rescue."

Oric continued to argue against the idea, but Josh would have none of it. "We are wasting time. Let us get about our business."

"Nay, lads, have some sense!" advised Ichtheus. "If you walk through the village at this time of day, you can say goodbye to secrecy. Every man and his dog is out there at present. I suggest you wait until the early hours of tomorrow morning. You can set off before daylight and make the most of your climb before sunrise. Then lie low near to the castle until nightfall."

Oric reluctantly agreed and resigned himself to kicking his heels around Archie's cottage for the rest of the day.

The sleepless night dragged by, and Oric arose long before dawn. Ready to get on with the task ahead, he tied Parzifal to Archie's table. "Keep your eye on the dog. Given half a chance he will run after me."

Armed with daggers and axes, the grappling hook and rope slung around his torso, Oric crept alongside Josh through the silent village. Leaving Skelgut before anyone had arisen from their beds, they crossed the swollen ford at Brundle Brook. At the foot of the mountain, they deliberated over which route to choose.

"If we climb the secondary track we are unlikely to meet any Lockton Castle inmates," said Oric. "And that part of the mountain is not easily seen from the castle. The going is steep and treacherous, but I am game if you are."

Josh nodded.

Arriving at the bottom of the mountain, they began their ascent in the half-light of early dawn.

Walking up the lower slopes of the mountain proved easy, but the track soon degenerated. Late summer rain caused waterfalls to tumble over rocks at every turn, soaking the boys to their skin. Rounding a steep corner in the track, a substantial landslide blocked their way. Josh leaned back as far as he dared to check the extent of the obstacle. "How in God's name do we get around that?"

Oric grimaced, and wrung water from his tunic. Refusing to admit defeat, he unwound the rope and grappling hook from his torso. "Where there is a will, there is a way," he stated and hurled the grappling hook with all his might. It latched on to a rock protruding out of the landslide part-way up. "I shall climb as far as the rope goes and then you follow me."

"Are you crazy?" Josh exclaimed.

"Aye – you could say that. Crazy in love with your sister."

Josh bit back a retort. There was no arguing with a man obsessed. "How do you know the hook will bear your weight?"

"Only one way to find out," said Oric, giving the rope a firm tug. The rock crumbled and the hook dislodged. Moments before Oric tumbled down the slope, the grappling iron caught on to a more substantial rock. Taking a deep breath to calm his shredded nerves, Oric tugged the rope again. This time it held, and he moved slowly, hand over hand in an upward direction.

Terrified, Josh kept his eyes on Oric's shadowy figure. When he reached the half-way point, Oric beckoned for Josh to follow.

The grappling hook broke loose again, and Josh catapulted downwards. Oric lurched after the rope and looped it around himself and a different, larger rock. Taking up the slack, he groaned as Josh's weight threatened to drag his arms out of their sockets.

Josh dangled from a narrow ledge, thanking God it was still too dark to see how far down the valley floor lay. He scrabbled with his feet to gain purchase on firmer ground and clung to the rope until he became dizzy. Shale rattled off the ledge and on to his upturned face. More small stones rolled past his body and plunged down the near-vertical slope.

"Are you alright?" came Oric's muffled cry from above.

"Ain't nothing broken as far as I can tell, though I almost suffered heart failure with fright. Is the rope properly secured at your end, now?"

"Aye, I think so."

"Think ain't good enough. Make sure that grappling hook is latched onto something more substantial this time. There is nowt but fresh air directly below me."

"Hang on tight and I will pull you up. Get some purchase on the rock face with your feet if you can, for you are nearly too heavy for me to lift."

Oric hauled on the rope until he thought his eyes would pop out of his head with the strain. When Josh's round face appeared over the ledge, Oric leaned down and grabbed his friend by the arm.

His muscles screaming for mercy, Josh made a last, valiant effort and heaved his body up on to the ledge beside Oric. For several heartbeats they clung together like a pair of limpets on a rock.

"Sheesh! I never want to get that close to meeting my maker again for a long, long time," rasped Josh, loosening his hold on Oric at last.

Thoroughly shaken but still determined to pursue their goal, the boys prepared to carry on.

Oric freed the grappling hook and hurled it upwards once more. It disappeared around the curve of the landslide and, unable to see what the hook had latched on to, Oric gave the rope a vicious tug. Satisfied it would take his weight he continued slowly upwards.

Nearer to their destination, streaks of dawn silvered the dark sky. "Not far to go now," Oric panted, moving toward a row of windswept bushes beneath the plateau upon which Lockton Castle stood. "We shall lie low under this greenery for the rest of the day. Once the inhabitants of the castle arise, we may hear something to our advantage."

Oric spent the longest day of his life listening, chewing on hard biscuits, and dozing. The moment darkness fell, he was up and raring to go. Half way across the plateau in front of the castle, the moon sailed from behind a cloud. Bathed in silver light, Oric and Josh crouched low to the ground.

"Dear Lord, this is all we need," muttered Josh. "We are lit up like a pair of mummers on a stage!"

Mercifully, more cloud soon blotted out the moon. "That is a good omen," Oric whispered. "Hopefully darkness will now prevail until we get over the wall."

Oric recalled the last occasion he had entered the castle by devious means. At the time he had no idea of his rightful tenure of the Lockton Estate. Ironically, as the verified lord, he was gaining access to his own castle in a secretive and demeaning manner once again.

They swam across the moat, silently grateful for Rory's begrudging efforts to clean the stagnant water. Soaked to the skin they stood well away from the main entrance, staring up at the castle's battlements. Oric hurled the grappling iron once again. This time it hooked into a robust castellation where it remained firmly wedged. They waited for a few heartbeats to make sure the clang of iron against stone had not alerted anyone within the castle.

All remained quiet and, one after the other, Oric and Josh climbed the rope. The moon reappeared from behind its cloud, illuminating the pair sitting atop the battlements.

"Quick, let us get down before we are spotted," whispered Josh. In a panic, he pulled up the rope and dropped it down on the inside of the wall."

Safely on ground level once more, the boys hugged the black shadows inside the bailey. "Where do we begin looking?" Josh asked.

About to reply, Oric tripped and fell on top of a prone body. "What goes on here?" he gasped, immediately feeling for a pulse in the person's neck. A faint flutter confirmed that the fellow lived, and Oric rolled him over on to his back. "We have to get this fellow somewhere less public. If I can bring him round, he might be able to impart some useful information."

"Do you not see who it is?" growled Josh.

Oric took a closer look. "The poor fellow is so badly beaten, I can barely make out his features in this poor light."

"'Tis the crest on the fellow's doublet I recognise, not his face," said Josh. "The emblem is faded, but that rampant black serpent on a red background is Sir Ragnald's coat of arms. I think Rory is the only man who did not get rid of items bearing that insignia."

"Od's blood!" growled Oric, peering more closely at the man's chest. "Why has the poor fellow been beaten in this barbaric way? Since he is out here, perhaps no-one is in his wheelhouse. Keep him quiet, Josh, whilst I investigate."

Josh snorted. "That will not be hard to do – the fellow is out cold."

Sticking to the dark side of the deserted bailey, Oric crept around the wall with his dagger at the ready. He made it to the wheelhouse without incident. The door stood ajar and a small lantern burned within the room. Judging by the overturned bed and pools of blood on the floor, Rory's assault had taken place inside this room – but why was he now outside? Oric righted the bed and returned to where Josh waited beside Rory's prone body. "Quick, help me carry him inside so that I can administer to him."

For the first time since he could remember, Oric carried no medical supplies. Now, faced with a seriously wounded man, he could do little to help him save wash the blood from his face. Rory's breath rasped, bloody snot bubbled from his smashed nose, and a trickle of darker blood ran from the corner of his mouth, indicating serious internal injuries.

"We cannot stay here," said Josh, "'Tis only a matter of time before someone will want the portcullis opened."

"You worry too much, my friend. Joffrey and his men will be abed by now. By all accounts, they made a raid on Skelgut a short time before we arrived in the village, there will be vittles aplenty to last them a day or two. I doubt anyone will need to venture out of the castle immediately. Rather than blunder around with no inkling of where to look for Dian, let us wait a short while to see if Rory regains consciousness."

The injured man groaned under Oric's ministration, and he opened one swollen eyelid with difficulty. He took a deep, shuddering breath and spat out globs of blood.

"Pass me your water container, Josh, and I will give him a drink."

Oric assisted Rory into a sitting position. "Take a sip of water, then you might be able to tell me why you have been so brutally beaten, and who did this to you."

Rory sipped a little of the water and winced as the cold liquid stung his battered lips. "I helped Dian to escape..." His voice trailed off with the exertion.

Oric dropped the pot of water in shock. "Dian has escaped?"

In severe pain, Rory lowered himself back down on to his bed. "Lovely girl," he gasped. "Prison... life. No good..."

"Where she has gone?"

Coughs racked Rory's body, and more blood trickled down his chin. "Dunno," he rasped. "Side... gate." Here, a faint smile flickered around his mouth. "Doretta locked in turret...Key in moat...Joffrey..."

"How did Joffrey link Dian's disappearance to you?" asked Josh.

"Gatekeeper...copped a beating."

"I know not how to reward you," replied Oric.

"Dian... always kind..." Rory struggled, as his voice became a tortured whisper.

"We have to get him away from here," said Josh. "If we leave him, Joffrey will come back and kill him for sure."

"No need," said Oric sadly. "The poor fellow is on the point of death."

Rory's breath rattled and stopped. Oric pulled a thin blanket over the gatekeeper's broken body and made the sign of a cross.

Grabbing the key from a hook on the wall, Oric peeped out of the gatehouse door to make sure no-one had entered the bailey. "Come, Josh, we must make all haste away from this place, for we are now on borrowed time."

"What about the grappling hook and rope? It will be a sure giveaway that some intruder has been in the castle."

"Never fear, long before Joffrey discovers who the intruders were, I shall have gathered forces to arrest him. But first we must seek Dian."

Dance Macabre

Lornika Fentwhistle banged on Archie Pender's door. "Open up! We know you are hiding someone within."

Parzifal barked loudly several times at the disturbance.

"You ain't got no dog, Archie Pender!" yelled Annie Brody. "And we seen those extra animals in your back yard, and an old cart."

Archie raised his eyebrows at Ichtheus and Cordelia. "What shall I do?" he mouthed.

Ichtheus sighed and drew a hand across his brow. "We had best talk to them. They are unlikely to go away until they get some answers to their questions."

Shambling to the door, Archie wrenched it open.

Outside the cottage, a semicircle of people gathered behind Lornika Fentwhistle.

"What do you need to know, woman?"

"We believe Oric is back in Skelgut. Is he here for good, or what?"

"Joffrey is ruining our lives." cried Desdemona Whittle. "If Oric is here we want him to stay."

A general babble of agreement drowned out Archie's reply.

Ichtheus stepped out into the street and held up his hand for silence.

"See, I told you something was going on," said Lornika Fentwhistle, pointing her finger at the apothecary. "He is the medicine man from Bayersby Manor. Him and Oric are near inseparable so, if he is here, I will wager the Lord of Lockton is around somewhere."

"Be silent!" Ichtheus retorted, "and I will tell you the truth. Yes, Oric is back, but he needs absolute secrecy to achieve his aim. I am asking you all not to repeat anything I say to anyone outside the village. Oric has a plan and, if Joffrey suspects anything untoward, many lives could be lost." Ichtheus omitted to mention Dian's incarceration. "Oric is on his way to Lockton Castle as we speak. He plans to scout the area in secret and, once he ascertains how many men Joffrey has at his disposal, he will muster his own supporters. It is my belief Oric plans to arrest Joffrey and bring him to justice for his felonies."

"What are we supposed to do in the meantime?" demanded Jeremiah Brody.

"Carry on as normal but sharpen your weapons. Be prepared for action when Oric returns."

The villagers dispersed, muttering amongst themselves. They agreed to support Oric in any endeavour he chose to help rid the district of the tyrant, Joffrey.

Archie plopped down on the wooden bench outside his cottage and mopped his brow. "Oh dear me. Will there ever be an end to all this upset?"

"Not 'til somebody puts a stop to Joffrey's antics," growled Hamish, appearing from the side of the cottage. "Now the villagers know we are here, at least we no longer need to hide ourselves away like a bunch o' criminals."

"When will Oric and Josh return?" asked Cordelia.

"I doubt we shall see them until long after dark," replied Archie. "Hopefully they will have Dian with them, and all three in one piece."

Ichtheus darted a glance at Cordelia. "Since we have time on our hands, what say we make use of the day and visit your cottage?"

"I would like that, for I am concerned how well my chickens have fared in my absence. The sooner I can move back there the happier I shall be."

"Dear lady, I doubt it is safe for a woman to remain alone in the middle of the woods during these troubled times." Ichtheus peered at Cordelia from beneath his bushy, white eyebrows. "I suggest you stay with Archie until the unrest dies down."

Prepared to take Ichtheus' advice, Cordelia turned to Archie. "Would you mind?"

"Pleased to oblige, Mistress, I shall be glad of your company."

Hamish harnessed Braccus to the cart in readiness for the journey. Ichtheus and Cordelia climbed aboard, and the pair set off.

Ichtheus drove slowly through the woods but, deep in conversation with Cordelia, the time passed quickly. Entering a clearing, he was surprised to see how high the sun had risen.

"Look," said Cordelia, pointing ahead. "I can see the front of my place beyond the next group of trees… Oh, my goodness, I can smell smoke! No-one lives hereabouts except for me; the fire must be on in my hearth."

"Maybe we should leave the cart here and continue on foot," suggested Ichtheus, also smelling the smoke as they drew nearer to the cottage.

"Good idea," whispered Cordelia. "Let us do that, and approach with caution."

Not only did smoke drift from the cottage's roof hole, angry voices issued from within.

"There is never any peace around this place. You behave like a madman, raving on about hell and damnation, morning, noon, and night. For the love of God – shut your mouth!"

"You would do well to pay attention to my words, you objectionable heathen." A loud crash followed the angry retort.

"How dare you hurl vessels at me! I will not have it!"

"Move out if you do not share my philosophy. I found this cottage and finders is keepers, so I deem this place belongs to me." More sounds of breaking pottery followed.

"I ain't going anywhere, so you had best get used to my presence. I warn you, if you do not cease your prattle, I will cut out your tongue whilst you sleep. And if you threaten to burn my prisoner at the stake once more, I will set fire to you."

"Ye gods," gasped Ichtheus, "I know those voices! 'Tis the fellow who poisoned Sir Edred, and the crazy priest from St Griswald's church."

Ichtheus' suspicions were confirmed when the cottage door burst open and the furious altercation continued outside.

Amery dared not allow the priest to see he was afraid, for if he allowed the fellow to get the upper hand, goodness knows what he might do next. He planned to poison Father Chrispian, but he had not yet found the right plant for the job.

Wearing nothing but a loin cloth, Father Chrispian danced around his plump adversary, waving his arms above his head like a demented monkey. Stick thin legs pumping, pasty white skin with a mat of black hair upon his chest, he looked preposterous. He grabbed a two-pronged pitch fork from against the cottage wall and began jabbing at the fat man's backside. "If you fail to heed my warnings, you will surely burn in hell."

Trying to protect himself with his bare hands, Amery jumped about. His rolls of soft fat wobbled and his face turned pink with the effort. Eventually he managed to grab hold of the pitch fork, and he hurled it back inside the cottage. A bucket of cold water stood by the door and he threw the contents at Father Chrispian.

The cold water caught the priest full in the face and he staggered back, gasping and spluttering.

"Consider your ablutions complete and cover yourself!" yelled Amery. "Get out of my way, I need to take food to my prisoner, always assuming you have not gobbled up all of last night's rabbit stew."

Were it not such a serious situation, Ichtheus would have laughed out loud. Instead, he gave Cordelia's hand a gentle tug. "Come, dear lady, we must hasten away from this place. If that pair catches sight of us, I dare not think what they might do. We do not have the strength to ward them off."

"I wholeheartedly agree," Cordelia whispered back. She gathered up her skirt to ease her swift departure. "Who do you suppose the prisoner is?" she asked, when they arrived safely back at the cart.

Ichtheus stroked his throat and grimaced. "I have no idea, but I cannot imagine the privations the poor wretch has suffered. Much as I would like to investigate, I am loath to risk our lives by looking. Since Trundle and the priest are wanted men, we will return with reinforcements to arrest them. They will both go before the magistrate when next he visits Skelgut. I have no doubt he will pass the death sentence on them both. But it will be down to Oric to make the final decision."

Dian huddled in the back of the henhouse, listening to the argument between her captors. Weary beyond imagination, her head lolled forward on to her chest, but sleep eluded her. The food provided once each day was barely enough to keep body and soul together, and her stomach grumbled constantly. But hunger was far from her main concern. Each day the crazy priest added more branches to his ever-growing pyre around the stake he had hammered into the open ground behind the cottage. His mumblings about ridding the district of witches terrified Dian, for she feared she might become Father Chrispian's victim.

Repulsed by the man, Dian attempted to conceal herself behind a spindly elderberry bush that grew in the back of the henrun. But her efforts were in vain. Father Chrispian entertained himself by thrusting a long-handled pitch fork in and out between the stout wooden planks that served to protect the chickens from wolves and foxes. Dian dodged from one side of the enclosure to the other to avoid being jabbed with the fork's sharp prongs.

"Do not imagine Amery Trundle will prevent me from setting you alight, witchy girl," cried the priest, a length of silvery drool hanging from his bottom lip. "If I knew where he hides the key to this accursed structure, I would seize it then kill him whilst he sleeps." Father Chrispian grasped the bars of Dian's cage and shook them, but they remained impervious to his efforts. "One way or another, girlie, I will see you atop my pyre."

Her worst fears realised, Dian covered her eyes to shut out the sight of the madman.

-oOo-

"Who dragged the gatekeeper's body onto his bed and pulled a cover over him?" Joffrey demanded. "I beat him senseless and left him outside on the ground to die."

Cadwin gave his battle-axe a vicious swipe with a sharpening stone. "I dunno! Maybe he came around and crawled back into his filthy-rat hole by himself."

"I doubt that very much, I broke his legs as well as his thick skull."

A low rumble came from the men lounging around Lockton Castle's bailey. Rogues they might be, but few of them had the stomach for the inhumane punishment Joffrey dished out to anyone he thought might go against him. They shifted nervous glances at each other, but no-one put up his hand.

Feeling a prickle of apprehension, Joffrey chose not to pursue his line of questioning any further. He needed to keep on the right side of the few men he had in his employ, for he might need their services sooner rather than later. Besides, did it matter if some soft-hearted fool had dragged the gatekeeper out of sight? "Get a burial party together before the corpse begins to stink. Find a spot under the walls, dig a hole, and drop the cur into it."

Leofrick stepped forward. "I will see to it, sir." He nodded at a couple of his cronies, and all three went off in search of shovels and a suitable place to dispose of Rory. Moments later, they returned at a gallop. "Master Joffrey," yelled Leofrick. "I believe someone has secretly entered the castle."

"What makes you think that?" growled Joffrey.

"There is a grappling iron embedded in the battlements, and a length of rope hanging from it. That would suggest someone has entered the castle illegally – would you not say, sir?"

Joffrey ignored Leofrick's insolent smirk. "Show me the place."

At sight of the offending piece of equipment, Joffrey's prickle of apprehension turned to fear. "Get that hook and rope down from there. Throw it in the hall before the culprit uses it to escape."

Rather than spook his men, Joffrey pretended a nonchalance he did not feel. "Some local lad probably accepted a dare from his peers to prove that he can scale the castle walls undetected. I suspect he will be long gone; nevertheless, make a search of the castle in case some stranger skulks in the shadows. If you find anyone, bring him to me and I will flay his hide."

Pacing the bailey, Joffrey's worries increased. What if Oric had scaled the castle wall? What if he had rescued Dian? Now he no longer had the girl to use as a bargaining tool, he regretted killing Rory. The fellow had stayed on in Oric's employ after Sir Ragnald's departure from the castle, and he might have known something useful.

Joffrey clenched his teeth. It would not do to allow the men to see that he was perturbed. Craven cowards all, they would likely run away at the first sign of trouble. He could not afford to lose one of them.

Putting on a cheerful face, Joffrey confronted his men. "We are not due in Skelgut for a few days. Rather than sit about on our backsides, what say we practise siege activities. Not that I am expecting trouble," he hastened to add, "but it will be good for us to be ready in the unlikely event we ever need to barricade ourselves in."

Leofrick did not believe a word his master said. Nevertheless, he decided to go along with Joffrey's little game. He enjoyed a comfortable billet at the castle, but at the first sign of trouble he would be off.

-oOo-

Winded after their mad gallop down the mountain, Oric and Josh burst into Archie's cottage.

"Dian has gone," the boys both spoke together.

"What do you mean gone?" stuttered Ichtheus. "Do you know where she is?'

Oric chewed on his lip. "No, not exactly. According to Rory, he allowed her to escape and has paid for his act of kindness with his life."

"Oh, dear Lord," cried Cordelia. "The poor man. Who killed him?"

"Joffrey beat Rory to death for allowing Dian to escape. But punishment for that act of brutality can wait. My major priority is to search for Dian – she is out there somewhere, and I mean to find her." Without further ado, Oric made for the door.

"Wait!" Ichtheus chased after Oric and squeezed his arm. "I know Dian is your major priority, but there is another situation we need to deal with as soon as possible. Perhaps we can combine both things." Ichtheus explained the discovery of Father Chrispian and Amery Trundle in Cordelia's cottage. "The tension between the pair is terrible and I am concerned that one or the other of them might leave. It would be a tragedy if either one of them escaped justice for the evil acts they have committed. My guess is, to avoid recapture, Dian will have made for the woods. She could easily have become lost so, in my opinion, the woods are the best place to begin our search, and at the same time we can arrest Trundle and the priest."

Deliberating over what to do for the best, Oric tugged at the neck of his tunic as if it had suddenly grown too tight. "I am sorry, Master Ichtheus, we do not have the manpower to pursue both causes. Right now, Dian is my priority."

"Oh, I think you might be surprised. Manpower is not lacking."

Forgetting his manners, Oric snapped. "Do not be ridiculous, we have Hamish who is crippled and unable to walk far. Archie, who is likely to suffer heart failure under such pressure, and," Oric rolled his eyes, "you, master Ichtheus, and Cordelia. Josh and I are the only able-bodied members of this group."

Ichtheus allowed Oric's unusual rudeness to pass. "I think you underestimate the loyalty you have engendered amongst the villagers during your brief tenure of Lockton Castle."

"What would they know? They have no idea of what is going on."

"Again, you do them a disservice. They are not fools, and word soon spread of your return to Skelgut. They were also curious about the animals, and my cart in Archie's yard. This morning, a deputation of visitors banged on Archie's door, demanding an explanation."

"But I said Dian's imprisonment at the castle must be kept secret!" Oric, now in a fury, stood with his fists clenched and his chest thrust out. "How dare you disobey my orders?"

Overwhelmed by Oric's outburst, Ichtheus brought a shaky hand to his forehead. "I understand your distress but please hear me out, lad."

"Make it quick for I have no time to lose." Foot tapping impatiently, Oric waited.

The other four people in the room stared askance at Oric. No-one had ever seen him so angry.

"We are the only ones who know of Dian's situation," said Ichtheus, "though I feel we should tell the villagers now. The more people willing to search for her, the sooner we are likely to find her." Seeing a slight give in Oric's angry stance, Ichtheus hastily continued. "Everyone in the district is keen to help you oust Joffrey, so I believe you will find manpower aplenty. Rather that stand here arguing, I suggest we send word to your supporters and get started on both causes."

CHAPTER TWENTY-EIGHT

Operation Clean Up

Delighted to see their beloved lord back in Skelgut, the villagers were quick to answer Oric's call for assistance. More people than he could ever have imagined turned up at the designated meeting place outside Archie's cottage. They came with horses and carts, some rode donkeys, others were on foot, all eager to do what they could to help. They broke up into separate groups and set off in different directions to search for Dian.

Oric asked the burliest of villagers to accompany him, as he intended to arrest Amery Trundle and Father Chrispian. They would not give up without a fight, and Oric wanted to make sure they had no chance of escape.

Sensing the urgency of the occasion, Jester behaved like a perfect gentleman, and Oric loved him even more. Parzifal ran ahead of the men, only his feathery tail to be seen waving in amongst the tall grasses by the wayside.

At Ichtheus' insistence, Oric made straight for Cordelia's cottage. Long before they got to their destination, a bitter smell of charred wood assailed their nostrils.

"What funny business is this?" said Ichtheus. "The woods could surely not have caught alight, could they?"

"I very much doubt it," replied Oric. "But, to be on the safe side I will ride ahead. I do not wish to see anyone trapped by a forest fire." He whistled to Parzifal and tied him to Ichtheus' cart. "Please keep an eye on him, Master Ichtheus. I do not want to risk his life by taking him with me."

"Since there ain't no sign of fresh smoke," said Walter, "I think the smell is coming from another source."

"You could be right," replied Oric. "Nevertheless, everyone must remain at safe distance. I will whistle when all is well."

Jester picked his way through the forest, and the smell of burning intensified. Wild animals and birds sensed when something was amiss, and the woods sounded eerily quiet. A little further on, the source of the smell became horribly apparent. Ahead, a burned-out building smouldered. Oric swiftly dismounted. He tethered Jester to a tree and went to investigate. Approaching the building, smoke seared his throat and he coughed.

"Help me."

The plaintive plea caused Oric to hold his breath. Surely no-one had lived through the inferno. He ventured as close to the charred ruins as he dared and yelled. "Is any one there? Shout out if you can hear me."

"Yes, yes, I am here," cried a female voice. "I am behind the cottage."

Oric raced into the back yard. Before him stood the stoutest henrun he had ever seen. Inside, a ragged-looking woman clung to the wooden planks.

"Hold on, I will have you out of there in a trice." For the life of him, Oric could not think what she was doing in the henrun.

The woman sobbed and, coming closer, Oric's heart almost failed. The woman was Dian!

He tore at the door, but a huge padlock prevented it from opening. Forcing his hands through gaps in the planks, Oric seized her arms. "Dian! Dian! My dearest love, what has happened to you?"

Choked with emotion Dian failed to utter another word. Tears of relief made white tracks down her filthy cheeks, and she lay her head against the planks.

Dian's pitiful condition filled Oric with a fury he had never experienced before. Gently stroking her hair, he murmured soft words of love to her. "My darling, darling girl, I thought I would never see you again. Are you hurt?"

Dian lifted tear-filled eyes to look at Oric. Every moment of horror she had experienced drifted away at the sight of his strong, handsome face.

"I want to hold you close," cried Oric. "But first I must get you out of here."

The planks resisted Oric's assault and, in desperation, he went in search of a suitable implement to break into Dian's prison. No tools survived the cottage fire, and he was obliged to whistle for help. Within moments, people swarmed into the clearing.

Never without his axe, woodman Sedrick soon chopped Dian free.

Unable to wait a moment longer, Oric gathered her into a deep embrace, pressing her body close to his own. Regardless of the amused audience, he smothered her face with kisses. "I will never, never, let you out of my sight again. I am going to marry you even if I have to make you my prisoner first."

Aware of her disgusting body odour and matted hair, Dian blushed scarlet. Horribly embarrassed, she tried in vain to push Oric away. "I have been made prisoner twice already and I am not keen to repeat the experience. Stay clear of me – I am dirtier and smellier than the filthiest of fish wives."

Light headed with relief that Dian had suffered only superficial ailments, Oric pressed her even more tightly to his chest. "You look and smell like an angel to me."

A light tap on his shoulder brought Oric back to reality. "When you have finished trying to crush this poor young woman to a pulp, I suggest you take her back to Skelgut and allow her to bathe, enjoy a good meal, and get some sleep. She looks utterly exhausted."

"Wait!" cried Dian. "What of Amery Trundle and the priest. They were both within the cottage when it burned. Did they escape through a window, for they never came out of the door?"

Ichtheus looked at Oric over the top of Dian's head. "No," he mouthed, shaking his head. In a louder voice, he added, "Do not fret over that pair, my dear. Allow Oric to take you to Cordelia, she will look after you."

A cold chill invaded Ichtheus' stomach, and he called out to Oric once more. "Please allow me to inform Cordelia of the destruction of her cottage. I wish to break the news gently, for she will be devastated."

"I will," promised Oric. Sweeping Dian up into his arms, he carried her over to where Jester stood waiting, and lifted her on his back. The gelding whinnied softly but remained still. Oric climbed up behind Dian and, holding her to him, he tapped Jester's flanks with his heels.

Leaning back against Oric's warm chest, the motion of the horse soon lulled Dian to sleep. Oric rubbed his cheek against her hair. He was the happiest man on earth and he felt ten feet tall.

To allow Dian and Cordelia breathing space, Hamish

and Archie moved their bedding into potter Manluss' workshop. Oric and Ichtheus accepted Desdemona Whittle's offer to bed down in her cottage. They soon regretted their decision, for the woman talked non-stop until bed time, then she snored and grunted like a prize porker until morning.

After the first night, Ichtheus packed up his belongings. Always the gentleman, he smiled sweetly at Desdemona and thanked her for her hospitality. "Oric tells me my snores are insufferable and, like as not, I kept you awake all night. To save you further disruption I shall take up residence in Master Pender's hay loft."

"What?" Backed into a corner, Oric opened his mouth to disagree then, at sight of his mentor's meaningful expression, he thought better of it. *Wily old fellow, now I must come up with a suitable excuse to escape.* He gave Desdemona a sickly smile. "Yes, Mistress, I must also leave your charming cottage." Unable to think of anything better on the spur of the moment, he added, "My dog pines without me and, since he is not allowed inside your dwelling, I must join Master Ichtheus in the hay loft. Thus, my dog can sleep alongside me." For good measure, he added, "I dare not leave my horse for long, either. He becomes difficult when I am not there to tend him."

Desdemona simpered over Ichtheus. "Of course, you must please yourself, Master Apothecary, however, should you change your mind I am more than willing to put up with a little inconvenience in exchange for your most interesting company." Sniffing expressively, she eyed Oric. "As for you, young man, I find your choice of bedfellow very strange, and I should be glad if you would remove yourself from my residence forthwith."

Outside the cottage, Ichtheus squeaked and snuffled with laughter. "Well done, lad. No doubt she will tell the entire village that you prefer the company of animals to humans."

Oric punched Ichtheus gently on the arm. "Thank you very much. But I would rather claim an antisocial reputation than spend another night under that woman's roof."

Clean and fed, Dian slept all night and most of the following morning. When she awoke, Oric was her first caller.

They sat together at Archie's table sharing a plate of oat cakes drizzled with honey. Oric reached for Dian's hand but she pulled away, a prim expression on her face.

Oric sighed. "What is troubling you now?"

"You are still a lord and I am still a ladies' maid. I have told you time and again, a match between us is unthinkable."

"But after I rescued you, I thought you might love me just a little."

"Of course, I am grateful to you for saving me, but I cannot marry you."

"Ye gods, woman, what can I say to change your mind?"

"Nothing, for my mind is made up."

"Will you at least agree to rekindling our friendship?"

"Yes, I suppose that will be alright as long as we avoid becoming too familiar."

Familiar! The word screamed silently inside Oric's head. *If only she knew how familiar I would like to become. I want us to have lots of children and become a family.* He breathed deeply to steady his emotions, "Very well, if friendship is all you are prepared to offer, then I must accept your decision with good grace. At least we can talk to each other again. Would you care to tell me exactly what happened after Joffrey seized you on your way to Roxbrough with Lady Myferny?"

Oric's invitation to share her woes opened a flood gate. The more Dian talked, the more furious Oric became. Near the end of her story, he was on his feet pacing the cottage.

"So help me, I will kill that bastard once I get my hands on him."

"Woah, lad. May I assume you are referring to Joffrey?" said Ichtheus, entering the cottage in time to hear the end of Oric's statement. "Calm down. You need a cool, level head and plenty of back-up to best that soulless fellow. I suggest we call a meeting with the villagers and plan a strategy."

-oOo-

Disgruntled by the extra work, preparation for a possible siege and the thought that one might occur, Joffrey's men began deserting the castle. They sneaked away one-by-one, after dark, until only Cadwin, Leofrick, and a handful of the laziest men remained. Not caring one way or the other, Leofrick and Cadwin omitted to inform their master of the dire situation.

Joffrey spent his days looking through Lockton Castle's ledgers, planning exactly how much he could bleed from the villagers for his own benefit, without quite causing them to starve. He dined alone in his private quarters, preferring to avoid contact with his uncouth employees. Not until most of them had gone did he notice that the bailey was unusually quiet. Concerned, he called his two main men into the Great Hall.

Cadwin and Leofrick stood before their master, neither one keen to break the silence.

"Well?" Joffrey barked. "Who is going to speak first?"

Leofrick looked at Cadwin, and Cadwin shuffled about with his eyes downcast.

"I instructed you to drill the men in the art of defence, but I see no evidence of that happening."

The two men remained mute.

Joffrey slammed his large ledger shut. "For the love of all that is holy – will one of you tell me what is going on?"

"Er, we ain't got no men to instruct, bar one or two wastrels," Leofrick ventured.

"Where are all the others?" demanded Joffrey, a sinking feeling invading the pit of his stomach.

"Gone," snapped Cadwin.

"And I am off an' all," stated Leofrick. "I done all your dirty work for little or no reward. Now the girl has escaped, you ain't got no bargaining tool. Oric of Lockton will be after blood, and it ain't going to be mine." He tapped a finger to his brow in a mock salute, turned on his heels, and sauntered out of the Great Hall.

Cadwin watched his colleague depart but said nothing.

"I will promote you to Steward of the castle if you stay," promised Joffrey.

"Thank you for nothing," sneered Cadwin. "'Tis only a matter of time before Oric reclaims his castle, and I guarantee he ain't going to keep me on." He spat a glob of phlegm on to the floor. "If you value your life, I suggest you be long gone before he gets here." With a similar, derogatory salute to Leofrick's, Cadwin left the Great Hall for the last time.

Joffrey paced up and down, his worst fears realised. With nobody to back him, he stood no chance of repelling Oric and his men. *Best to cut my losses and leave. But first I will gather up all the valuables I can lay hands on.* He lifted down a sword and scabbard, one of several, from a bracket on the wall and fastened it around his waist. His next call was the bailey.

A few bleary-eyed fellows lolled around in the sunshine, drinking ale and playing cards. Filled with uncontrollable rage, Joffrey drew the sword and whipped it back and forth. "Arm yourselves, there are weapons aplenty in the Great Hall. Stand by me and I shall reward you."

Joffrey harnessed his horse to the only cart left in the

stables and led the beast around to the back of the bailey. Furtively returning to the castle, he began removing everything of value he thought would fit into the cart. Thanks to his father's earlier tenure of the Lockton Estate, few original treasures remained, but Oric had accumulated one or two new items since his takeover. Joffrey seized them all. He would need all the help he could get for his next venture – whatever it may be.

Passing through the hallway on his way to the turret room he had commandeered for himself, Joffrey noticed the grappling hook and rope bundled up on a chair. *Might as well take that, too. It might come in handy.*

Coiling the rope with the grappling iron around his waist, Joffrey ascended the spiral stairway to his bed-chamber. Cutting all ties with Lockton Castle would be no bad thing. He was leaving with more wealth than he had had upon his arrival. Once he moved to a new district he would soon find another weak-minded land owner to ensnare in a fresh web of evil.

Whistling softly, Joffrey unlocked a trunk at the bottom of his bed and removed a pouch heavy with silver coins. Clutching the pouch in his left hand and the sword in his right, he took one last look around the turret room to make sure he had left nothing of value behind.

Sounds of clashing steel came from the bailey, and Joffrey grinned. The men had clearly taken him at his word and were practicing combat. But that was no concern of his. Soon he would be gone.

Outside a dog barked, causing Joffrey to halt momentarily halfway down the stairs. Since Doretta had departed with her animals, no canines remained at Lockton! He slowed his steps, opened the outer door, and peered down the stairs. The bailey below seethed with armed men. A large grey wolfhound, teeth bared, made sure no-one escaped. In the centre of the melee, Oric brandished a sword and shouted orders. Joffrey had not expected to see his arch enemy quite so soon.

Glancing up, Oric spotted Joffrey. He took the stairs up to the main door two at a time.

Too late to retreat, Joffrey drew his sword.

CHAPTER TWENTY-NINE

Oric Gets His Man

Oric thrust his weapon like a man possessed, and Joffrey had no choice but to parry. Sparks flew from the blades as they clashed together. Oric thrust again and again, the fury of his onslaught driving Joffrey back into the castle's hallway.

"You stinking lump of dung," yelled Oric. "I will make you pay for all the misery and death you have caused."

On the defensive, Joffrey tried to stop Oric's sword blade from slicing though his flesh. Out of practice in hand to hand combat, his shoulders burned like fire.

Another furious downward thrust from Oric forced Joffrey to drop his guard. Seizing the opportunity, Oric brought his sword down on Joffrey's left bicep, drawing blood.

Joffrey grunted with pain and dropped his pouch of silver. The coins jingled as they hit the floor.

Furiously swishing his sword from side to side, Joffrey crossed the hallway in reverse until his heels grated against the bottom step of the spiral stairway. With nowhere else to go, he ascended the stone stairs backwards.

Restricted by the narrow stairwell, both swordsmen were obliged to make do with vicious upward and downward thrusts. Their sword blades periodically struck against the stonework causing more sparks to fly.

Oric's supporters were, by now, the victors in the bailey and Joffrey's deposed men chose surrender over death. Josh and Sedrich raced up the stairs after Oric but there was nothing they could do to help. The spiral stairway provided only enough room for the two assailants facing each other and, in the heat of the conflict, Oric had no intention of stepping back to allow someone else take over his position.

Momentarily disappearing behind the central column, Joffrey gained the advantage.

Oric charged around the bend, straight into Joffrey's raised foot. He lost his balance and toppled head over heels down the stairs. Seizing his opportunity, Joffrey turned tail and ran for the turret room. Once inside, he turned the key in the lock a mere heartbeat before Oric could barge in.

Josh and Sedrich surged up the stairs behind Oric. "Let me get at him," cried Josh. "'Tis time he paid for what he did to my sister."

"Break down the door," yelled Oric, heaving for breath.

Panic overtook Joffrey. He could hear thuds as someone applied their shoulders to the door. *It will only be a matter of moments before the timber caves in. Dear Lord, what shall I do?* Three storeys up – to jump was not an option. Then he remembered the rope and grappling hook. Pulling a heavy cupboard against the door to gain some extra time, he raced up the last flight of stairs to the open, castellated area above his room. He threw down his sword and removed the rope from around his waist. Gusts of wind buffeted his body, and he almost lost his balance. Securing the grappling hook to one of the battlements, he twisted his legs around the rope and began the dizzying descent to ground level. Not daring to look down, he prayed the rope was long enough. Six feet above the moat he let go, plopped into the water, and swam across. On the other side of the moat, he faced an almost sheer wall of mountain. Not daring to venture around to the front of the castle, he had no choice other than to begin an ascent.

The turret room door burst open under the combined assault of Josh and Sedrich. Oric pushed them aside and, brandishing his sword, strode into the room. "Come out and face me, you miserable knave." Oric slashed his sword under the bed but encountered nothing.

"He must be on the ramparts," cried Sedrich.

Oric raced up the last few stairs. Stepping outside the first thing he saw was the grappling hook. He sheathed his sword and looked down, raking the area below for sight of Joffrey.

"There he is!" Josh pointed to a spread-eagled figure, inching his way up the mountain behind the castle.

"The fellow looks like a fly caught in a spiderweb," laughed Sedrich.

Had Joffrey heard the woodman's comment, the irony of his situation would have struck home like an added blow.

Oric grabbed the rope before either Josh or Sedrich could stop him and began to climb down.

With no head for heights, Sedrich turned green.

Josh patted Sedrich's back, "Worry not, lad, we need not follow our lord and master down the rope. Had he spared time to think, he could have made the descent just as quickly, and far more safely, down the stairs. Let us do that and meet him at the bottom."

Joffrey's wound throbbed, and blood dripped from his sleeve each time he dropped his hand below shoulder level. Pain slowed his ascent and he began to panic. On the point of blacking out he reached a ledge part way up the mountain and crawled on to it. He lay flat on his back and took several deep breaths. Feeling a little better, he rolled on to his stomach and peered over the edge. Oric was nowhere to be seen.

Observing Joffrey's ascent as far as the ledge, Oric chose a fissure in the rock to the right-hand side of the near-vertical slope. More secure foot and handholds aided his climb and, hidden from sight, he soon by-passed the place where Joffrey lay.

Heads tilted back, Josh and Sedrich watched the drama unfold.

Wind buffeted Oric's body the moment he left the sheltered fissure. His sword constantly got in his way and he reluctantly unbuckled it and let it fall. Easing his way slowly across and down toward the ledge, he jumped the last few feet and came face to face with his enemy.

Joffrey drew a dagger from his boot cuff and stabbed repeatedly at his opponent.

Oric jerked away from the blade, missed his footing, and slipped off the ledge.

"Oh, dear Lord!" wailed Sedrich, covering his eyes. "Oric has fallen."

Josh's stomach lurched with fright. "Quick, fetch a rope. We must climb up there and help him."

Joffrey watched and waited but he could no longer see Oric, for a rocky overhang blocked his view.

The wind threatened to blow Oric away but, catching hold of tough clumps of grass to steady himself, he managed to push his toes into a narrow crevice. Like an adder slithering along, he eased himself back on to the ledge. Silently unsheathing his dagger, he jumped on to Joffrey's back and held the sharp blade to his throat.

Joffrey all but soiled his breeches with fright. Unable to move under Oric's weight, he begged for mercy.

At that moment, Josh appeared on the ledge, round eyed with fear and red in the face. "Are you alright, Oric?" he panted, out of breath after his hasty climb. "Here, I fetched you a rope."

Suddenly exhausted, Oric handed Joffrey over. "Tie him up. He sickens me, but I cannot bring myself to kill him."

Step by careful step, Oric and Josh made their way down the fissure dragging Joffrey along between them. At the bottom they were greeted by a group of cheering serfs and villeins. "Hand him over to us," yelled Jeremiah Brody. "We will tear him limb from limb."

The crowd moved in and Joffrey cowered behind Oric. "Do not let them near me," he begged. Bleeding profusely, he presented a sorry sight.

"I would hand you over for less than a crust of bread," spat Oric, "but unlike you I have scruples. Josh, attend to his wound and lock him in the castle dungeon. Let us keep him in chains until the magistrate's next visit to Skelgut."

-oOo-

Life in Skelgut returned to normal, and Oric moved back into Lockton Castle. Ichtheus accompanied him, planning to stay and help his friend for a short while.

Cordelia's cottage remained uninhabitable, and she gladly accepted Oric's invitation to reside at the castle until another suitable dwelling could be found. Eager though she was to return to Bayersby Manor, Dian was obliged to wait until Ichtheus was ready to escort her home. She maintained a cool but cordial relationship with Oric, keeping out of his way as much as possible. Loving a lord for a person in her lowly position was out of the question, but adore him she undoubtedly did. Because she loved him she could not bear to subject him to the ridicule he would suffer from his aristocratic peers if she encouraged a serious relationship. Regardless of her strong feelings, she would not allow herself to indulge in a frivolous affair.

Hamish protested that he was too old to take over Ned and Joe's positions of Steward and Reeve but said he would do his best until they returned. In their absence, he organised the daily work schedule and kept a kindly watch on the village folk. Each day a gaggle of serfs volunteered to come up from Skelgut to perform the various tasks needed to keep the castle going.

-oOo-

August drifted in on a heatwave, bringing crowds of flies that buzzed around the villagers' dung heaps and cesspits. Streams dried up, and the lake receded. Ducks and geese bobbed about in the shallows, adding their droppings to the villagers' already fetid water supply. Disease spread throughout the community and Oric, Ichtheus, and Cordelia worked together, tending the sick. Vomiting and loose bowel movements were the main cause of distress. After two small babies died, Oric spent sleepless nights poring over his medical journals, concocting new medicaments to try to prevent the loss of more children.

September brought cooler weather, people recovered their health and strength, and the harvesting of winter crops of wheat and rye began. Soon after, spring grains of barley and oats were added to the bountiful harvest. Every able-bodied villager worked in the fields from dawn until dusk.

Toward the end of the month, the travelling magistrate made his annual visit to Skelgut. Oric went into the castle dungeon to let Joffrey know.

"I will receive the death sentence for sure," mourned Joffrey.

"Do you truly believe you deserve anything less?" demanded Oric, unlocking the manacles that held Joffrey fast to the wall. "Frankly I shall be glad to see the back of you."

Escorted by an armed guard, Joffrey suffered the indignity of being dragged through the village on the back of a cart. The magistrate waited in the village centre and, upon the prisoner's arrival, ordered him to stand before a jury of countryfolk. "You are charged with the heinous crimes of murder, violent abduction, imprisonment, the ill-treatment of an innocent party, and theft. What do you have to say for yourself?"

"Not guilty, your honour."

Howls of anger erupted from the villagers. Most had witnessed the hanging of forester Barda and they wanted to see Joffrey's blood spilled.

The jury of local folk took no time to bring in a verdict of guilty, and the magistrate condemned Joffrey to death. "You shall be suspended from a gibbet in a public place until you are near to death. Thenceforth you shall be cut down, disembowelled, and your innards thrown on to a fire. Your head will be severed from your body and impaled on a stake for all to see. Take the prisoner away!"

"Wait!" Oric stepped forward "As lord of this manor I exercise my right to commute the prisoner's sentence to hanging only."

An angry roar erupted from the villagers. "After all the

upset this fellow has caused, we want to see his guts spilled," yelled Jeremiah Brody.

"Have you not seen enough brutality?" demanded Oric. "Magistrate, see to the transportation of the prisoner to the Yaracumb gaol. The hangman employed therein will see that he meets a just and swift end."

Master Plunket pushed to the front of the crowd, his pasty, pimply face wobbling with righteous indignation. "You are robbing us of our entertainment. The fellow could be made to linger on for several days before he dies."

Oric eyed the village hypochondriac with distaste. "If that is the kind of community you choose to live amongst, Master Plunket, then I suggest you move elsewhere. Criminals must be punished for their crimes, but I will brook no needless brutality in my district." Turning his back on the subdued crowd he addressed Joffrey. "Be thankful I have spared you an agonising death, but after that I have no sympathy for you." Oric stood back to allow the magistrate's men to bundle Joffrey back onto the cart.

"You allowed the fellow to get off too lightly," said the magistrate in a low tone only Oric could hear. "I maintain the wronged deserve to vent their feelings." In a louder voice he announced that he planned to repair to the inn for a bite to eat. "The prisoner will remain shackled to the cart. If any law-abiding citizen has rubbish he wishes to dispose of, now would be a good time to do so."

Joffrey all but disappeared under the quantity of refuse the villagers hurled at him. When the magistrate reappeared, ready to leave, many people followed the cart to the end of the village street. "Good riddance to bad rubbish," they all chanted.

CHAPTER THIRTY

Guwain Meets his Match

Oric, Ichtheus and Cordelia sat together in the Great Hall enjoying breakfast. "'Tis time I returned home to Bayersby Manor," Ichtheus announced. "You can manage very well without me, now the sickness in Skelgut is under control. No doubt a queue as long Bayersby's jousting lists awaits my ministrations at home. Dian is keen to return, too. No doubt she will be needed to help look after Lady Myferny's new baby after she travels home from Roxbrough."

"I shall miss you sorely, Ichtheus" sighed Cordelia. "I have enjoyed your company more than I can say."

"Why not accompany Dian and me, dear lady? I have a mind to set up an apothecary's shop in Kilterton. Perhaps you might consider joining me in a partnership? I believe we could work well together."

"I can think of nothing I would like better. But where would I live? With no place to call my own, I would feel like a ship without a rudder."

Ichtheus patted Cordelia's hand. "My time at Bayersby was spent frugally therefore my savings have accrued. I am considering a shop with a two-room dwelling to the rear. You would be most welcome to share the premises with me."

"Wonderful idea, Master Ichtheus," said Oric. "Together you make a formidable medical team. The folk of Bayersby and Kilterton will be lucky to have you close by." He rose to his feet and dusted bread crumbs from his tunic. "And, speaking of medicine, the last bout of illness in Skelgut put paid to most of my emergency supplies. I must away to consult Josh about topping up with fresh herbs."

Taking advantage of the glorious late-summer weather, Josh hoed weeds from between rows of lavender, rosemary and sage. Heady perfume wafted from the late-flowering lavender plants, and bees buzzed amongst the hazy blooms.

Oric trailed his fingers through the greenery, enjoying the plants' fresh smell. "Good day to you, Josh. My word, the garden is a credit to you. May I gather some fresh herbs today?"

"Take whatever you want," said Josh, laying down his hoe. "Whilst you are here I would like to ask a favour of you."

"Go ahead, my friend," said Oric, snipping a few sprigs of sage, "I am all ears."

Josh cleared his throat and looked Oric in the eye. "I want to return to Bayersby for a short while. I am soon to wed Faylinn, and I need to help finalise the preparations. She is a local girl and most of her friends and family live in the district. Naturally she wishes to be married with her loved ones around her. You are my closest friend; would you be my supporter at the ceremony?"

"Indeed, it would be an honour," said Oric, blushing with pleasure. "But I am not sure I can spare time away from the castle at present."

Josh's disappointment was palpable, and Oric suffered a pang of regret. But, since Ned and Joe were both still at

Bayersby, who would look after the castle in his absence if he agreed to Josh's request? Back in the Great Hall, he talked over his concerns with Hamish.

"Och, I know not what ye are worrying about, laddie. The harvest is gathered in, and the epidemic of sickness seems to have passed. I can hold the fort with Archie's assistance whilst ye are away. No doubt the villagers will also help us keep things in order. Therefore, ye have no reason not to visit Bayersby Manor for a wee while."

Unable to come up with any further reasons for staying, Oric acquiesced. "Very well, I will take a short holiday, but I will not stay away long." He trusted Hamish and Archie but, having just reclaimed his inheritance, he was not keen to abandon his home again.

-oOo-

The first shades of autumn coloured the trees with splashes of gold and red as the five friends set forth for Bayersby Manor. Oric invited Dian to ride pillion on Jester, but she demurely refused, choosing instead to sit in the back of Ichtheus' cart. Cordelia took her place on the driver's seat beside Ichtheus, and the pair chatted non-stop for the duration of the four-day journey. Josh rode alongside Oric on a sprightly mule, babbling happily about his forthcoming nuptials. Oric answered his friend when he deemed it necessary.

Swept away on a wave of excitement, Josh barely noticed Oric's melancholy.

Try as he might, Oric could not lift himself from the deep pit of sadness that weighed him down. He loved Josh, but he felt envy bordering on jealousy over his friend's ecstatic happiness. Dian's continued polite, cool demeanour helped him not at all.

Blissfully unaware of any sad undercurrent, Parzifal trotted along the track after his beloved master, keeping well away from Jester's hooves.

Night-time closed in a little earlier each day, and Oric smelled a hint of frost. He hugged Parzifal close for warmth, wishing the dog was Dian.

On the evening of the fourth day, Bayersby Manor loomed out of the autumn mist.

"Alleluia!" shouted Josh, kicking his mule into a canter. The moment he entered through the Bayersby gates and dismounted in the compound, Faylinn hurled herself into his arms.

A knife twisted in Oric's gut as he witnessed the reunion between the two young lovers. *Lucky, lucky fellow.*

Lady Myferny, already back in residence, showed off her new daughter and Oric admired the beautiful baby girl. "What shall you call her?" he asked.

"Edredina after her father." Lady Myferny stroked the baby's fuzz of red hair. "She already looks so like dear Edred."

A feeling of shame overwhelmed Oric. How selfish was he, indulging in his own misery? Not only had this poor lady lost her husband, she had a baby to bring up alone, not to mention a bad tempered, recalcitrant son to deal with.

Upon entering the Great Hall, Oric was amazed to see Guwain seated at the head of the communal table rather than in isolation on his dais. He was not in his cups, nor were his clothes spattered with food. In fact, his demeanour had changed markedly for the better.

"Ah, Master Ichtheus, Oric, what a pleasure it is to see you both." Guwain beamed in welcome. "Please join me for a bite to eat."

Oric and Ichtheus exchanged puzzled glances. What

had brought about such a sudden change of personality in the young man?

Chatting to their friends later in the day cleared up the mystery.

"He has been introduced to his future wife," giggled Faylinn. "When Lady Myferny was in Roxbrough, her brother-in-law helped to select a young woman from a wealthy family of merchants. By all accounts, the new bride's father is happy to pay a handsome dowry in exchange for a title for his daughter."

"Good gracious," laughed Oric. "It seems you have infected someone else with wedding fever. Have you met the young lady yet?"

Faylinn gave Oric a knowing wink. "Oh, aye, that I have. She ain't been here for long, but Master Guwain seems to be lapping up her attention like a tomcat with a dish of cream."

"Her name is Teresa, and she has beautiful black hair and dark eyes." Joe rolled his eyes, the expression on his young face saying it all.

"She ain't half a looker." Ned curled his fingers and blew back and forth on his nails. "I hear the lady has Spanish blood and, no doubt, a temper to match. Guwain panders to her every whim."

"Maybe 'tis just a big act he is putting on," tittered Joe. "I cannot wait to see what happens after they are married."

"If Guwain's new lady-love carries on as she is doing now, it will be good for Bayersby, and good for us all," said Bannulf. "She is clearly her father's daughter, for she has a well-developed sense of business. I now have a meeting with Guwain and Teresa each morning. Guwain remans mute most of the time, but Teresa manipulates him into making decisions when necessary. No-one, not even Sir Edred, controlled Guwain the way Teresa does. The young woman is highly ambitious and I foresee Bayersby Manor going from strength to strength."

"She sounds like a saint," said Cordelia. "Surely the young lady has some flaws."

Faylinn widened her eyes, "If she has, I have yet to spot them. She is strict but kind to the serfs, and she has become firm friends Lady Myferny. 'Tis wonderful to see them both chatting and laughing together as they work at their distaffs and spindles."

Happy days drifted by. Mornings dawned fresh and cold, and darkness fell swiftly in the late afternoon. The big inglenook fireplaces in the Bayersby kitchen and the Great Hall belched warmth from huge, flaming logs. Many a sing-song occurred in the servant's quarters and happiness exuded from all and sundry.

Josh and Faylinn's wedding activities faded into insignificance beside those of Guwain and Teresa's grandiose plans. Teresa's large family arrived from Roxbrough along with Lady Myferny's sister Elfine and her husband. The two couples had many children, and the Manor rang with youthful laughter and the sound of running feet. Ichtheus found himself the butt of many a prank. When Demzel, Lady Myferny's younger sister, arrived from Yarracumb with her merchant husband and two spoiled daughters, Ichtheus' resolve to move into his own premises in Kilterton redoubled.

Teresa involved herself in everything, getting to know each of her servants individually. Dian's workload doubled with the care of Teresa, Lady Myferny and the new baby girl. She admired Teresa enormously and the two young women chatted freely together. Sitting before the fire in the Great hall, Teresa with her embroidery and Dian with a pile of mending, Teresa brought up a subject she had been agonising over since Oric and his small entourage arrived at the manor.

Taking a deep breath, she confronted Dian. "You are in love with Oric, are you not?"

Dian flushed red to the roots of her hair. "Good gracious, Mistress Teresa, whatever makes you think that?"

"'Tis as plain as the nose on my face, dear girl. The way you look at him every time he comes near is a complete giveaway. And, if I am not mistaken, he feels the same way about you. So why do you shun him?"

Tears of misery prickled Dian's eyes and she dashed them away angrily. "Because any relationship between a lord and a ladies' maid is not proper."

Teresa's peals of laughter echoed throughout the room. "Oh, my dear, do not let that come between you and a good relationship. Look at me – I come from the humblest of stock. My father was nought but a hard-working shipwright in his youth. In his free time, he built a small boat of his own and sold it for a profit. He built another two boats, and so on until he was able to leave his employment and work entirely for himself. Soon he had a fleet of merchant ships and here we are today, common, but rich. That is why he is so eager for me to gain a title to bring what he calls 'respectability' to the family name."

Dian became pensive as she mulled over Teresa's words.

"I hope you are thinking of changing your ideas," said Teresa. "You and Oric are made for each other."

"Do you really think so?" At Teresa's nod, Dian hurried on. "But I have pushed him away so often he no longer approaches me. I cannot suddenly fall into his arms and beg him to marry me, it would not be seemly."

Leaning forward, Teresa gently stroked Dian's forearm. "You would like to marry Oric, would you not?"

Dian, her face now wreathed in smiles replied with a resounding, "Yes!"

"Oric will fall over himself to propose if you give him half a chance," said Teresa. *And I will make sure he knows of Dian's change of heart.*

CHAPTER THIRTY-ONE

Happy Times

Aidie Kirtle, the Kilterton haberdasher, arrived at Bayersby Manor with a cart-load of fine fabrics, braids, and trims. Since money was no real object, Teresa wanted her wedding to be the finest the district had ever seen. Bolts of fabric spilled in glorious jewel colours from one end of the Great Hall to the other.

Entering the room, Guwain stopped abruptly at the head of the long table. "Good gracious what are you about, dear heart?" He fingered a particularly splendid swatch of pure silk. "I suspect this will cost a pretty penny." He sat down on the bench beside the table.

Teresa immediately plopped down on to his lap. She curled a lock of his hair around her finger and dropped a soft kiss on the tip of his nose. "I know I am being extravagant, but a girl only weds once. Mistress Kirtle has kindly brought her samples up from the village, so I can choose a suitable fabric for my bridal gown."

Hardly able to believe the exotic beauty would soon be his, Guwain was prepared to give her anything she desired.

Eyes flashing with mischief, Teresa cuddled in close to Guwain's chest. "I have a suggestion that you may or may not like, but I am going to put it to you anyway."

"Go ahead, I am happy to listen."

"You know Oric and Dian are in love, do you not?"

"Er, yes..." Guwain wondered what was coming next. Although he had made his peace with them both, he continued to feel a certain reserve on their part.

"Well," continued Teresa, "I am planning on letting Oric know that Dian is amenable to his advances. If things go according to plan, I was wondering if you would object to them getting wed at the Kilterton Priory and holding their wedding feast here at Bayersby Manor."

Slightly taken aback, Guwain eyed his fiancée. "If that is what you think they would like, then it is fine with me. I wish you luck dealing with Oric, he can be as stubborn as a mule when he chooses. Besides, I am not sure that Oric and Dian have forgiven me for my... er... not so charitable treatment of them when they were my servants."

"Oh, I doubt Oric will take much talking around this time," Teresa trilled, flapping her hands at Guwain. "Now, if you do not mind, I have women's business to attend to so kindly make yourself scarce."

A few days after her chat with Guwain, Teresa strolled in the garden, looking at suitable greenery to make her wedding posy. A little warmth remained in the late October sunshine, and she enjoyed a moment of reflective solitude. At the beginning of the year, marriage was the last thing on her mind and now here she was, but one moon from committing herself to a youth who had been a total stranger a short time ago. Admittedly she had been wooed by the idea of a title but, strangely enough, she really liked her groom to be. He was a little on the short side, but what he lacked in stature he made up for with good humour. Given time, she was quite sure she could fall in love with him. Absorbed in her thoughts, Teresa did not see Oric arrive in the garden.

"Good afternoon, Mistress. I trust you are well. Hopefully my presence is not disturbing you. I am here to gather herbs for Master Ichtheus, it will take me but a moment."

"You could not have chosen a better time, for I would like to talk to you." Teresa brushed fallen leaves from a garden seat and invited Oric to sit down.

"Do you wish me to help with your wedding arrangements?" Oric asked. "I know it is a busy time for all concerned and an extra pair of hands may be welcome."

"'Tis a wedding I wish to discuss, but not mine in this instance. Yours."

"I have no plans to marry, Mistress. Whatever gives you the idea that I have?"

"A little bird told me you are in love with a certain ladies' maid."

"If you refer to Dian then, yes, you are correct. But she offers me naught but a chilly friendship." Oric stared at his boots. "She is under the impression my life will be ruined if we become romantically entangled. I am resigned to bachelorhood for the rest of my life, for I shall not marry anyone else."

Teresa's dark eyes sparkled. "What if I told you Dian may have had a change of heart?"

"What!" Oric's head snapped up. "How so?"

"We had a little chat together a few days ago, and she is most certainly in love with you."

"Yes I know that, but she will not marry me."

"Were you not listening to me?" said Teresa, tapping Oric on the cheek with a sprig of lavender. "I said she has had a change of heart. Now I suggest you go and find her and propose to her before she has time to change her mind."

Grabbing Teresa's hand, Oric bent his fair head and kissed her fingers – then, just for good measure, he kissed her cheek, too, "You wonderful, wonderful lady. If Dian agrees to marry me I shall forever be in your debt."

Teresa watched the handsome young lord run over the flower beds, in too much of a hurry to traverse around them.

-oOo-

Ichtheus and Cordelia travelled into Kilterton to view the shop Ichtheus had in mind for his business. The premises, situated in the centre of the village, boasted a drop-down shutter which could be wound up from the inside on trading days, otherwise it acted as a safety device to keep out would-be thieves. Ichtheus had obtained a key to open the shop door from a helpful neighbour.

"Who does this place belong to?" asked Cordelia.

"An unscrupulous moneylender named Esica Figg," replied Ichtheus. "During his tenure of the property, he added extra rooms at the back. But his shop has stood empty since he died."

"If Master Figg is dead, to whom do we pay rent?"

"According to my enquiries, the fellow owned the shop outright. Some considerable time has elapsed since his death and I doubt anyone will turn up to claim the shop now. As far as I can ascertain, the man had no family."

"It is quite a substantial property," said Cordelia, poking her head into all the nooks and crannies the shop had to offer. "It will need a good scrub and painting with lime to make it habitable, but it appears to be structurally sound."

Clasping his hands loosely behind his back, Ichtheus

followed Cordelia around the empty rooms. "Once we are up and running, I foresee a very comfortable living, especially if we offer more than just herbal remedies."

"What else do you have in mind?"

"As well as the dispensation of medicaments, I am quite capable of offering the same medical services as a barber-surgeon." Ichtheus rocked back on his heels. "Of course, we will still be within easy reach of Bayersby Manor should our services be required there. And, if necessary, I can always perform haircuts and beard trims if we need a little extra money."

"I can make rose-water and gewgaws for the ladies," cried Cordelia, getting into the spirit of things. "And I am told my preserves are second to none."

-oOo-

Oric tore through Bayersby Manor shouting. "Has anyone seen Dian? Come on – someone must know where she is."

Enjoying a quiet ale beside the fireplace in the kitchen, Bannulf jumped to his feet. "Ye gods! What has bitten him on the backside? I ain't seen Oric this agitated in many a long moon."

"I think my sister is in the Great Hall with Faylinn," said Josh. "They have begun work on Mistress Teresa's wedding gown. Faylinn is excited because the mistress says she can choose some material for her own gown, too."

Oric paid his friend scant attention as he charged past. Taking the stairs three at a time, he arrived at the Great Hall doorway and burst through.

Golden fabric pooled around Dian as she plied her needle. She made Oric think of a beautiful jewel in a crown. "Put away your sewing," he said. Taking hold of her hand, he dragged her out of the Great Hall, down the stairs, through the kitchen, and out into the compound. Making for the only place he thought would be private, he entered Jester's stall.

The big black horse turned his head to see what the fuss was all about and, seeing only Oric and Dian, he swiftly returned to his hay-filled manger.

"What in God's name is…" Dian failed to say another word, for Oric had his arms around her, pushing her against the stable wall with his mouth locked firmly upon her lips.

After several long heartbeats they broke apart, trembling and gasping for breath.

"Now tell me you do not want to marry me," Oric yelled, shaking Dian until her chestnut-coloured curls tumbled about her face. "I swear if you turn me down again, I will kill us both!"

Dian's knees buckled, and she slid down against the wall until she sat in a heap on the straw. "I, I, I…"

In a trice Oric was down beside her, kissing her again and again. "I adore you, I want you, I cannot live another moment without you. Will you be my wife?"

Years of pent up emotion spilled from Dian's hazel eyes. She raised her face to Oric's, and he tasted her salty tears. "Yes!" she managed between his hungry kisses. "Yes, I will wed you!"

A round of applause erupted from the stable door where Ned, Joe, Josh and Bannulf stood in a semi-circle.

"Please forgive the interruption, Oric" said Josh, trying to keep his face straight. "But you acted in such an outrageous manner, I feared for my sister's life. I truly believed you meant to do her harm."

Red faced, with bits of straw sticking out of her hair, Dian giggled. Already on his feet, Oric offered his hand and pulled her up.

"I managed to save myself," said Dian playing the coquette. "However, had I not agreed to wed this fellow, I am sure he would have followed through with his threat to kill us both."

"Maybe we should break the happy news to everyone else in the Manor," suggested Bannulf. "One or two folks are somewhat concerned over your peculiar behaviour, Oric."

Unable to keep their hands off each other, Oric and Dian returned to the Great Hall with their fingers entwined.

Teresa glanced up from her needle and thread. "Now that you two have overcome your difficulties, it is time for practicalities, do you not think?" Dian thought her mistress looked like a well-fed pussy cat.

"Thank you for making me see sense, Mistress," said Dian. "I cannot believe how silly I have been." She gazed lovingly at Oric. "Now I have come to my senses, I will never let this fellow out of my sight again."

"I am pleased to hear it," said Teresa, putting down her needle, "but, back to practicalities. What do you think about celebrating your nuptials in Kilterton Priory? Dian's family and most of your friends live in the district, it would save them making the long journey to Lockton Castle for the ceremony. Father Franciscus has also suggested that Josh and Faylinn marry the day before. That way you, Oric, can still be Josh's supporter."

"It seems you have it all planned, my lady," said Dian, dropping a small curtsy. "But am I worthy of getting wed in the priory?"

Teresa's hoot of laughter filled the Great Hall. "Worthy? Did you not hear a word I said to you earlier? Of course, you are worthy." Her dark eyes twinkled wickedly. "Once we are wed we will both be members of the landed gentry and people, if they feel so inclined, can curtsy to us." She erupted with more gleeful chortles, "Though I must say I am not keen on the habit."

"What is the to-do about?" asked Ichtheus, entering the Great Hall with Cordelia. "It looks as if celebrations are about to take place. If so, may Cordelia and I join in? We have made the decision to take over Esica Figg's old shop in Kilterton."

CHAPTER THIRTY-TWO

Web of Romance

A stickler for getting things right, Ichtheus urged Oric to visit Dian's parents in Kilterton to ask Eadbald Coles' permission to wed his daughter.

Dispirited, Oric shrugged his shoulders. "The fellow could not care one way or the other, he will be interested only in what is in it for him."

Ichtheus regarded Oric from beneath his bushy eyebrows. "Even so, courtesy dictates…"

"As it happens, Dian and I have a meeting with Father Fransiscus this afternoon. If you insist, I shall call at the Coles' place and talk to Eadbald – if he is home."

Dian rode a grey pony, kind courtesy of Teresa, alongside Oric on Jester. As they drew away from Bayersby Manor, Parzifal's mournful howls faded.

Dian giggled. "That dog is such a baby. The moment he loses sight of you, he cries."

"He will just have to make the best of it, for he cannot accompany me everywhere I go." Oric reached across the gap between them and squeezed Dian's arm. "Do you have any idea how much I love you?"

"Of course I do." Dimples indented Dian's rosy cheeks as she smiled. "If only I had not been so silly we might have been wed long since."

Entering the village, Oric and Dian made straight for her parents' cottage. The Coles had lived alone since Dian's younger siblings had moved into Oric's moorland hut above Bayersby Manor, and their tumbledown home had fallen into a shocking state of disrepair.

"One would never guess my father is Kilterton's odd job man!" stated Dian. "I am ashamed of him."

"Let us get this formality over as quickly as we can," said Oric, rapping sharply on the cottage door.

"Who is it?" quavered Frida. "We ain't got no money, and our daughter ain't here."

Oric looked askance at Dian. "What is she talking about?"

"Mother, it is I," called Dian. "Let me in."

The door opened, and Frida dragged her daughter indoors. She tried to shut Oric out, but he was having none of it. He put his shoulder to the door and forced his way into the dank cottage.

"Thank God you are here, girl. The merchant who paid money for you visited us this morning. He said we had to have you ready and waiting to leave with him when he gets back later in the day. Otherwise we must return the money he paid us. If we fail to honour our agreement one way or another, he says he will cut off our ears."

Infuriated, Oric pushed Dian behind him. "I am here to tell you that Dian and I are to be wed, and she is moving to Lockton Castle with me. If you wish to save your ears, you had best repay the money you owe."

Eadbald Cole lurched drunkenly out of the shadows at

the back of the room. "I already spent the merchant's money and, since I ain't planning to lose my ears, Dian will go away with him as arranged."

Thunderous knocking on the door made them all jump.

"That will be him," shrieked Frida, giving Dian a push. "Go on, off you go."

"Dian is not going anywhere, except with me," snarled Oric. Wrenching open the door he glared at the short man standing on the Coles' doorstep. "What do you want?"

Somewhat taken aback by the young man's aggressive attitude, the merchant stood on tip toe to eye Dian up and down over the top of Oric's shoulder. "I paid good money for yon wench, and I ain't leaving without her," he bellowed.

"In that case you are going to be sorely disappointed! I am Oric, Lord of Lockton, and the wench belongs to me. Unless you remove yourself from these premises forthwith, I shall have you charged and incarcerated for threatening behaviour."

"What about my money?" demanded the merchant.

"Next time you pass by Skelgut, call in at Lockton Castle and I shall reimburse you."

Overawed by the young lord's haughty presence, the merchant nodded his agreement. "I will be out that way next new moon and I shall look forward to completing our transaction then."

Eadbald greased up to Oric, thinking he might extract a promise for more money for his daughter. He held out a grubby paw and put on his best smile. "If you want our Dian, you will need to pay me a fair sum."

"I am not seeking a servant," roared Oric. "I came here in all good faith to ask you for Dian's hand in marriage. I believe, in that case, it is you who will owe me money in the form of a dowry. Providing you give us your blessing, I am prepared to absolve you of that obligation."

Eadbald agreed to Oric's request with indecent haste. He already saw himself in residence at Lockton Castle and, as father of the bride, he imagined a life of luxury might lie ahead.

Frida twittered on about suitable clothing to attend her daughter's wedding.

"That proved easier than I anticipated," said Oric giving Dian a leg up onto her pony.

"So, I am naught but a wench who belongs to you, now, am I?" said Dian tartly.

"Oh, good gracious, no... er, of course not," mumbled Oric, blushing brick red. "I did not mean it to sound like that, I was merely..."

Seeing Oric's horrified expression, Dian burst into gales of laughter. "Worry not, I am only teasing you! Quite honestly, I care not what you said or did, just so long as you got rid of that horrible merchant fellow."

"The sooner I can call you my wife the happier I shall be," said Oric. "Now, let us find Father Franciscus and organise our nuptials." He slanted a look at Dian. "But, before we do that, I want you to make me a promise."

"Oh, yes, and what would that be?" Dian asked, a doubtful look upon her face.

"I beg you not tell Master Ichtheus that I omitted to ask your father for your hand in marriage. If he discovers that I demanded, rather than requested the honour, I will never hear the end of it."

"I promise," giggled Dian. "I have been thinking about our nuptials quite a lot lately. Since Josh and Faylinn are to be married soon, what do you think about making it a double celebration? Josh is my brother, he is your good friend, and I have become uncommonly fond of Faylinn. Mistress Teresa is keen to provide the feast at Bayersby Manor afterwards so what do you think about my suggestion?"

"It is a wonderful idea," said Oric. "Let us see if Father Franciscus is prepared to conduct both weddings at once. Then, of course, we must ask Josh and Faylinn if they agree with our idea."

Kilterton Priory stood on a rise, commanding fine views over the village. The young priest knelt at his devotions before the altar but rose to his feet when he heard the priory door creak open. Seeing Oric and Dian framed by sunlight in the doorway, he strode down the aisle with his hands outstretched in welcome.

"I have been expecting a visit from you," he said, smiling from ear to ear. "Josh and Faylinn were here not long ago, making the final arrangements for their nuptials. They told me your good news. Including Mistress Teresa and the young Lord of Bayersby, it seems I am to conduct three weddings in quick succession."

"Aye, but two of them might be performed together," smiled Dian. "If my brother Josh and his bride are in agreement, we would like to make our wedding a double celebration."

"Let us hope they will," replied Father Franciscus, delighted with the idea. "I have already tacked Josh and Faylinn's notice to the priory door to inform every one of their forthcoming ceremony, now I must add yours. You know not of anyone who would object to your union, do you?"

Oric and Dian looked at each other. "I think not," said Oric, replying truthfully for them both.

"That is good news," beamed Father Franciscus. He blessed both young people and chased them off to organise everything.

"Our next job is to inform our friends of the arrangements," said Oric, grasping hold of Dian's hand. "Let us make Uther our first call."

Busy in his shop, the old cobbler was delighted to see the young couple. "Come away in, I was just about to have a sup of elderberry wine, will you join me?" He bustled about, seeking drinking vessels, and returned with three pots, brimming with sweet crimson liquor. "I believe I owe you an apology, Oric."

"You do? Whatever for?"

"I fear the Committee of Law let has you down. Despite our vigilance, we were unable to help you in any way. Regardless of our negligence, I am glad to see you have your friend back safe and sound." Smiling at Dian, he added, "I dare not imagine the harrowing time you must have endured."

Dian kissed Uther's leathery cheek. "Please do not concern yourself any further. I have put all that unpleasantness behind me. Now Oric and I have something wonderful to tell you." Dian went on to explain the arrangements that were being made, and invited Uther to the wedding.

"I have a favour to ask of you," Oric chipped in. "Because I need to return to Lockton Castle as soon as possible, everything is being arranged in rather a hurry. I have no time to ride south of the village to invite Egglebart, Etheldrida, Sir Oswold, and Lady Malla to our wedding. They will be at the next market in Kilterton for sure, and I would be most obliged if you would pass on our invitation. I cannot get married without four of my oldest friends in attendance."

"It will be my pleasure, lad, and many congratulations." Toasting the youngsters' good health, Uther promised to make each of them a pair of kid slippers as a wedding gift. He was not so pleased to hear that Oric intended to invite Tewdric Bascoomb, the Kilterton butcher. "I suppose that means his horrible wife, Helled, will be present," he grumbled. "That wretched woman gets more disgruntled with every passing day. I know not what ails her for they are not short of funds.

I might suggest they donate a beast for your wedding feast." He sniggered wickedly. "That will put the cat amongst the pigeons. Tewdric will oblige gladly, but first he will need to run the gantlet of that mean harridan he is married to."

On the return journey to Bayersby Manor, Oric and Dian talked non-stop, discussing their plans. Warmed by Uther's home-made wine, and just a little tipsy, Oric kept reaching across the gap between Jester and the pony Dian rode, touching her hand to make sure she was real and not a figment of some beautiful dream.

Over the evening meal in the Great Hall, Oric broached the subject of a double wedding with Josh and Faylinn. They were thrilled at the idea and joined in enthusiastically with everything Oric and Dian suggested.

"Under these changed circumstances, Josh, I cannot be your supporter on the day," warned Oric. "I am afraid you will need to find a replacement."

"The same applies to you, my friend" replied Josh. "I will ask my younger brother. He is nearby, living in your old hut on the moor. But who will you ask?"

"Judging by my two friends' antics over there," said Oric, nodding towards Ned and Joe, "I need not look too far. If I do not ask them they may well both suffer an apoplectic fit."

Genevieve, pale, thin, and shy was reluctant to accept Faylinn's request to act as flower girl. "You need someone far prettier than me," she protested.

Cries of disagreement came from Dian and Faylinn. After some gentle persuasion Genevieve changed her mind.

"Thank goodness for that," sighed Dian. "I plan to ask my two younger sisters to accompany me, and they are as wild as a pair of spring hares. I need someone calm and sensible to keep an eye on them." She became pensive. "My entire family, apart from Josh, is a problem. I know mother is a foolish woman, but she has been downtrodden all her life and I think looking to her own survival has been her priority. As for father, I believe he drinks to blot out his wretched lifestyle. Since the children have all left home, I fear my parents believe they have nothing left to live for."

Having no family of his own to worry about, Oric wondered if he could do anything to help the beleaguered Coles. "What say we invite your mother and father to live at Skelgut? There are still one or two empty cottages in the village. If they are willing to move, you could keep an eye on them. Perhaps Eadbald could start afresh, and your mother might make some new friends who would be willing to help her make a new life."

Tears brimmed Dian's eyelids as she nodded. "You are a good, kind man, Oric. I wonder if I truly deserve you?"

Oric tut tutted and gathered Dian up in a hug.

CHAPTER THIRTY-THREE

Grand Celebration

In the days leading up to the wedding, Bayersby Manor underwent a transformation. The Great Hall looked like a dressmaker's establishment, as fabrics for the brides' and flower girls' dresses were chosen and worked upon. The kitchen became a bakery for masses of pies and sweetmeats. Mistress Foley, the Bayersby housekeeper, ran herself ragged overseeing the preparations. A pig arrived from Kilterton kind compliments of Tewdric Bascoomb, and Oric wondered how many hoops the poor butcher had to jump through to get around his wife, Helled. The porker, prior to being spit roasted on feast day, was stowed away with the rest of the food in the manor's cold larders.

Teresa insisted that her nuptial arrangements with Guwain were temporarily laid aside. "Our wedding is not until the following full moon. We shall have plenty of time to organise everything once we get you four married off."

The constant racket of Lady Myferny's squalling baby, rumbustious children, guests, and wedding fever gave Ichtheus a permanent headache. He spent much of the time trying to hide away in his apothecary's quarters, longing for the peace and quiet of his own shop with only Cordelia for company. Men were already at work in the establishment, lime-washing the walls, building work benches and installing a pair of braziers. It would not be too much longer before Ichtheus achieved his dream.

-oOo-

The end of November brought the first few snow flurries of the season, and Oric worried that he might not be able to return to Lockton Castle if winter closed in. Lornika Fentwhistle prophesied that no more snow would fall until late January, early February and, for once she was proved right.

The wedding day dawned with a hard, white frost, bright blue sky, and primrose-coloured sunshine. Ice particles sparkled like precious jewels on the leafless branches of trees and shrubs. Hips and haws glowed red against a stark, frosty background.

Excitement reached fever pitch around mid-morning as the two grooms and their attendants mounted horses in the Bayersby compound. Oric rode Jester around to the window behind which he knew Dian and her attendants were preparing for the big day. At his loud whistle, Dian's face appeared in the narrow opening. Oric blew her a kiss and threw up a posy of lavender tied with a purple ribbon. "I love you," he called. "See you in church."

Amid ribald shouts and whistles from the male members of the manor, Oric, Josh, and their three attendants cantered their horses away from Bayersby toward Kilterton.

The inn overflowed with drinkers when the boys strode in for pre-wedding pots of ale. Oric, head and shoulders taller than his friends, looked magnificent. The wide sleeves of his cream linen shirt showed cleanly against the dark green of his doublet, and a matching cap sported a long feather. His freshly-washed hair shone like a golden beacon. Pale, tight-fitting breeches, tucked into calf-high brown boots, showed off his muscular legs. Similarly attired, Josh also looked wonderful, though his choice of dress was a little more subdued. Ned, Joe, and Josh's brother danced attendance upon their masters.

Oric raised his pot of ale and winked at Josh. "Here is to us both. In a very short time we shall be brothers-in-law."

At the designated time, Oric and Josh rode to the priory. All their friends awaited them outside the building, stamping their feet and blowing on their frozen fingers. Greeted warmly by Father Franciscus, the two grooms and their attendants took up their positions on the priory steps to await the arrival of Dian and Faylinn.

Moments later, the sound of jingling bells announced the arrival of the bridal party.

A large cart drawn by two magnificent oxen pulled up in front of the priory. Garlands of holly and ivy decorated the sides, and the five girls seated within looked like beautiful flowers.

The ladies of the manor followed behind on their individual horses, each accompanied by her partner. Children brought up the rear in a series of smaller carts.

First to step down from the big cart was Faylinn, her rosy face wreathed in smiles. She had chosen a deep russet-coloured gown, which complemented her bridegroom's attire.

Dian's gown took the watchers' breath away. Shimmering golden satin billowed around her, and a froth of lacy petticoats peeped from beneath the folds of fabric as her father handed her down from the cart. A criss-cross of laces held the bodice together, finishing in a neat bow at Dian's slender waist.

Both brides wore coronets made from green larch sprigs and scarlet holly berries. Dark brown cloaks lined with white rabbit fur kept the young women warm. Their flower girls, all three in matching light-green tunics, carried baskets full of dried rose petals which they scattered on the ground before the brides. Ned and Joe, chests thrust out like pouter pigeons stood one either side of Oric. Parzifal, held firmly under Ned's control, looked splendid with a bright red ribbon tied in a bow around his neck.

Everyone assembled on the priory steps and the ceremony began.

Father Fransiscus addressed the guests. "Does any person present have just cause to prevent the marriage between Oric, Lord of Lockton and Dian, daughter of Eadbald and Frida Cole? If so, speak now or forever hold your peace."

Someone in the crowd coughed, and Oric's heart almost stopped. *Please God, let nothing go wrong at this late stage.*

Father Franciscus waited for what seemed a lifetime. No-one objected, and he carried on.

"Does any person present have just cause to prevent the marriage between Josh, son of Eadbald and Frida Cole, and Faylinn, currently employed by the Lord of Lockton?"

No objections were raised.

Father Fransiscus turned his attention to the two young couples. "Have you committed any crimes or transgressions you deem reason to prevent your marriage?"

The four all shook their heads vehemently. "No, Father," they chorused.

"Then let vows be exchanged."

Following the priest into the priory, Oric and Josh knelt

before their brides. They promised to love, honour, and cherish until death did them part. Oric slipped his ruby ring on Dian's fourth finger of her left hand. It was too big, but Oric had promised to have it made smaller as soon as he could find time to visit the goldsmith in Yarracumb.

Josh had a silver ring set with a garnet for Faylinn.

The girls promised to love, honour, and obey 'til death did them part.

Father Fransiscus made the sign of the cross and blessed them all. "You may now kiss your brides," he said.

Folk arrived at Bayersby in dribs and drabs throughout the afternoon. Thus, began the biggest party the manor had ever seen. Jollifications went on far into the night until the two young couples were eventually led to their chambers and put to bed. With the closing of the heavy drapes the newlyweds were finally left on their own.

-oOo-

Next morning, Bannulf crawled out of his bed, hanging on to his head with both hands. He shambled into the Great Hall in search of a pot of ale. Ned and Joe, seated at the table, looked similarly off colour.

"By heck," rasped Ned, hoarse from singing, "that was a noisy night. I ain't danced like that since I was a youngster. I swear I know not which hurts most, my head or my feet."

Joe tittered. "Well you did choose to dance with the biggest girl in room. Judging by the size of her feet and the times she stomped on your toes, I am surprised you ain't got nothing broken."

Genevieve and Mistress Foley appeared to be the only two people not nursing sore heads. They served breakfast to the newlyweds in bed, sparing them the sight of their sick and sorry friends. Making the most of a little peace and quiet, they failed to surface until mid-afternoon. Then began the business of packing up in readiness for the journey to Lockton Castle.

Shortly after dawn the next day, Oric announced that he was ready to leave Bayersby. Egglebart, Etheldrida, Sir Oswold and Lady Malla, all of whom had followed the bridal party back to the manor after the wedding, were also keen to return to their smallholdings south of Kilterton.

Etheldrida promised to keep an eye on Dian's parents and they sat, prim and proper in their crumpled wedding outfits, in the back of her cart.

Amidst much chatter, a few tears, and many hugs the friends parted company, promising to visit Lockton Castle in the New Year, weather permitting. "Please bring my parents with you," cried Dian. "We will have a cottage repaired and cleaned, ready for them by then."

Ichtheus and Cordelia each hugged Dian. "Be happy, darling girl," said Cordelia. "You have a wonderful man for a husband, and he has a beautiful bride."

"Well, lad," said Ichtheus, struggling to control his emotions. "'Tis the parting of the ways at last. I cannot find the words to say how much I will miss you." He pulled Oric into a fierce embrace. "Make sure you take proper care of that young Lady."

"Aye, I will Sir." Oric hugged his old mentor in return. "And I shall miss you, too. Not only have you been my teacher, you are like a father to me and I thank you from the bottom of my heart. You and Cordelia will always be welcome at Lockton Castle, please be sure to visit us soon."

Faylinn and Genevieve travelled in a cart pulled by Oric's donkey, Otty. Josh sat astride a mule with two full panniers,

Ned and Joe both rode donkeys also carrying panniers.

Oric lifted Dian on to Jester's back and the traitorous horse turned his head to gently nuzzle her foot. The big black animal seemed to love her, and Oric wondered why his own relationship with the horse remained so unpredictable. Jester proved his wicked temperament by head butting Oric as he walked by. Parzifal yelped as he narrowly avoided a nip on his backside.

Standing in Bayersby Manor's gateway, Guwain, Teresa, and Bannulf laughed uproariously. "I hope you have better control over your new wife than you do over your horse," Bannulf howled.

Climbing up behind Dian, Oric slid his arms around her. "Here begins our wonderful new life together, my darling. I wonder what adventures lie ahead for us both."

THE END

If you enjoyed Oric's adventure, I would absolutely love it if you could let the world know. There are two easy ways to do this.

Firstly, if you bought this from an online bookstore, please leave an honest review for this title on the online bookstore you bought it from, it really helps other people find it.

Secondly, if you have a Goodreads account, please review it or add it to a book list, so other people can discover and enjoy it too.

www.ingramcontent.com/pod-product-compliance
Lightning Source LLC
Chambersburg PA
CBHW061017120726
47910CB00006B/1982